The Two Faces
of Dr. Collier

The Two Faces of Dr. Collier

Elizabeth Seifert

Thorndike Press • Chivers Press
Thorndike, Maine USA   Bath, England

This Large Print edition is published by Thorndike Press, USA and by Chivers Press, England.

Published in 2000 in the U.S. by arrangement with Spectrum Literary Agency.

Published in 2000 in the U.K. by arrangement with Ralph Vicinanza Limited.

U.S. Hardcover 0-7862-2590-4   (Candlelight Series Edition)
U.K. Hardcover 0-7540-4197-2   (Chivers Large Print)

The text of this Large Print edition is unabridged.
Other aspects of the book may vary from the original edition.

Set in 16 pt. Plantin by Minnie B. Raven.

Printed in the United States on permanent paper.

British Library Cataloguing-in-Publication Data available

Library of Congress Cataloging-in-Publication Data

Seifert, Elizabeth, 1897–
 The two faces of Dr. Collier / by Elizabeth Seifert.
  p. (large print) cm.
 ISBN 0-7862-2590-4 (lg. print : hc : alk. paper)
 1. Physicians — Fiction. 2. Middle West — Fiction.
 I. Title.
 PS3537.E352 T93   2000
 813'.52—dc21   00-028687

The Two Faces
of Dr. Collier

Chapter One

My name is Lissa, and I think I have a story to tell — a story about me, about a town, and about two doctors: one who could have been a good doctor, and another who surely will be one.

The town is called Two Bridges, because we actually do have two bridges which cross our river. A placid, brown river it is, most of the time, but which can rise and spread itself, and talk loudly and roughly.

I came to Two Bridges in April, which is a beautiful season in the mountain country. The sun is warm, the trees have spangled out into new green leaves which blow and dance in any little breeze. There is green grass, flowers everywhere, and young animals to play in the meadows. Lambs jump straight up on their four little feet, colts toss their heads and run wildly from nothing to nothing, and young possums ride across their mother's back when she comes to the low birdbath for a drink.

I came to Two Bridges to rest, though that is not a natural thing for a young woman to need to do. I am — that is, I have been — a concert pianist. You've heard of me; you've heard and seen me play — on records, the concert stage, on TV.

At fifteen I was a prodigy; I attended and graduated from a prestigious conservatory with all that meant in work, concentration and self-discipline. At no more than twenty I was acclaimed in this country and in Europe. I was known for my playing of the classics — most of them the old classics. I was trained to play them, I trained myself, and I became adept. Without any gimmicks or flashy self-arrangements, I was able to make the playing of that wonderful music popular and exciting. The people and the critics were kind to me. I became a fad, though I did make every effort to keep myself an honest musician. The critics talked of the youthful emotion and intensity I gave, but I think a great part of my success was because the classics have a great deal to give to an audience, though there is always appeal when they are adequately performed by a pert young girl-woman with thick and shining auburn hair. My habit of pushing my dark glasses up on top of my head became a trademark; the album covers showed this, and sold as many records as did Chopin, Debussy and Liszt. At thirty I was known everywhere — New York, San Francisco, London, Tokyo . . .

At thirty tragedy struck my life and everything was changed. The concerts, the talk-show appearances, the crowds — all this was immediately behind me.

For the last time I was to leave the concert hall with the excitement of a successful performance still bubbling in my veins, for the last time a way was made for me through the people crowded on the sidewalk. For the last time there was the ride to the airport with my manager talking, with sleepy me only half listening. For the last time I went across the wide concrete apron to the boarding steps of the plane. The wind was too high to use the motorized lounge. Two men held me by the elbows. . . . "You're a little one," said the airport official. "You could blow away."

But the plane itself was big, strong-looking, and warm. In the dark of midnight, only the wind and an occasional slap of sleet against my face indicated a storm. The plane took off on time, as I remember. I kicked off my shoes, refused a drink, and lay back in the chair, determined to sleep for the hours it would take to arrive.

Where we did not arrive. Later I was told that we hit a weather front, the plane lost altitude, regained some of it, then shuddered

— and went down.

I was one of the "lucky" ones. I escaped with what was called "slight injury." Now I will grant that a crushed shoulder is more "slight" than death. But to me it meant months of pain, surgery, and fear. To all intents and purposes, I had lost my right hand and arm. I went through all the business of muscle-saving splints, tendon surgery, massage and exercise. The doctors assured me that I would, with time and patience, regain use, if not facility. Oh, the words they used! *Facility,* indeed.

What those words all meant was that I would never again play the piano well enough to entertain an audience. I would never push my dark glasses atop my head, swish out on the concert stage, hear the applause across the footlights, tuck my green lamé skirts prettily between the bench and the piano — and —

Which was the only *facility* I wanted as I listened to the panel of doctors who were telling me things I did not want to hear.

I was discouraged, I was frightened. It was not a matter of money. My earnings over ten years had been well managed and invested; there was insurance. But there was little life and hope ahead for me, or so it seemed. I had had no romantic attachments. That could come later, I had always told myself. I had no family — a grandmother had raised me, and had died three years previously.

So what did I have? A helpless arm which still could pain me, and a long, long life ahead. Doing what? At night, bad dreams of crashing planes, and too-long days filled with reading, aimless shopping, talk with people kind enough to listen to me. . . .

But I did have one particular doctor, my specialist — a kind man, large and well scrubbed, and understanding. Fortunately he had been blessed with a grandfather who lived in the Ozarks.

And the doctor would, with great kindness, take time to sit in the corner of my room high up in the hospital building in that bustling city, with at least a dozen people who needed his care more than I did — he would still take time to talk to me about the Ozarks and his grandfather — a bearded man who farmed on land too thin to support crops, who fed beef cattle, and walked into the woods each morning, fished the streams nine months out of the year, hunted deer and quail, counted the wildflowers to be found on a spring morning.

Dr. Kohl would look out of that high window across the towers and the canyons of the city, and he would talk to me about the summers he used to spend on his grandfather's farm. I listened, and I too could smell the hot sun on a hayfield, hear the greeting bark of an excited dog, ride bareback on an old mare . . .

"There was time in those hills," said Dr. Kohl. "Nerves did not exist. One could see the sky, hear the rain on the roof close above your head, sit all day and watch the brown river flow between its banks . . ."

He sold me. I had to go somewhere and do something. "Get well first," he cautioned me when he transferred my case to a specialist in St. Louis. "Give those old green hills a chance."

I had already started on my plans. I would find a place to stay in the Ozarks; there were numerous resorts with hotels and lodges, and eventually I would find a home in a town "with a doctor," where I would establish myself, read, enjoy the peace and quiet, and get well — bones, muscles, nerves, and heart.

Hope and interest built up slowly, but they did build. I got books about the Ozarks, maps, brochures, lists of resorts and towns — road maps.

I had to start somewhere, and from my first sight of it, the name Two Bridges intrigued me. I considered other places — a resort on a big lake, a quaint older town . . .

But eventually it was to be Two Bridges. And when I went to see it, I found the town to be a quiet place, just such a one as had been suggested to me. In fact, it was a beautiful town. The river was brown to dark green because of the vegetation and the overhanging bluffs. Two Bridges was built on the side of a roundly sloping hill; advance reports said that it would afford me any of the simpler pleasures. Well, simple was the sort of pleasure I could take and, I hoped, enjoy. My first inspection verified the river, the trees, the rolling hills, and peace. One drove into Two Bridges along a rather steep road from the main highway, down to the main street of the town, with the river dark behind the elevators and the barge dock. The air was clear, the farms and the fields — pastures, cornfields, even tobacco and beans. Cane. I was to learn about those things much, much later.

For the first days it was enough that these farms and fields were close at hand to be looked at. It was enough that springs abounded in the area and were reputed to be healthful. I did not care about healthful things but, given my first glass of spring water, I knew that the cold, clear water was a joy. Driving about, I did not see any wildflowers except those on the side of the road, but the woods were there, and the flowers would be, too. Even from the road the dogwood and the Judas trees, the flowering crab, seized my senses, and I told myself solemnly that I was happy.

For all the springs, the river, and the beauty, the town had never quite become the resort that the old-timers had dreamed it would be when they built the hotel — a matter of towers and bay windows, a creaking cage elevator, and deep leather chairs in the lobby. I came soon to believe that the town never had really wanted to be a resort. The six thousand people who lived there liked to have space to move about, and clear air to breathe. The big, splashy resorts were at the lake, the large department stores and boutiques could be found in the city. In Two Bridges, the people had what they needed, and they liked living in their homes. . . .

Those homes. I remember my first view of the big Gothic houses. The first one I saw was the Bedford house, standing still among its farmlands, a red brick handsome edifice of white stone framed windows, sloping gabled roofs; it had become the County Historical Museum. When I first saw it, I said I wished I could live in such a house — no less than fifteen rooms, high-ceilinged — but there surely would be a magnificent staircase. (And there was.) As well as window seats, cupboards in the kitchen that would smell of cinnamon and sugar, and —

I liked the gingerbread porches on some of the houses I saw that first time — the Edward Hopper houses with their tall, Gothic windows, towers and bays. But I deplored one new and self-conscious river-colonial with its oversupply of green shutters, white columns, and wrought-iron balconies. It was the Langan home, I was told. And from the first, this set things off wrong for me with the Langans.

The Langan home, all the houses, had wide lawns that were green and smooth, flower beds that glowed with color. One could drive along a street under tall trees between these houses and come to a place where a ravine would unexpectedly drop away. But even there would be great patches of jonquils, the side of the slope carpeted yellow with them. It was that sort of thing which convinced me — that, and the vista to be had across the hills. I stood at one place, below and around me were the dark trees, and across the valley there arose still another hill, its slope rounded in the sunlight, its age-old rocks serene and safe. Yes, I would live in Two Bridges. If things worked out well, I would stay there. Besides the big homes, there were vacation houses, A-frames and others, down along the river, some weathered cottages built on stilts against flooding. There was David Masters' handsome windowed house cantilevered out over the river, its open deck inviting me to bask there in the sun even before I knew there was such a person as David Masters. And there were, in at least three places, clusters of tents, jerrybuilt shacks which young people had assembled and called communes. Some of these people were students at the small college twenty-five miles away, some of them planted gardens, fished and told all who would listen that they were living "back to nature." As they were.

Two Bridges had old brick sidewalks and thick hedges trimmed to a razor sharpness. The large homes had gazebos smothered in wisteria vines or rambler roses. In April, iris bloomed magnificently everywhere. But best of all were the trees. Big trees, small trees, hardwooods, flowering trees — trees and trees and *trees!* I fell in love with the town because of the trees, and because of the house that was to be mine.

This would do, I told my friends who had brought me to look at Two Bridges. I would be close enough to the city and the specialist there. There was a doctor in Two Bridges. The town had no hospital, but there was a nursing home, a retirement home, which the doctor attended.

In my innocence I thought that would serve. Talking to the townspeople in a restaurant and at the filling station, the doctor seemed to be popular.

I found him to be a likable, lively young man, interested in my case, in my problems, and charming about everything. I counted myself a judge of men, and I liked Roger Collier.

I remember that one of my friends asked about amusements. What would I do to fill the time in a place like Two Bridges? Now, I have to think back to that question put to me so long ago, such short months ago, and ask it again — because there were amusements.

Not the theater, nor concerts, not the great stadiums or museums.

But there was time to read books, to take walks, to savor peace. There was time to watch the boats go up and down the river — the barges, the government boats, the canoes, the houseboats, some of them luxurious, some utilitarian homes for a fisherman and his family. There were the john boats in which guides escorted the outland fishermen who sought our sort of amusements.

Quarter horses were raised in the district — bred, raced, bought and sold, displayed at shows, sometimes a great distance away. These horses made pretty pictures in their fenced pastures.

There was a nine-hole golf course, and some tennis courts. The householders made an amusement — a passion, really! — of their lawns. The talk of zoysia was the one thing that could supersede gossip at almost any gathering. The people played bridge knowingly, skillfully, but with indulgence for the duffers, too. There were Friday night dinner groups of friends who met at the hotel or in the different homes.

For the kids, there were school events, and always the river, water skiing, fishing, as well as the communes with guitar music, and work in the organic vegetable gardens.

There was one of these communes — six young girls lived together in a frame house down the hill from me, and I enjoyed them. Invited to do so, I visited them. They had a ridiculous old piano, and it was on that yellow keyboard that I made one of my first tries at playing. A miserable performance, but I was thrilled about it. It was fun to be with these young folk.

I was even invited to come and live in their

18

house. But my answer had to be a hesitant "I'm afraid not," followed with the confession that I was a coward.

I quickly made friends and was introduced to other amusements. For one group, jogging was a stern pastime. A dozen people — ages varying from twenty to sixty — went past my house every evening, rain or shine. Single joggers were to be seen in the morning mist or late in the evening. A neighbor who was a coach at the high school always waved to me as he passed.

And of course there were the Langans, who proved to be amusing, if by amusement you mean a frequent subject of thought and consideration, or time spent with them or avoiding them. I first encountered Mrs. Langan in the beauty parlor; she was a talkative woman, anxious that I be informed as to her family's wealth and influence in the community. Within a week or two, I realized helplessly that Mrs. Langan was always to speak of me as "poor Lissa."

I soon found that Two Bridges could provide an occasional cocktail party, sometimes a dinner. These social events were nicely done, with white-coated waiters, flowers, silver and crystal, though they could be casual affairs of cushions on the floor, spaghetti kept hot on a warmer, and gay talk. In both cases, sometimes the parties were fun. Sometimes . . .

The first big party to which I was invited was called a cocktail buffet. I tried to refuse the invitation extended to me by Mrs. Langan over the telephone. I said that I was one of those supernumerary women-alone; no party needed us. But she overrode me. Tee was to be my escort, she announced. That was all arranged. I had not met Tee, though his garrulous mother had made me well acquainted with her family. Her husband, who had made a fortune in feed mills and storage facilities for grain throughout that part of the state. Supposedly retired, he still kept a lively interest in the business. Mrs. Langan, like her husband, was a small person, abounding with energy. Both of them were talkative. There was a daughter Diane, mother of three small children. And there was Tee — Leroy T. Langan, Jr. He was to escort me to the party at the Langans' home.

I found the party to be a very large affair, with the living rooms so crowded with guests that the din of voices became intolerable. I found Tee to be a swarthy young man, perhaps thirty-five, who was determined to impress me. He plied me with small glasses half filled with ice and the liquor of my choice, or stemmed glasses of champagne.

He talked about music, and once during the evening he demonstrated his own musical ability by joining the small orchestra and playing the trumpet. Well enough.

The buffet dinner was spread in the dining room, a lavish display of sliced ham — "raised on our farm" — sliced turkey, salads, vegetables, relishes —

Small tables were produced, and folding chairs. There still was the noise — I think we talked of music. Tee, I discovered, was not a drinker. But, Lord save us, he was dull! For the first time, for a rare time, I made use of my recent invalidism and asked to be allowed to leave early.

Tee escorted me, and at my front door he kissed me, promising to see me again, and often.

Not if I could help it, I determined. Not if I could get into my front hall and manage to keep him out!

His mother always spoke of Tee as a virile man. "I don't ever expect him to marry; so many girls and women are crazy about him."

Not me. I found him a pompous fellow, and a deadly bore. I would have condemned Two Bridges for Tee if I had not met other pompous bores and attended other deadly parties in other and, supposedly, more sophisticated places. There, the trick had been to refuse to go to such affairs. I could also use that device in the Ozarks.

However, many of the parties were not boring. Many were fun, and stimulating. I well remember the first barbecue. In Two Bridges society, barbecues were as ritual as church attendance. And, in fact, the first one I went to was given by a retired bishop.

He lived in a big, converted barn almost on top of a mountain. He did amusing writing on a variety of subjects — cooking being one of them — and an invitation to one of his barbecues was never refused. One did not become bored at the Bishop's parties, though one certainly did eat too much. His salads! His spit-roasted meats — a pork shoulder basted with sweet-sour sauce, Cornish hens crackling brown — served with rich, purple-grape wine he had made himself.

Well, enough about our amusements. Perhaps the assortment sounds dull; but thinking about their variety and their appeal, I asked myself: we who call ourselves city folk, what more do we have in the way of amusement and companionship? Do we have as much?

★ ★ ★

Before the plane accident, before that incredible night of terror . . . "Take off your shoes, put the pillow on our your lap, bend forward and grasp your ankles . . ." the sickening lurch and drop of the helpless plane — the noises of ripping metal, the darkness that was terrifying, the explosion of light that was not to be borne — the prayer for an end to the horror, well knowing what such an end could mean . . .

The moments of stunned unconsciousness and the awakening to cold, to some movement about me, to the groans of those who were alive but hurt — darkness did not let me see — the onset of pain — *I* was hurt! And I could not move! *I could not move!*

Rescue came, of course. And I am alive, where many are not. And I should be able to forget the terror of that night. I have been advised to put it out of my mind. But then I have also been advised to face the memory, to think the thing through, the whole bit, how cold I was, how my arm hurt and became numb, how I wanted to lean my head on something firm, then the pain in my shoulder might go away. I have been advised only to look and think forward. To build my life anew.

One can do all these things. But one

cannot do just one of them. So I remember how things were before the plane accident.

And before it, as young as I was, I had often considered giving up the complications of public life, the constant travel, the pressures that were put upon me to please the audience, to please the critics, to please musicians greater than myself. The work, the long, relentless hours of practice. The sketchy sort of home life possible for me. An apartment, a suite in some hotel where I was "resting." A house rented for two months in Florida. The interviews wherever I went, the record sessions. The restricted and carefully supervised social life I knew. The sort of clothes I must select, have fitted, wear and discard — both in concert and while I "relaxed" — always subject to public view. Even the friends I made must be a matter of thought and consideration; impulsive liking could not be the deciding factor. I must constantly establish the contacts that were essential to my career. Oh, the many, many things that had to be considered and which, I told myself before the accident, I was ready to abandon. I made plans. I would give up my career. I would find an occupation. Perhaps I could serve as a companion for a retired composer, with peace and quiet the chief inducement for my choice.

So I would dream. Wistfully.

And then, when I was thirty, perhaps at the peak of my attainment of success, fate took me at my unspoken word, and I found myself set down into such peaceful surroundings as I had dreamed about. There was not even a piano in my new home; all was to be calm, all was to be peaceful, without pressures or striving.

And what did I find in this Utopia? More excitement, including love — I had had no time for that before! — than I had ever known out "in the world."

When I was considered to be healed of my injury, the bones patched and returned to their former shape, the flesh grafted and sewn and restored to what it should seem to be, when only convalescence and recuperation lay before me — not invalidism, I was cautioned — I was to select some quiet place in which to live. There I would need to recover muscle tone and nerve tone, as well as the use of my arm. Such a place must have an available doctor. And it was determined, by Dr. Kohl, that Two Bridges did have such a doctor, a graduate of a good medical school where his own record had been excellent. This man already owned the apparatus which would be needed for my care and treatment, or he would make room for, and learn to operate, the gadgets which the specialist would recommend and which I would buy.

We were all reassured when Dr. Collier agreed to care for me, but defended his right to purchase and keep any apparatus that would be required. This position made him sound good.

Dr. Collier. Roger. Called Raj . . .

That pleasant young man with the deep and comforting voice, the warmly intent eyes. Not an excessively handsome man, though surely his thick brown hair and his smile were attractive. He had a charming Swiss-chalet office building tucked into the side of one of the many hills that marked Two Bridges. There was an open fireplace in the waiting room, the windows were diamond-paned.

Raj and his mother, a tall, handsome woman of sixty, and his really beautiful wife Sarah — Sally — lived close to the house which was to become my home. Raj was the only doctor in Two Bridges, but the town was lucky. One doctor for six thousand people was a better average than was known across the country as a whole. We were a rural community, and we were really fortunate to have a well-trained young doctor all to ourselves.

Just about the first thing I did on coming to live in Two Bridges was to make an appointment to see the doctor. "Yes, of course, Miss Bartels, come this afternoon — oh, about three." That was Mae Ward, the nurse-receptionist, whom I was to come to know very well — a brusque, businesslike woman who usually had too much to do.

I had determined where the doctor's office was, and I walked down the hill to it that spring afternoon pleased with the picture which the building made. Tall trees towered above it, there were tulips as bright as a patchwork quilt along the walk to the door.

That door opened into a hall-like place where there was a desk, filing cabinets, a chair against the wall. To the right was the patients' waiting room and the fireplace I have mentioned, sparkling windows and comfortable chairs, magazines on a table.

"Doc's held up," one of the women in the room said to me. "Emergency."

I smiled at her, selected a magazine and sat down.

"Ward's helpin' him," the woman continued. "That's the nurse."

"They're putting a cast on somebody," said the second patient.

"Resorter," added the first one. A certain tone, I would learn, was reserved for the non-natives of Two Bridges.

I nodded and opened the magazine. I could wait, certainly. I even speculated a little as to the injury to the resorter. "Fell down the hill," I finally concluded, pushing up my dark glasses.

"That's a pretty shade o' hair you got," said my companion.

I looked up. "Thank you."

"I don't suppose you'd tell a person . . ."

At first I did not understand. Then — "Oh, it's my own," I said.

"G'wan!"

"I'm afraid it is," I insisted. And I was glad when the nurse came to the desk in the foyer. "You're Miss Bartels," she called to me. "The doctor will get to you pretty soon," she assured me.

The two waiting women went in, and must have left by a rear door, because I didn't see them again. Then the doctor himself came out to fetch me. He smiled at me, and went to the desk to talk softly to Mrs. Ward. She nodded, rose, and went off into the depth of the building.

The doctor then gave his full attention to me. I had already decided that I liked his friendly face, his size — strong-seeming and muscular. At that stage, anyone with a strong, well body was enviably handsome to me.

The doctor wore a white jacket, and he asked me to come back to his office. "We'll get acquainted today," he said amiably. "And I'll show you around. We have a patient in the treatment room." He seated me in the chair facing his desk, and sat down in his own chair. A glance about the room showed it to be a comfortable place, creamy-colored walls, some photographs, some certificates or diplomas, framed and hung. The doctor's desk was a large one, the top bare except for a framed photograph of a dark-haired woman and a row of books between book ends that were crystal in the shape of a leaping fish.

The doctor was telling me about the patient "which held you up," he said. "She is a guest on a houseboat tied up downriver. Two weeks ago she broke her arm, and the problem today was the cast which was so tight that her fingers were blue. This was done in —" he hesitated — "by a city doctor four hundred miles from here," he continued. "I removed the cast and put on a looser one, but she already has partial paralysis in that arm."

"Oh, dear," I murmured, rubbing my own injured arm.

"You seem to be having good medical care," he reassured me. "While this patient —"

"You think the tight cast caused the paralysis?" I asked.

"I think it could have. And perhaps I should have told the poor woman that it had. Then she could have taken on from there."

"You mean a lawsuit?"

Dr. Collier looked rueful. "Oh, a disclosure of possible cause shouldn't in any way seem to be an endorsement of legal action. The trouble is, if one says anything to bring such action to mind, the patient gets agitated. . . ."

"Why not?"

He laughed. "Why not, indeed. But then it's up to me to say something like 'I think your previous doctor must have used his best judgment at the time he put on that cast.' We fellows have to walk a thin line between saying 'Don't sue' and castigating the other fellow."

"So you don't say anything."

"Well, even a raised eyebrow is often enough to tip a patient off that something wrong has been done. I do believe I said the first cast was too tight. But it's not my place to make legal judgments. I certainly don't want those lawyer fellows coming around making diagnoses for me."

He smiled at me. "Now! Let's take a look

at your arm and shoulder."

"And I'll watch for a raised eyebrow," I told him.

"You do that." He lifted his voice and called "Ward!" very loudly.

The nurse came at once, took me to the examining room, set me up on the end of the table and helped me take off my blouse. She was brusque, gentle-handed, and humorous.

"I hear you fell out of an airplane," she told me.

"Oh . . ." Then I laughed. "For all I know, I did," I agreed.

Dr. Collier came back, and with firm, gentle fingers, he examined my injured shoulder and arm. He had been sent copies of my records and consulted them as he examined me. Dr. Kohl had suggested the course of treatments, and he said he was going to follow that procedure.

"But the exercise bit is going to be your department," he told me.

"Yes, I know. I am both fearful about using my arm and lazy . . ."

"Dear me. Then we'll have to prescribe for that!"

I was liking my latest doctor as I had not liked some of the other individuals whom I had dealt with. Good doctors, but with personalities that did not appeal. Roger Collier was young — within five years of my own age, I decided. He seemed assured and knowledgeable, and his manner was solicitous, interested. Yes, I liked him.

He helped me put my blouse on and suggested that I use the fingers of the injured hand to fasten the cuff. I tried. Then, smiling, he did the job himself. "This all goes on your bill," he assured me.

"I've been told that I'll regain use of my hand," I said, watching his face.

"Oh, you will," he said quickly — confidently. "Now! Let's make a tour of the Collier Medical Center."

He was being whimsical about his "office building," but I found it complete and well equipped, comfortable and attractive. We drank a cup of coffee in what he called the hideaway lounge, a small room with comfortable furniture, a small TV, and magazines. Here, I judged, he and Mrs. Ward could retreat for a time of relaxation. I could imagine his office setup duplicated and occupying the whole floor of a tall glass and steel structure in the city — such medical setups as I had visited for various reasons since my injury. Everything seemed to be in this office; there were two examining rooms, a laboratory, the treatment room — Raj called it the chamber of horrors — where there was everything from the EKG recorder to the whirlpool bath and various diathermy and exercise apparatus which I would come to consider as my personal property. There was even a small X-ray machine which looked modern and correct to me. He spoke of his nurse-technician, an R.N. whose husband was a government engineer stationed at this point of the river. That was why she was available in Two Bridges. His lab and X-ray technician, he told me, was a science teacher at the local high school who gave the doctor several hours, most days, and was on call at other times.

Back in his office, the doctor gathered all the plates and record transcripts together. "I'll study them many times," he assured me.

I said something about his having a well-equipped office.

"Yes, I do," he agreed. "The thing — the main thing — I don't have is — are — other doctors to consult with. But that will come. One of these days in the not-too-distant future, we'll have a clinic, and even a hospital. I plan to build one, you know. It will serve this general district. There is a small hospital at Burton, but that is twenty-five miles away. We need something right here."

I thought he intended to start building his hospital within weeks. It was much later that I discovered that Raj would often talk about his hospital project, and sound just as enthusiastic and realistic each time. But at no time had he ever achieved anything concrete in the way of a hospital or a clinic.

We drank our coffee and he talked about the work he did in the office he had. "The work we have to do," he amended. "It's only a cottage office," he reminded me. "But here I have to take out tonsils, set bones. I can deliver a baby, and occasionally do. I perform many sorts of minor surgical things — d and c's, remove a hematoma . . ."

And he also did abortions, illegally, I was later to learn.

But even when I began to hear tales about Raj, I still liked him. That first day, I liked him very much, and on going home, I lectured myself about the silliness of a woman who fell for her doctor. I knew better than to do such a thing!

But he was a friendly person, and I felt that he was really interested in the course of therapy which had been aligned for me. He set up schedules for me; there was to be the whirlpool, the diathermy, even ultra-sound. I was to see him at fixed intervals. He got a large sheet of paper and concentrated on this plan of treatment. It all could be done in the office, even the exercises, at least at first. He wanted to be sure I was doing the right ones, and correctly. He spoke of the need to keep my whole body in balance. Yes, he would supervise me, or supervise those who assisted me.

"No, no!" he assured me. "You won't be in our way! Of course not!"

He was a delightful man, warm, and I believed him when he said, "We'll take good care of you."

Since I have made side remarks, not so complimentary, I will say, too, that that promise was one which Raj Collier made and scrupulously kept.

His first gift to me, and a continuing one, was the feeling of security, without which I could not have known the life I was to know in Two Bridges.

As it was, I could entirely enjoy my new home — a really, lovely house, low to the ground, built of soft red brick, ivy-grown, its red-tile roof spangled with the small leaves and the shade from the tall trees which towered above it. The specialists in New York and in St. Louis had advised me to get a home, preferably not an apartment, and to do my own work in it, to take care of myself, and thus acquire both strength and confidence in a place where any failures would not be public or humiliating.

I had a cleaning woman who came in once a week and did what I called "swamp me out," though as time passed I learned to pick up things, to sweep and dust, wash dishes. I had a boy for the yard work, though I supervised him and, later, began to do some work myself. Beyond their expert, strong help, I did my own housework, thanking the grandmother who had taught me what to do and how to do. I knew what a proper home should be. So I swept and dusted, made the bed — with one arm that is not easy. I planned balanced meals, shopped for food, and cooked. I did the dish washing, and I even did the ironing. Did you ever try to fold a sheet and iron it with one hand? You use the other one if you possibly can!

But the result was that I had my pretty home, and I came to love it with a satisfaction I had used to know in accomplishing a sparkling arpeggio or a satisfying running bass.

At the beginning, I became acquainted with, and acclimated to, the town largely through Denny — Dennis Marion — the eighteen-year-old boy who cut my grass in the summer, raked leaves in November, shoveled snow, sometimes, in the winter. Dennis was a "nice" boy. I liked having him around, and I liked the way he let me use my arm, clumsily, to help him. He would see me pick up a basket of grass clippings and leaves, holding it grimly with my weak hand as well as the strong one, his eyes would be concerned, but he accepted the fact that I must do these things without help, and certainly without skill. He would bring an extra pair of clippers and say, "How about helping me with these borders, Miss Lissa? I have a heavy date and I want to get through." He held the clippers toward me, and his smiling eyes forbade me to take them in my left hand. "You're no southpaw," he would tell me.

Actually, naturally, I was not, though in a year's time I had learned to use my left hand.

I was no help with the clippers, not that first time. I could scarcely bend my fingers around the handles, and the pressure I exerted was negligible, but I obediently crawled around the edge of the grass, with Denny watching me and talking to me.

At first, he talked about himself. He wanted, most in life, he said, to play basketball. Since he was only five feet ten, that was an impossible dream. His next passion was cars. He urged me to buy a car.

"I'm not checked out to drive, Denny," I told him.

"Man, I'll drive for you!"

"I'll bet you would."

"Lots-a great ladies have chauffeurs."

I laughed at this bold flattery. "Not this great lady," I assured him. "I can also imagine the car you think I should buy."

He grinned and went to move the hose spray. He was working, I knew, to buy his own car, though his father made him spend some of the money he earned on clothes. "He argues that if I don't have time to cut the grass and stuff at home, he doesn't have the time to buy me sweaters and Levis."

"I think that's right, Denny," I told him.

"Yeah, it's right, I guess. But maybe I wish he wouldn't be that kind of father."

"He's good to you. You told me that he lets you drive his car."

"Yeah. I get it one night, on weekends. But it's a square car, Miss Lissa, and he won't let me do one thing to soup it up."

"I think that's right, too. He probably doesn't want the back of his head jerked off on a quick start."

Denny laughed at the picture. I had met Denny's father; he and his son were exactly alike — swarthy men, of stocky build. Denny wore his black hair cut thick and full atop his head, down to his collar in the back. Mr. Marion clung to a crew cut.

Denny talked about me. He'd heard that I was the Alicia Bartels who played the piano and made records.

"Not any more, Denny."

"That's too bad. You had a thing going."

"Yes, I did."

"I played some of your stuff at the record store. It was sweet."

"You didn't like it."

"I realize you knew your ivories, but there wasn't much jive, you know?"

"I played it the way the man wrote it."

"Yeah. That's what I mean."

I liked Denny. I liked talking to him, about himself, or about me, about the town. He was a pleasant person to have around, though he was not always dependable. He could cut half the lawn and trim it neatly. Then he could fail to show up to do the other half for as much as a week. This irritated my friends for me, and some of them suggested that there were other yard boys.

"But not as good talkers," I argued.

Only through Denny and his talk could I have so quickly become informed about Two Bridges and the people who lived there.

From his math teacher to the Rector of the church, from Dr. Collier to the man who ran the fruit store, I got to know them all, and intimately, quickly. Tee Langan, the Bishop who lived in a barn — Denny knew them all.

It was through Denny that I came to "know" and then to meet Clare and the other girls who lived in the commune down the hill from me.

Clare was not Denny's girl, he assured me, though he sure wished she was. "I can't afford a chick like that," he said. "She earns her own bread, you know, and that makes things tough for a school kid."

"But if she likes you, Denny . . ."

"Oh, she likes me. We have dates when I can afford it. But — well, some guy with his own income, or a fellow like Mike Singley — he's on a basketball scholarship, you know. And he's due for the big time."

So that was the basketball hang-up.

"Clare doesn't seem to be the kind of girl . . ."

"Who considers a guy's income? Aw, Miss Lissa, you dames all consider that!"

"Well, I can't judge this Clare without so much as ever seeing her."

"I'll take you down to meet her."

"Bring her up here, maybe?"

"Okay. I've told her about you."

That I had played "sweet" music, no doubt, that I had some pretty stodgy tastes and ideas . . .

But he did bring Clare up to see me. Together they walked up the hill one summer evening; there were clouds in the northern sky. We would probably have rain. But I was enjoying the sunset when they came up the walk.

Clare, I decided at once, was a bit older than Denny. Yes, she had graduated from high school a year before. She was a very pretty girl with a madonnalike, serene face and shining black hair which she wore long and straight; it made a thick cape upon her shoulders and framed her face as an oval of loveliness. I was interested in the commune where she lived and in the other girls who shared the home. Three girls had regular jobs, two worked by the hour, one at a gift shop, one did housework. Clare herself worked part-time as a secretary to Mr. Masters.

So it was partially through Clare that I came to know David — a very, very big thing in my life.

I lived up the hill from the girls' commune, a house that looked as if a child's blocks had been erratically piled together,

41

leaving openings here and there for doors and windows. The roof sloped steeply on one side, and was almost flat on the other. The girls had painted the front door a bright orange, and where they had no curtains, one of them had painted bright abstracts upon the glass of the windows. Their small lawn was devoted to a vegetable garden which alternately flourished or succumbed to weeds. The furnishings of the house had been acquired in various ways. "What's left over from rummage sales," Denny explained to me. For a long time I could not decide if these girls were foolish or brave to live as they did. With one exception, each had an ordered parental home, and three had the opportunity for an education, to weigh against their sometime hardships in the commune.

I came to know the girls by watching them from afar, by encouraging Denny to talk about them, and gradually by accepting their invitations to come down or to stop in.

"We've cooked up a mountain of beans, Lissa," they would tell me.

So I would take a cake or some cheese down and eat supper with the girls, demanding my right to help clean up afterward. They encouraged me to talk about the life I had used to lead, the people I had known, the places I had seen. The girls were planning — or hoping — to spend the summer after next in Europe — hostel travel. I could tell them about things to see, food — but not, I confessed, about the practical things they wanted to know — cheap lodgings, the safety of sleeping bag and hitchhiking travel.

"You'd have fun," I admitted. "But I wouldn't have the courage to do it."

"Not with your arm," Clare consoled me.

"Oh," I protested, "I'm braver with this arm than I ever was wrapped in cotton wool the way I used to be when I traveled."

Somebody asked what cotton wool actually was.

The commune was below me, and up the hill, above me, was the Bridell-Collier home, seeming to rise from the low roof of my own dwelling. This was a large, square, wooden house, old-fashioned, complete with tower rooms, deeply sloping roofs, and Victorian gingerbread. I was fascinated by the sight of it and my imaginings of what the inside of such a house might be.

My curiosity was due to be satisfied, because I met Sally Collier very soon, and within a few days I also met her mother-in-law, who was "Mrs. Collier," of course, but who was always spoken of and known as Mary Bridell in the town where she had been born sixty years before.

I first met each of them over the hedge, and later Mary came to call formally upon me. Sarah, or Sally, I saw frequently at her husband's office. She seemed to help out there, kept the books, things like that.

The two women made me feel at home in my own house, much in the same way as Raj had made me feel secure in his office.

All three Colliers said that I would soon become a part of the town, and soon, indeed, I did.

Deciding upon Two Bridges as the town where I would live and the house which I would occupy was a two-pronged undertaking. Had I not liked the town when I saw it, I would not have signed the lease on the house which had been secured for me through one of those agencies that make it their business to find such things, whether it be a castle on the Rhine or in Scotland, a chateau in France, or a flat in London.

Finding a house in an Ozark town where there was a competent doctor, I suppose, was not too difficult.

So, in beautiful Two Bridges, there was my lovely home, all furnished and ready. On my part, I qualified for occupancy. I would take care of things, I would keep the house in repair, and replace any breakage. I had no children.

The home had been that of a woman whose husband, a long-time invalid, had recently died. For a time she wanted to travel, and she would, perhaps, decide to live elsewhere. So I could use her home, and come to cherish it. It was an entirely modern house, with every modern gadget and convenience known to electricity and plumbing. It was well built and was furnished with many family antiques, chairs, sofa, tables and lamps. Beautiful old china plates — Dresden, French and English — were hung on the walls, along with family portraits, some of them primitives in which I rejoiced — and loved.

In the dining room there was a Karastan rug, glowing, beautiful. In the library was gray-brown shag carpeting. The rest of the rooms were wall-to-wall carpeted in a glowing dark red, with a pink and blue flowered design which would have delighted my grandmother, a great believer in Axminster or Wilton carpets.

This was to be my home, Chippendale furniture, a Stubbs painting over a fireplace, and good neighbors. The Colliers above me, the commune girls below me, both house-holds loyal and watchful. Next door lived the high school coach and his family, especially the five-year-old who came to visit me. "I'm Jimmie next door," he announced himself. "Do you know Jimmie behind? He has red hair." And did I also know Jimmie who lived across the street? "But he's old." Jimmie across the street was twenty-five.

My friends from what I was soon considering as the "other world" had helped me determine the place I would live and the doctor who would care for me. And though I had heard of him through Clare, they also sent David Masters to see me as an attorney.

One afternoon he presented himself on my doorstep, that handsome, reserved man in his brown flannel — or tweed? — or cashmere? — suit, his quiet face and fine dark eyes. He told me who he was, and presented his card. He mentioned my friends in the East. . . .

And the first thing I said to David was: "But I don't expect to need an attorney!"

He laughed and said he hoped I was right. But since my friends had introduced us, could he come in anyway?

Of course he did come in, and in the half hour he stayed, I found the man fascinating.

Not in the way I found Raj charming, but as a reserved, quiet man whom I wanted to like me.

We talked — about music, and the river. He told me that he was attorney for the lead mining industries that flourished in our part of the state, he had a home in Two Bridges as well as an office and an apartment in St. Louis. I mentioned that I had met Clare.

"She's a nice girl. I am hoping that she can learn to spell."

I said I had seen his house; the deck must be great for sun-bathing. He agreed that it was, winter and summer.

"Do the winters get rough here?"

"They can, and the floods in the spring. I welcome them if they close the roads and I can't get back to the city."

"But if they keep you from getting here?"

"Oh, that's different. Then I heatedly deplore the weather."

He departed with my saying shyly that I was sorry I had said I didn't expect to need him.

"That's all right," he replied. "I'll be around anyway."

It was, really, only a few days after my arrival in Two Bridges that Mary Bridell came to call upon me, and rather formally, at that. Mary is a tall woman, not pretty in any

47

sense, but with so much dignity, so much strength in her face, that one had to call her handsome. That afternoon she wore a well-tailored dress of creamy linen, a white hat upon her head, white gloves — and she laid an engraved calling card on the table in the foyer.

I offered her tea, and she accepted. I had just that morning selected china and silver, put them upon a small tray, in readiness for just such callers. It was difficult for me to pour boiling water into a teapot and to carry the tray into the living room, though I managed it without mishap. I poured the tea with my left hand and carried the cup and napkin in that hand to my guest. I hoped she had not detected that I was trembling.

I took my own cup and sat back, shaking with relief.

Meanwhile, Mrs. Collier had made small talk, telling me about the woman who owned my home, with an anecdote or two about various items such as the portrait of the owner's grandmother.

"She was a mean person; once she got tired of dusting and caring for the vases, pictures and knickknacks. She had them all packed into boxes and put into the basement. Then anyone could dust the room with a sweep of a cheesecloth rag."

"I'm glad someone rescued the pretties," I said.

"Yes. A house should not look like a corner of a furniture store. Miss Bartels, I understand you are a pianist."

"Oh . . ." I could feel the color pouring into my face.

"If you're as good as they say, Two Bridges could use you." She didn't identify "they." "We don't have any good musicians here. The young people learn to do two chords on the guitar, and they think that's music. We both know it isn't. But if you are a musician, you'd be such a help on programs, or you could give programs on your own. Do you play the organ, Miss Bartels?"

I sighed and shook my head. "Please call me Lissa," I urged. "I . . ."

"I saw you in church Sunday, and as you could tell, we badly need an organist. Have you met the Bishop?"

At that time, I had not. So Mary Bridell told me at length about him. "He had to retire when he was seventy, and usually those people, if they survive at all, go about helping out where they can. But not our Bishop. He comes to service — he won't even wear a collar — but beyond that he tinkers about up on his mountain. He does some writing, and he also does what he calls farming. If he didn't have a pension, he would starve to death, though Raj says he raises fine tobacco. What good is that, I ask you, now that cigarettes have become a dirty word? Well — what was I talking about?"

"You were talking about my playing the organ," I said, laughing.

"Oh, yes. Would you?"

"I'm afraid not, Mrs. Collier. Perhaps your son should have told you why I am living in Two Bridges."

"If you are a patient, he wouldn't tell me one thing. That's an ethic he keeps to the letter!"

"Yes. Well, you see . . ." So, as swiftly as I could, and as simply, I told her about my shoulder and arm.

She was shocked. She called the whole situation a tragedy. I was so young . . . To have that sort of talent — and training, she supposed — then to have it all taken away. Yes, it was a tragedy.

"It was," I agreed.

"I'd rather have died."

"Oh, no, you wouldn't, Mrs. Collier!" I assured her. "You're too full of life yourself. You'd fight like a tiger if . . ."

"Did you fight?"

"I suppose I did. I suppose I still am fighting, though more like a kitten than a tiger.

And I hope to play the piano again sometime. Though for now . . ."

Mrs. Collier looked about the room. "Lydia Bell never did own a piano," she said. "But I have one up at our house. It's a square, and old, but it is a good piano. You can use it to practice on whenever you want. Just come up the hill — and come on in. Whether I'm at home or not. You'd be welcome."

"Well, thank you very much, Mrs. Collier. And I'll probably accept your kind offer when I am able. Just now . . ." I explained about the doctor, and the treatments, the exercises, speaking enthusiastically about the way Raj had co-operated with the specialists, about his warm understanding of my problems. "He's made me feel sure that, with time, I'll overcome this handicap."

This pleased the doctor's mother. And she talked happily, frankly, about her son. She was a forceful person, this tall Mary Bridell, and bluntly honest in all she said. I could tell that she was very proud of her only son. She admitted that he had faults. For one thing, she supposed he drank a bit more than he should. Though men did. . . . But, at least, since he drank, he didn't do like Tee Langan, who was teetotal when his parents were present, and drank everything in sight when they were not.

51

"I have met Tee Langan," I murmured.

"Of course you have. He's a terrible bore, isn't he? All the Langans are terrible bores."

I giggled. They were.

"Raj isn't a bore, ever, and I suppose that's commendable. But about some things, he's lazy."

"Oh, now, Mrs. Collier! I have found Dr. Collier interested in me — attentive — and very, very nice."

"Oh, yes," said my visitor, leaning forward to set her cup and saucer on the table. "Raj is nice," she agreed. "Charming, in fact. He began that when he was still in his bassinet. And I'll agree that he's not dumb. He graduated with honors, Lissa, both from college and from medical school. But do you know? He could have gone far in his profession if it weren't for that laziness I mentioned. But, no, sir! The minute he got his M.D., he came back here to Two Bridges — *Two Bridges!* — and started in practice. He never did an internship, let alone the rest of it that's supposed to take several years. This state allows medical school graduates to practice without an internship, and that's what Raj did. He came back here right away. Because of me, he said."

"Did it please you?" I asked, curious only. I was in no position to judge a man for doing as Raj had done.

"Oh," said Raj's mother. "Of course I was glad to have him here. I am a widow, and he's my only child. My only family, really. So I built and equipped an office for him, the way he wanted it. The town needed a doctor. The only other one we had was a hundred and six — anyway, he was doddering. He's died since Raj came. But I couldn't tell you if I really was pleased to have Raj do the way he did about not taking the training other doctors take, and which is supposed to be necessary. That could have been a mistake. Patients accepted Raj — but that's partly, at least, because they had no choice. I don't entirely blame my son. The greatest mistake probably was that there was money available. My husband's business was sold to a corporation, Raj had some money of his own, and I had a lot of it to spend on what I thought would please my son. I've come to believe that, past the age of twenty-one, sons do better on their own."

She sounded sad, and I was glad when she changed the conversation and soon took her leave. But of course the things she had said and suggested stayed with me. I thought about them.

Beyond listening to him, I did not really

encourage Denny to talk to me about these new friends of mine. But he did talk — oh, about all sorts of things. This could include information as to where home-grown strawberries were available. "I'll pick you some!" he offered. "If you had a car, I could drive you out there to get them."

When I repeated that I didn't believe I needed a car, he said that some of my friends would drive me.

Maybe even the Doc. "He gets around the whole neighborhood, you know."

"Does he make house calls? Out in the country?" I asked the boy.

"Well, not exactly house calls. I mean, say you get sick with something and have to stay in bed, he doesn't come around every day or so and hold your hand."

"You haven't been sick much, have you, Denny?"

"Gee, no. Not doctor-sick. I catch cold, and last year I got mono — that threw Mom for a loop."

"What's mono?"

"Mononucleosis. You get it from kissing the girls."

"Why, Denny!"

He grinned at me and went on raking the grass clippings. "Doc does quite a bit of hunting and fishing," he continued his dis-

54

course. "He'd probably take you to the strawberry people."

What did that have to do with hunting? "I don't really need that many strawberries, Denny."

"No, I guess not. But Doc's mother — Miss Mary Bridell — she drives a car, and I just know she goes after strawberries. Lettuce, beans — all the ladies get that kind of stuff out in the country."

"Why do people call her Miss Mary Bridell?"

"Gosh, I don't know. She's Mrs. Collier all right, but she lives in the Bridell house, and the Bridells used just about to own and run Two Bridges."

I'd heard that they did. "Has her husband . . . ?"

"He's been dead since I was just a little kid."

Ten years, maybe. The Bridells had long been people of substance, though not extraordinarily rich. I had heard that Mary Bridell had met her husband-to-be when she was a student at a girls' college. He was an older man, twenty years older, and already eminently successful in the aircraft industry. He had married Mary Bridell, and for the time he lived, the Colliers used the Two Bridges house as their summer home.

When he had died suddenly of a heart attack, Mary and her son had returned to live in the big house. Their stock in the Collier industries had become enormously valuable during the years of burgeoning air travel and plane manufacture.

"Mr. Masters could tell you all about Miss Mary's husband," said Denny.

Mr. Masters already had told me about the Collier family, the things I knew.

"I liked Mr. Masters," I told the yard boy.

He sat back on his heels. I had asked him to scrabble leaves and trash out from under the boxwood hedges. "He's supposed to be a really swell guy," Denny told me.

"Isn't he?"

"I don't know. Nobody knows him too much. He works for the lead company — if lawyers work?" He looked up questioningly.

"Anybody who can do what I can't do, works," I assured Denny.

He grinned. "Like raking under the hedge? Well, yes, I guess that's work."

"Mr. Masters has an office in St. Louis," Denny continued. "And he has one room at his house here fixed up like an office. Down on the ground, that is. His house is built on levels. Well, you can walk right into his office from the ground one. I know because Clare works there when he needs her. He keeps his boat on that level of his house, too. And his car."

"He is a very attractive man," I said.

"I guess. He's older, of course. Older'n Doc."

I looked up. "Not much. But what difference does that make?"

"Only that the dames, and the chicks, they go for Masters, and I can't figure why."

I could have told him.

"He don't fall for them," said Denny. "You can't hardly get Mr. Masters to go to a party or anything. He sometimes has somebody at his house — not a party. Just one or two people. He's friendly but he doesn't warm up, if you know what I mean."

I thought I did. He didn't have Raj Collier's outgoing charm. He didn't have Tee Langan's aggressive virility. David Masters was his own man, and he planned to live his own life as he wanted it lived.

"He and Bish are friends," Denny told me.

"The Bishop?"

"Yeah. He's an oddball, too. Looks like a big kewpie doll, and makes wine and stuff. Lives in a barn."

I must, I decided, get to know the Bishop. I hoped, in that way or somehow, I would get to know David Masters, too.

Chapter Two

It was by these measures that I learned about my new home. About the neighbors, and my new friends. I have since decided that it was a good thing that I found these people so interesting. My curiosity about them and their lives kept me from thinking too much about my own life. I did the things I was supposed to do mainly because I wanted to see more of the folk, to find out more about them.

They were interesting people, though perhaps almost any tightly knit community could turn up groups just as interesting. Perhaps not. . . .

For one thing, my new friends were stationary. In my past life I had had few friends. Of course there was my manager and my personal maid, both of whom had been killed in the airplane crash. But I really had had no *friends* — people whom I saw or could see every day. None whose life threads tangled with my own the way, from the first, the interests of these new people had become my interests. I became vitally concerned in Denny's efforts to get a car. If

David Masters had few intimates, could I become one of them? If I found the Langans crashing bores, did not other people? Why then were the Langans invited everywhere? Why was the simplest invitation from them considered to be a royal command?

I didn't feel at all bound to them. And yet I saw a good deal of the Langans. I refused a date or two with Tee, pleading my need to rest "more than I am doing."

But when the Langans' Lincoln rolled into my driveway and Mrs. Langan came up to my front door, followed closely by her husband, of course I admitted the callers. I seated them in my living room, and I offered them refreshment, which they refused.

For ten minutes Mrs. Langan talked steadily, fast, breathlessly about the woman, Mrs. Bell, who owned the house where I was living. Wasn't I afraid I'd break things? She had such lovely china and glass. . . .

I made some sort of answer. I didn't use things that could not be replaced, though, actually, I didn't break many things. "I'm careful," is what I think I said.

"How are you doing?" Mrs. Langan asked me then.

"In what way?"

"I mean, recovering the use of your arm. Does it pain you?"

"Sometimes, yes."

"Ought to go to Arizona," said Mr. Langan. "I had arthritis so bad, couldn't walk. Began to spend my winters in Arizona, cleared the whole thing up. I can even ride horseback."

"My situation isn't exactly like arthritis, Mr. Langan."

"I'll bet Arizona would help you."

"I like living here. I like the trees, and the river. And, anywhere, my case promises only a slow cure."

"I hear Raj Collier is giving you treatments."

"I go there for therapy. To his office."

"I'd think you'd want a better doctor, Alicia." Mrs. Langan spoke very firmly.

It was none of their business, but I answered anyway. "The specialist in New York and one in St. Louis have set up a program for me, Mrs. Langan. Mrs. Ward, in Dr. Collier's office, gives me the therapy treatments. I will, at intervals, be checked over by the specialist."

"I think you'd do better to go back and forth to the city. Couldn't you do that?"

"Not for daily exercising and whirlpool treatment. Please don't worry."

"But Tee said you weren't able to go somewhere when he invited you."

I tried to laugh. "That was temporary fatigue, nothing to indicate a failure in my medical treatments, Mrs. Langan."

"You should get out, you know. See people, and have fun. Tee is really upset about your health being at the mercy of a scamp like Raj Collier."

I gasped. *I* was upset that Tee — and his parents — should presume . . . I said something stiff about having, for years, made decisions for myself. I was sure my reply would offend the Langans, but I would not tolerate interference.

The Langans were not offended. It took entirely different things to offend them, I was to discover. Evidently they had decided to take me under their protective wing, and some small objection on my part would not require notice.

But I still would not let them dictate my choice of a doctor. Dr. Collier's credentials had seemed good enough for the men in St. Louis. He was giving me good care, I felt sure. Dr. Kohl had warned me that my progress would be slow. "Don't judge it day to day, Lissa. Think about it in terms of weeks, or months even. Ask yourself, are you better this month than you were last? Things like that."

So I didn't worry about the scamp part of

the Langans' advice. My relationship with Raj was purely professional. He seemed adequate there.

By then I knew that the townspeople recognized that their doctor had his faults. When I heard someone laugh and call him outrageous, I did wonder why. In what way was Raj outrageous?

But scamp — even outrageous — if those charges were true, how could such a man continue . . . ?

The answer came quickly. It was obvious. Raj was all the doctor the town had. He had a pleasing personality, and he could do competent doctoring. I could figure an answer for myself, had I needed to do it.

But my neighbors provided me with those answers, and Denny did. "Doc's okay," he would say. "Anyway, he's all we've got."

It wasn't quite enough. And I would have pursued the matter further, got better opinions than those of the Langans or Denny, but I met with a strange disinclination among my new friends to speak of Raj in any detail.

The family of Jimmie next door, and David Masters — they talked of other things — many other things. But not much at all about my doctor. And that very omission came to bother me.

It was to Bish that I eventually put the direct question.

Bish. He has become so familiar a part of my life that it is difficult to present him as he first appeared to me. From almost my first day of living in Two Bridges, I heard about him. He was a clergyman. Past seventy years old. He had bought some acres of land on a hillside overlooking the town; there was a small house and a huge barn on the property. It was in the barn that Bish decided to live. He remodeled it, he closed some openings, cut windows in other places . . .

I heard much about his cooking before I tasted any of it. I saw him on the street before I met him. A very big man, six feet five, I believe, and muscular. His head was almost entirely bald, and his skin was as pink as a baby's. I'd see him in church, and I enjoyed the way he sang. The vicar of the small stone church had no voice to speak of.

It was after a church service that the Bishop first spoke to me. He introduced himself, saying that he was a superannuated clergyman. His bright blue eyes denied any thought of age. He said he knew that I was a pianist, and if I could prove I didn't put a candelabra on my piano or play the *Warsaw Concerto*, he would like to be my friend.

I told him that I needed friends but I

would also be happy to be able to play any concerto, and he enfolded my two hands in the warmest grip I had ever known. He walked down the sidewalk beside me, and told me to keep trying. "Why don't you bake cookies?" he asked. "That is a task that thrives on ten thumbs and no fingers."

I liked him; I wanted to know him. So I baked cookies, on the chance that I would see him again and could announce my triumphs — or failures. At first, the task did seem to be beyond my capabilities. But I persisted, and eventually I didn't always spill the flour; I didn't burn myself, or the cookies, all the time. My back still would ache, but that was tension, and I knew how to cope with such a back.

The Bishop invited me to a cookout and I went, enjoying myself very much. But there, too, I encountered the unwillingness, prevalent among some people, to say anything definite about Raj Collier. So — three or four days after the party — a casual gathering of friendly people about the stone-chimneyed cooking fire — we drank wine and coffee, ate hamburgers and corn-pone . . .

I had succeeded in baking at least two pans of oatmeal cookies without burning them, and on an impulse I called the

Bishop's telephone number, told him of my triumph and said that, if he came into town, I would give him some of the fruits of his advice.

"And talk?" he asked.

"But no *Warsaw Concerto*!"

He came later that same day, bringing me a great bag of lettuce from his garden.

"How will I ever eat all this?" I asked.

He spent five minutes telling me how to wilt lettuce, how to put leaves of it in the bottom of the pan when I cooked green peas. . . .

"And where are the triumphal cookies?" he demanded.

I fetched them, and he sat down at the kitchen table. I poured milk into mugs, knowing that he watched me alertly as I did it. He talked about his barn. "I came into town for nails," he said. "That old wood eats nails."

I said that he would have an attractive home.

"But not the way I wanted it. I wanted the living area up in the loft, with a great picture window looking out across the valley. But certain problems of construction — plumbing, electricity, supportive beams — have made me settle for that one enormous room on the stone-floored ground level, with less view and more practicality. I simply loathe compromise, don't you, Lissa?"

"It's the best I've been able to manage lately," I confessed.

"Is that what you wanted to talk about?" he asked me, taking another cookie. "These are good," he said. "I'd put a little more salt in if I were doing it. That's only one of my besetting sins; I like things salty. The doctors deplore it."

"Doctors," I repeated.

He shot me a keen glance. "You've had too many of them, haven't you?"

"Maybe just enough. And some of them have been really wonderful, Bishop!"

"Good. They should be. How is Raj Collier treating you?"

"He's been very kind. More than kind. He's interested, and generous with his time."

"But . . . ?" said the Bishop.

I frowned. "I've no right to bother you."

"Heavens, girl, I am an inveterate gossip."

I looked up at him.

"I love to hear things about my friends and my enemies. And you know? I listen so much, I hardly ever get to tell anything I hear."

I smiled at him. I had not suspected him of repeating what I wanted to say. I crumbled the cookie on my plate.

"Something's puzzling you," said Bish. "May I smoke my pipe in your pretty kitchen?"

"Yes, but we can go to the living room if you wish."

"In these boots? No, I like kitchens."

He got out his pipe, matches, a silk pouch of tobacco. He made quite a ceremony of filling the pipe, and the rest of it.

"I like Dr. Collier," I said to him slowly. "He's done very nice things for me. But, Bishop, except for a few people, I don't find anybody who wants to talk about him." I looked up.

"Those who do talk say . . . ?" he prompted, tamping the tobacco with a precise forefinger.

"Oh, that he's a scamp, a rascal — they even advise me to go to another doctor."

"In the city."

"Do you think you are making any progress with Raj's care?"

"It's a bit soon to expect much. But, yes, I am doing more things. For instance, six weeks ago, I couldn't bake cookies."

"Oh, I take credit for that!"

"Yes, it belongs to you."

"But — the thing that bothers you is that some of your friends like Dave Masters and

Mike Shannon, who lives next door to you, they don't have much to say, good or bad, about Raj. Is that it?"

I sighed with relief. "That's it," I confessed. "If *they'd* call him a rascal . . ."

"Or if I would."

I could only look at him helplessly.

He nodded. "Do you know Sarah? Raj's wife?"

"I've met her. In the yard, and at the office. She checks on my therapy when the doctor is out of the office. Isn't she lovely to look at?"

"Yes, she is. A smart girl, too. All right, my dear, I'll tell you a story about Raj and Sarah. What was it de Lawd said in *Green Pastures*? That he'd throw a miracle. Well, I can't do that, but I'll throw you a story."

"A parable?"

He laughed. "Not really. You know that Sarah helps in the office; she also reads Raj's books and keeps knowledgeable about the pharmaceuticals. You probably know, too, that Raj has a habit, a practice, of being away from the office for a few days at a time?"

Yes, I knew that. I'd seen him go. For the last days of skiing, he'd explained, just the week before. I'd seen his car depart, skis strapped to the top of it.

"He goes trout fishing," the Bishop was saying, "or he goes to attend a ball game — base or foot."

"I know," I murmured. "I suppose, as busy as he is, he needs to get away."

The Bishop nodded. "I suppose. Anyway, last spring, a year ago, Raj was gone on one of his expeditions. I was new to the neighborhood myself then, but everyone heard the story. Which was this: A young woman, downriver, who made her living by fishing, was at her work, aided by a sixteen-year-old boy whom she had hired. He was to operate the boat, I believe. At any rate, somehow or other, her slacks caught in the drive shaft, and the woman's foot became entangled in the engine's set screw."

I shuddered.

"Yes," agreed the Bishop, "it was, literally, a bloody mess. They were downstream, in a lonely spot — early morning — no help available. So the woman calmly, I was told, took her six-inch knife, with a jagged edge. Unable to get herself free, she — still calmly — sawed through the flesh and the bone, freeing her leg. Then she tore a strip of cloth from the shirt she was wearing, and tied a tourniquet about her leg to stop the bleeding. After this, she sent the boy out to find help. He located another fisherman around the bend of the river, not too far away. He came down to the boat and proceeded to take the injured woman up here to the doctor, a sixteen-mile trip. All this took about three hours, and no one had taught the intrepid fisherwoman that a tourniquet needs to be loosened occasionally.

"Arrived here at Two Bridges, the woman was brought — tenderly, I hope — up to Dr. Collier's office."

"But —"

The Bishop nodded. "But Dr. Collier was not there. Mrs. Collier and the nurse were. They detected that gangrene had already been established, and Sarah — our lovely Sally — undertook to do what she could to save the woman's life before sending her on to the nearest hospital. The muscle of the leg had been badly mangled, and must be trimmed away. She also found the strength and the skill to remove the leg just below the knee. Then she sent the woman on, having in the meantime summoned an ambulance. Further surgery, she felt sure, would be required. She was also able to predict a kidney condition that would and did develop because of a heavy loss of blood.

"The surgeon at the hospital spoke admiringly of the measures she had taken, but Sally does not want anyone to speak of the incident. Raj should have been there. Raj is a doctor, she is not."

I sat thoughtful. His story had revolted me in its details.

"And if they can't praise Sally," I finally said, "some of her friends don't want to discuss Raj."

The Bishop clapped his palms on the table and stood up. "I knew a pretty girl like you who doesn't play the *Warsaw Concerto* would be smart," he said.

He had not called Raj a rascal. He had not actually said that Sally was a good wife. But his story had answered a lot of questions for me.

I still thought that, while the doctor's absence might be an inconvenience, I could forgive those temporary departures. I knew that sometimes his patients became angry when they found him gone. But even they would eventually forgive him.

"Raj is young," these angry patients would say resignedly. "Anyway, he's all we have. I suppose we are lucky to have him at all."

At this time, with the Bishop's terrible story still raw in my mind, I was only puzzled about Raj Collier. I had come to realize that as a doctor he was greatly different from what I would have to admit were my idealistic ideas about what a doctor should be. As a child, as a girl, until my accident, in fact, I had known very little, first hand, about doctors. My health had been good, and there really had been no need to know these people.

But then had come the accident. For a year I was forced to live in a world peopled by doctors of all sorts, all ages, with all kinds of characters. Young doctors, old ones, handsome and even ugly, they filled my life. And I would speak mildly if I should say that the impression had been favorable. These men stopped my pain, therefore I loved them. They were always available to reassure me when panic seized me. "I'll get the doctor," the nurses would say. And sure enough, "the doctor" would appear at my bedside. He might scold me or laugh at me — I didn't care. He was there! And just to see his white-coated presence, to hear his cool, brisk voice, would let me go through that day or, more often, that night, and face the hours to come.

When I became discouraged — as I did many, many times — some doctor would sit down and talk to me, another might laugh at me and open ridiculous doors for my future, but in one way or another they did open those doors, they encouraged me to face life, and to believe that the future could be good. Of course I admired — and even worshiped — them.

I began to read books about doctors — fiction, biographies, and always I found that firm core of dedication, that admirable sense of responsibility, of self-abdication.

Their work, was painstaking, it was inspired — but it always had a true goal in view.

Until Raj.

Raj was different. He was kind to me, he was good to me. But . . .

Even Dr. Kohl had told me not to expect too much of the beautiful Ozarks. The people would be fine, he said. The living would be real, and satisfying. "We drive cars down there now instead of mules," he pointed out. "But you won't find caviar, or even beef Wellington, in your town."

So I came to Two Bridges expecting limitations. I found myself being pleasantly surprised by the services available — by the people I came to know — Bish, David Masters, the three Colliers. Even the Langans.

Raj himself explained to me that the medical service had its bare spots. He talked of the hospital and clinic which he needed. He said he wished there were other doctors. He told me that the people of the district took, or he himself sent, "big things" to the city specialists or to the large hospitals.

"I'm not an ear or eye man, for instance. I won't touch neurological or brain complications."

On my case, Dr. Kohl had brought in other specialists. I had spent too much time in a fracture bed not to realize that Raj's lack of a hospital was limiting. That lack explained all sorts of things. Had Raj possessed his hospital, Sarah would not have had to do surgery on the fisherwoman or send her on another long trip for treatment.

Having reached this conclusion and accepted it as a reasonable one, I discovered that some residents, even so-called friends of the Colliers, took every ailment and injury to the city. I could not understand this. Surely Raj, with his degree and his years of practice, could be entrusted with a migraine headache or a burned hand. There must be some personal reason why they went elsewhere for their family doctor, though in an emergency they would call upon Raj if he were available. I thought this unfair, but decided I should think about the situation before making too firm a decision concerning it.

I did do that thinking. As I did my housework, slowly, awkwardly, as I did my shopping, took my daily walks, or sat beside the whirlpool bath in the doctor's office, I thought. And I began to believe that I was figuring out a solution to my puzzle, a chart of the situation that satisfied me; I thought I had analyzed the nature of my new home. And with these points seeming to be in a satisfactory pattern, I thought I had some decisions which I could accept. I could go on living with these people and in this place according to my pattern, and would need to do no more worrying about it.

Then there came the day when I was sitting in the office waiting room ready to be given my therapy. I was reading the book I had brought with me, not paying much attention to the other patients who also were waiting. The doctor and Mrs. Ward were busy; I didn't mind delays of this sort; they would get around to me.

As I sat there, the telephone rang; Mrs. Ward was still back in the examination room laboring to undress and reassure a frightened child. Raj came to the door of the waiting room holding a wet X-ray plate in his hands, and he lifted an eyebrow to me. I nodded, went out to the desk, and picked up the ringing telephone.

The caller was Diane Ramsey. I knew her, but I was given no chance to identify myself. The Langans were all rather insistent talkers. Diane had something to say, and she said it quickly, completely. As she talked, I pictured the Langan daughter, a young woman about thirty, small, dark, often pretty. She was the wife of a prosperous young businessman, and was herself reputed to be an artist — well, at any rate, an artistic person. I took the message and, leaving the phone on the desk, I went back to find Raj and to tell him.

"Mrs. Ramsey says the baby is sick, Dr. Collier. He — she? — is running a high temperature. Can you go to the house?"

He shook his head. "In no way," he said tersely.

"Would you speak to her?"

He shook his head.

"Shall I tell her to bring the baby here?"

"No," said Raj. "Tell her I regret that I am busy for so many hours ahead. I would suggest that she take the child to her doctor in the city."

"But . . ."

He smiled at me. "Tell her," he said softly.

I went back to the desk, and I repeated Raj's message.

"Oh, dear," said Diane. "When I recognized your voice, Lissa, I thought you could get him to come out."

I frowned. "They're just awfully busy," I said. "I was here, waiting for a treatment, you know."

"Yes, but I thought you would feel friendly enough to the Langans to exert a little pressure. Well, I must run. Especially if I have to drive a sick baby clear to the city."

I was in a state. First, I'm afraid, because I was angry that Diane, that the *Langans,* would feel — Why, I wouldn't *try* to influence Raj's decision one way or the other. And certainly I wouldn't do such a thing because once or twice I had dated Tee! My goodness! I didn't even like the fellow! But I guessed my position on that would not be clear to the Langans.

I was so upset about this that I sat for five minutes staring at my open book, not seeing one word, before I remembered the sick baby and the mother — no matter who she was — who would have to drive the child to the city on a hot day. Why wouldn't Raj . . . ? He had refused even to talk to Diane. As for going to the house or letting her bring the child in . . . She probably wouldn't have wanted to take her turn, but even then — Didn't all doctors take care of all sick babies?

I have a mobile face; I've never been able to conceal my emotions or even my thoughts, so Raj detected my "state." He himself that day got things ready for my therapy, which was to be heat-diathermy. I must lie just so on the table, the doctor must be sure I was comfortable so that I wouldn't move for thirty minutes. The machine must be centered, adjusted, and centered again.

Doing this, Raj talked to me, explaining why he didn't think he could make it for the Langan baby. "They take everything to the city, Lissa. The births of their children, a case of hives. They — each member of that family goes there for flu shots and gas pains. Anything they have time for. Of course when one of the kids gets the wind knocked out of him because he fell off the barn roof, or when the baby runs a temperature, they do think about consulting me."

He didn't have to explain to me. "I understand," I said. "But . . ."

"I am busy," he pointed out. "I do keep busy without folks like the Langans. And don't bother to ask them about this situation, Lissa. I can tell you what Mom Langan would say to you. She'd say, 'We go to the city because Collier has no hospital.' Well, how in hell can we get a hospital for this town with their sort of patients? Of course we need a hospital. I don't like doing surgery and obstetrics here in the office. But I have to do some. I also could list fifty appointments a day, and into the night. I refuse to do that. I don't come into the office on Sundays, either."

"Though sometimes you do," I murmured.

I felt his fingers tighten on my shoulder. I could not see his face.

"I've heard you say you did," I explained.

"Yes," said Raj. "Yes. But I won't make a practice of it. Then —" he came around the table and I could see his downbent face as he adjusted the machine; his thick brown hair fell across his forehead — "take vacations," he continued his argument. "That's why I take a few days off now and then. Or I'd never get any sort of vacation."

"How do the patients manage when you're gone?"

He was ready to leave the room. "How would they manage if I'd leave here and go into some nine-to-five clinic-physician's job?" he asked. "Take a nap, Lissa."

"I'll try."

Then he again came closer to the table. "I can see this is worrying you," he said. "Are you involved with the Langans?"

I almost sat up, I was so shocked.

"Hold it, hold it," he said quickly. "I'd only heard that you were."

"Well, don't listen to things like that," I said crossly. "I am not *involved* with anybody."

"Do *they* believe you are involved, Lissa?" he asked softly.

I didn't answer him, so he left the room, and I did not sleep during that thirty minutes.

The Langans and what they believed — Raj Collier and the way he practiced medicine . . . Gee whiz! I could remember the time when I would have shrugged off such things as unimportant. But they were important to me now. And I wished I had had more experience with such matters.

As it was, I listened to what people were saying. I heard various things, among them that the Langan baby had recovered from her cold.

So — I would stop fretting about things I could not change and probably would not try to change if I could do it. I knew that Raj Collier had a busy practice. *I* thought he enjoyed that busyness. It spelled success. Being a doctor, and the son of Mary Bridell, automatically made a golden place for him in the community. I should accept that truth and not fret about the way people acted and talked.

Couldn't I decide that I did not like the

Langans, and not fret over what they believed or said?

I could try. There certainly were more serious things for me to spend my energies upon, and more rewarding people.

Sally Collier, for one. In the first place, she was a completely beautiful woman. She would have seemed so anywhere. I'd been "anywhere" and I could judge. She was my age, taller than I am, with a beautifully proportioned body which she carried naturally and well. Like the quarter horses I'd been shown, birth and breeding told in Sally. She had that enviably beautiful thing, a perfect oval face, and her features were set precisely in that high-cheeked, warm-skinned oval. Her eyes were a bit more gray than hazel, her hair was black, with rich brown highlights. In the office, she wore it smoothly twisted atop her head. Out of the office, she let it fall free, a rich and lovely frame for her lovely face.

I said to everyone that I considered her beautiful. Certainly she was the most beautiful woman in Two Bridges. When I said this to Denny, however, he disputed me. He thought the title belonged to Clare Thomson. I laughed at him. Clare was lovely, I agreed. Her hair was blue-black, and she wore it long, in a thick, clubbed cape. Her face was not quite the perfect oval, though she did have nice cheekbones.

And she was the object of Denny's affections. The boy was idiotically wild about Clare. He would talk about her at any time. I knew her. She liked to wear slacks, or very brief shorts, and turtle-neck pullovers. It was my private opinion that such a costume did a limited amount for any girl. But, yes, I admitted to Denny, Clare was lovely to look at.

"I wish she'd look at me," said Denny morosely.

"Doesn't she?"

"Oh, I don't mean *look*, Miss Lissa. Yes, she looks at me. Once in a while she'll let me buy her a cheeseburger or even take her out on the river. But — well, I've told you. She likes Mike Singley, and if you don't know who Singley is, ask Mike Shannon. He's the coach."

"I know," I said. That coach, a brown-limbed man who wore snowy white shorts and tennis shoes, who wore a baseball cap on his head and a red jacket called a warm-up — father of Jimmie next door — a nice person, Mike Shannon. He'd even explained to me how important basketball was to the rural small towns of the district.

"It's a game they can play not at all expensively. The boys practice with hoops on the barn door, they play in grade school, they certainly play in high school. Their families come to the games in town and charter buses to go to the out-of-town games. The women give chili suppers and bake sales to buy equipment. It's a community project; everybody is involved. When we get a good player like Mike Singley, he becomes a god to old and young alike. If he gets a college scholarship to play, and if he stays good, he'll make the pro teams. What more in the way of worldly success do you want, Miss Lissa? Well, anyway, what more does a local girl want?"

"A girl like Clare Thomson?"

"That's right."

And a boy like Denny could not compete. Clare preferred Mike Singley, and said that she did — which settled Clare for me, because the tall, ambling Singley was, in my book, a complete nonentity.

I argued the matter with the girls of the commune, with Clare. "Being tall," I said, "and having the ability to drop balls into a netting basket shouldn't be enough for a young man."

"He got a scholarship to college," said one of the girls.

"And he plays wonderful basketball," said another.

I looked at Clare. "Is that enough?" I asked her.

She flushed. "For a kid of twenty, it's more than most have," she said.

And for our town, among the available young men, what else was there? It seemed a waste. I was sorry, but —

Ten years ago, what had there been for Sally Collier in this same community? She had gone to college. She came from an old family; she could have left the little river and mountain town. Instead, she had married the glamorous rich boy of the town, the doctor-to-be — which was a mark of success, too, in that neighborhood.

Sally was not my first friend in Two Bridges. Though I met her quite soon, she had not immediately offered friendship to me. She had a reserved way about her. When everyone else was striving to meet and entertain the famous concert pianist, Sally was content with a friendly "hi" across the hedge or a gravely concerned "How are you getting along?" at the office.

But, gradually — she was interested in a book I was reading. She suggested another one she thought I would enjoy. I did enjoy it and we talked about it. When she noticed a burned and bandaged finger, I told her about my cookie baking, and she asked why

I didn't try bread. The kneading would be good for me. Oh, yes, she would show me how. . . . We spent a hilarious afternoon together.

So, a friendship developed.

It was Sally who gave me my little dog. I had never thought I wanted one, having seen too many traveling personalities with their yapping Pekinese, their rhinestone-collared poodles.

But Sally, one rainy evening, brought the puppy in, a sleek and handsome golden-amber dachshund, three months old, with liquid brown eyes and an inquisitive personality.

"I don't think you should live alone, Lissa," she told me, folding the blanket into the flat basket. "He already has a fine bark."

The puppy let me fondle him. I loved his silky ears, his wise, bright eyes, his independence. He sniffed at me, at my shoe. He explored my house, managing to push into closets, to look at Sally inquiringly when she called to him to "get out of there!"

"He's only getting acquainted," I explained for him. "What's his name, Sally?"

She looked quizzically at a dark spot on my red carpet. "Wouldn't it have to be Puddles?" she asked.

So, thanks to my friend, Puddles and I became a family, happy in the companionship. He loved his leash because it meant one of his bouncing walks; he loved the foot of my bed better than his basket; he had a comforting way of knowing when he should crowd into a third of a chair and sleep with his long head against my aching arm.

As for Sally —

I had already met her in the yard and in the office, we had baked bread together, and she had given me Puddles, when David Masters introduced Sally to me, and quite formally.

To begin with, I was taking one of my walks along the shadiest side of the street because the day was hot. Lawn sprinklers flashed before nearly every house, and the hum of air conditioners was everywhere.

Walking was a therapy for me; I had orders about holding my head up, my shoulders back, and swinging my arms. I was to step boldly down from the curbstones, not feel my way like an old woman. I was to step out briskly. All of which I tried to do, but the bold and brisk part was quite a bit beyond me on such a warm evening.

I had decided to give up the effort and had turned back toward home when David Masters pulled his low car up to the curb beside me.

"I am making a collection of beautiful ladies," he said, leaning across the door. "I already have a gorgeous brunette. Could I add a glamorous redhead?"

I laughed and went to the car, pushing up my sunglasses to the top of my head. Sally Collier sat in the far side of the front seat.

"Miss Bartels, Mrs. Collier," said David formally. "She is Dr. Collier's wife. He married the best girl in town, you know."

"That was long before you came here," laughed Sally. "How are you, Lissa?"

I was fine, but I didn't say so. I just stood and looked at Sally Collier, pretty as a magazine ad in her smart, summer print dress. It was red, sprigged with a white vine; the round collar was white and small; her arms were bare.

And I looked as hard at David. I liked him so much! He was a handsome man, with a taut cleanness that would last through all the years of his life. It would have begun to harden even in his college days — the wide-apart, brooding gray eyes, the pleasant smoothness of his face. When angry, I knew that his features could settle slowly into a formidable, craggy expression. And, in a world of suntanned people, David's high-cheekboned pallor gave him, at moments, a romantic air that, to me at least, was exciting.

And I stood there, smiling foolishly at these two handsome people — people I wanted to like *me*. I couldn't think of anything to say but "I'm supposed to walk."

"Oh, never do anything you are supposed to do!" cried David. "Get in, girl, get in!"

I glanced at Sally, who smiled at me. "It's too hot to walk," she said. "You didn't bring Puddles."

"He's smarter than I am. He refused to budge."

David got out of the car and gently took my hand. I let him lead me around so that I could sit beside Sally. "We'll go back to your house," he said, "and you will squeeze some lemons and offer us a cold drink. Are you comfortable, beautiful brunette?"

There was something in his voice when he spoke to Sally, something in his eyes when he looked at her. I felt sure that he was in love with her. And why not? I loved her myself.

We went to my home. We got cold drinks, though not lemonade, and David played with Puddles.

They had a great time; David asked where I had acquired the happy little dog.

"Sally gave him to me. I believe Dr. Collier did marry the nicest girl in town."

Sally fished the cherry from her glass. "I

might not have married Raj," she said softly, "if David had asked me to marry him."

David stood up; his face was grave. "You should have seen that I did," he said quietly.

Sally sighed and brushed her hair away from her face. She looked tired. "We all make mistakes," she whispered.

For a long minute there was a complete silence in the room — a vacuum, as if the air had been drawn up the fireplace chimney. I found it unbearable, and I broke it by saying, much too brightly, "You know? That's what the doctor's mother said about him, about his not doing some internships. That it was a mistake . . ."

It was one of those inane, conversation-making remarks, but Sally lifted her head and looked at me sharply. "Did she really say that?" she asked. Every inch of her was tense.

I shook my head and almost ran from the room. "I shouldn't quote," I said unhappily. "I'm sorry."

Sally smiled at me. She even stretched out her hand as if she wanted to touch me, to reassure me. "I am glad you did quote her," she said warmly. "I thought Mary Bridell said such things only about our marriage."

I can't, even now, describe how I felt. I

was sure that Raj's mother liked Sarah. How could any mother not want such a girl for her son? And yet, in Sally's frankness there was both bitterness and sorrow.

David seemed not to notice what she said. He has a way of closing his face and looking down his handsome nose by way of withdrawal. All lawyers hate to commit themselves by expressing their own opinions.

So he rubbed Puddles' ears and finished his drink, and then walked around the room examining Mrs. Bell's portraits. Sally could tell him who the various ones were, with a few historical comments that made us both laugh.

In a half hour she said she must go "up the hill," and David said he must go down it, and they both left together. I watched them as they stood talking beside David's car, the light of the setting sun behind them, shining on David's silver blond hair. I thought how lucky Sally was to have two men like Raj and David in love with her. But she was that kind — she could always say the right thing, find the right suit and dress in a shop, serve the right food at a dinner party.

I envied her, and I loved her.

I hoped her marriage was not the unhappy one the evening's conversation would seem to imply. Just to suspect that disturbed me. Though, just about then, I had other things to disturb me. The fact was that the Langans were becoming a nuisance to me.

They were planning to take one of their frequent trips, this time to Canada, and they were insisting that I should go with them. Tee insisted.

I didn't want to travel. I'd had my fill of doing it when I was appearing at concerts and recitals all over the world. Now my arm would be a considerable handicap.

I tried to make these excuses to Tee. He refused to accept them. The handicap thing he dismissed quite easily. He would be there — every minute! I would not be jostled in crowds, he'd see that I had a comfortable seat in the plane, a comfortable bed in the hotel . . . And of course the matter of luggage need give me no concern. Puddles, he'd already planned, could stay at Diane's. She and her kids had all sorts of pets — dogs, cats, some ducks on the pond, even a young goat.

I cringed for my little dog's sake and tried to cut Tee off by saying firmly that I did not want to go to Canada with him and his parents.

He laughed at that and said he would not take "no" for an answer.

"What am I going to do?" I asked David

when he came around with some legal papers for me to sign. Gradually, almost all of my legal affairs were going through his office. We had got to know each other pretty well because of this need to see one another frequently. My sort of business was fascinating to him — an entirely new field.

"It's fascinating to the Langans, too," I assured him.

"They smell money."

"What *am* I going to do about them?" I asked. "I don't like them. I don't like Tee. I know I don't, because in my former life I knew plenty of young men like him."

"But you escaped from them without my help."

"You're teasing me."

His eyes smiled at me. "Just a little. Though, seriously, how did you manage?"

"By having a concert in Paris and leaving them — him — in San Francisco."

"That's discouragement, all right," he conceded.

"I don't want to leave Two Bridges."

"Great day, no! We couldn't survive that."

"He asked me to marry him, David."

David pursed his lips and stacked the papers he had had spread out across the table. "First time a man. . . . ?"

"Oh, no!"

"Is he the first man who has threatened to take over your life?"

I gave this some thought. "No," I said. "Though if a woman marries a man . . ."

David reached for his briefcase. "Don't ever marry a person you don't like everything about, Lissa," he said. "Choose someone you'd want to be with, always, even while washing your teeth." He shot me a glance.

And I laughed. "That wouldn't ever be Tee Langan," I assured him.

"Good. I don't think Tee would make any girl very happy and certainly not you."

I thought he was ready to leave, but he stretched his long legs out beneath the table and gazed out of the big window at my lawn and the bed of nasturtiums. "The other day," he said slowly, "the matter of Sally Collier's marriage came up here in this house."

"Yes, it did." And I had decided, rather wistfully, that David would always carry a torch for Sally.

"These young girls . . ." said David. "You know Clare, who helps in my office?"

"Oh, yes, I know her. My yard boy, Denny Marion, is her publicity agent."

David chuckled. "I'll bet. He hangs around my place like a moonsick calf. Poor devil. I know exactly how he feels."

"You'll not make me believe that you were ever a moonsick calf, David Masters, Esquire!"

"Esquire," he repeated thoughtfully. "That's your Easterner for you. Nobody ever uses it in these parts."

"Here I've heard you spoken of as Judge."

"I know. I don't rate that, either."

"You're just a bundle of frustrations, aren't you?"

"Mhmmmn. I thought I'd talk a little to you about Sally Bradford, Lissa."

"Was that her name? Did you know her then?"

"Yes. I was sent down here by my office — a very junior member of the firm — to do some things for the mines. She lived in an old, old house, red brick, as you drive into town."

"Oh, I know it!" I cried. "It was the first house I saw that excited me about Two Bridges. I told myself that I would like to live in that house."

"Well, Sally did live in it. That was her background — gracious living in a threadbare old house. The family money was almost all gone. But it was an old family. And the last daughter of it had led a protected life. She'd gone to a small girls' college, she knew how to manage a home, how to talk pleasantly — and she was pretty. God, was she pretty!" He almost groaned that last sentence.

I watched him. He sat relaxed, still stretched out, his head resting on the back of the Chippendale chair, his fingers rubbing a pattern in the waxed shine of the tabletop. I sat very still and let him talk.

"She was what I always think of when I hear or use the word 'lady,' " said David.

"Was?" I asked.

"Well, is, if you insist. Though marriage to Raj has brutalized that girl."

"Oh, now, look!" I protested. "I don't think she feels and looks at all like a brutalized woman." Though in my mind, too, were pictures like that of the fisherwoman who had lost her leg. But just the same . . .

"I believe she likes medicine," I told David. "She seems entirely happy when she works in the office, and she is very good down there. At home, she reads stacks of books and magazines, all on medical subjects."

"Perhaps you're right," David said. "I was trying to dramatize my story."

I smiled at him. "Go on. Tell it to me," I urged.

"If you'll quit interrupting . . . Well . . ."

He paused for a moment, his head back, his eyes still on the nasturtiums. "I hadn't more than begun to come here when I first met Sally and fell in love with her. But then, that first summer, Raj Collier, medical student, came here with his mother for their summer vacation. And this rich young man, engaged in a profession you claim interests Sally, gave the girl a tremendous rush. He played the whole bit, Lissa. He did nothing original, but it was all most effective."

"Like a Viennese waltz," I murmured.

His eyes brightened. "Exactly! He sent her yellow roses; he took her horseback riding through the woods in a gentle summer rain. He used even a canoe on the river by moonlight, naturally. The rain had stopped."

"And you were jealous."

"Damned right! I had to be. At Christmastime they were married, and I didn't see Sally for three years. Then they came back to Two Bridges to live with Raj's mother, and the office was built and opened."

"Was Sally unhappy?"

"She didn't show it. She doesn't show it now. But ten years ago, even before their marriage, I suspect that Sally knew who and what that boy was. The things he did. Maybe she thought she could be the necessary influence in his life.

"But now she knows — maybe she knew when she married him — maybe she discovered it within six weeks after her wedding — that her woman's body could continue to love Raj while her mind despised the fellow. He does the most incredible things, you know."

"I don't. I only know him as a doctor, kind and considerate."

"Oh, but, Lissa . . ."

"I've heard stories, yes. I wonder how he can leave his practice so often. But, first hand, all I know . . ."

"You women."

"I am not in love with Raj!" I said sharply.

"I know you are not. But Sally — she recognizes the weakness in herself, and I believe that is the one and only reason she stays with him."

"Does she know you love her?" I was thinking hard about the things he had said and suggested.

Then I looked up at him, and he was smiling at me. "Oh, Alicia," he said gently. "I am ten years older, too, remember."

He picked up his briefcase and I walked with him to the front door. "There aren't any children," I said, still thinking.

"No. No, there are not. Knowing that he has not made her happy, Raj thinks Sally is glad that they don't have children. I believe she is not glad. Raj comes from good stock; Sally's children would be fine."

I looked up at him. My face must have been troubled. "How does she *endure?*" I asked.

"I've given that some thought myself. She has friends who satisfy her and help her."

"You."

"I hope so. Bish and she are pals. And now there's you."

"Oh, I hope you are right!"

"I hope I am, too. But she likes you, and that's a gain. I don't believe she has other women friends. Then — you mentioned this. She does study Raj's medical books; she keeps up on medical matters in ways that he does not."

"I heard about the fisherwoman's accident."

"Yes. That was bad. But Sally took it. And she still reads the journals and works in the office."

"That's where I first knew her. I admired her. She is a fine person, David."

"As I told you, she's the best in town."

"Mary Bridell must have welcomed Sally as a bride for her son."

"No," he said slowly. "No, she didn't. Logic or reason did not enter into that event. And it still doesn't."

"But — why?"

"Because Mary Bridell fears Sally. Now, that should give you something to think about until half-past suppertime, Funny-face."

It did give me something to think about, and for longer than that.

There came a time when I saw Sally make Raj toe the line.

This happening involved one of the communes that were established in and around our town. One that I knew of was back into the hills a way, but there were several down along the river. The one in which Clare lived was the most stable, the most respectable. Hers was really only a house where a group of girls, most of them employed, chose to live rather than with their families. But there were communes in old fishing shacks. There was at least one small tent colony. The town deplored these establishments. The health of the occupants and their moral behavior were deplored. They were somewhat closely watched because of drug traffic and drinking by minors. Almost any crime committed in town was grounds for suspicion that the commune dwellers were guilty, and perhaps they were in many cases. They didn't have money; in our society one could not live without money. Some of the "families" were issued government surplus food, and this practice, too, was condemned by some.

That day I was in the office, seated by the whirlpool tank, when the call came in. Mrs. Ward came back to tell Sally who was in the therapy room; she often kept me company there while she performed other tasks, like making up sterile bundles of instruments and towels which she would take to the autoclave, or she would be checking boxes of drugs which had come in, perhaps getting pipettes, beakers, test tubes ready to be washed and then sterilized for the technician who came in the late afternoon. Sometimes we talked, sometimes I read my book while she concentrated on what she was doing.

That morning we had talked a little — about inconsequential things, I suppose. I don't remember an item. I had my book propped at reading level. Sally was counting under her breath.

We both were a little startled when Mrs. Ward popped in. She is a brusque, large woman, very kind, of course, but she does move vigorously.

"There's a hippie out front," she told us. "He says the doctor is needed down at his shack."

I could only stare at her in disbelief. Sally set her tray of glassware to one side. "I'll talk to him," she said.

Raj was not in the office; I knew that.

Mrs. Ward said something about the hippies, the commune dwellers. "They smell," she concluded. "Old socks and rancid oil. *Pee-whew!*"

I laughed in spite of myself.

Sally came back into the room. She was wearing a blue denim dress that morning; it had a red leather belt. "Mrs. Ward will finish with you, Lissa," she said. "I am going down to see what is wrong. I only hope it isn't childbirth. These kids don't have any pre-natal care, proper or otherwise. They are diseased, undernourished . . ."

She was gone.

I had another fifteen minutes. Mrs. Ward came, when the buzzer sounded, and took me out of what she called "the pot." She was helping me dress and telling me that I could rest for a while on the couch in the doctor's office, because he wasn't there.

"Where did he go?" Though by then I knew better than to ask such things.

"I hope Sally knows," the nurse said grimly. "I've run out of places to tell people. Besides, in this town, folks know if you are at the barber's or the dentist's — if you are."

I, of course, said nothing. But I hadn't any more than made myself comfortable in the deep armchair in Raj's office when I heard Sally come into the building and speak to Mrs. Ward.

She came quickly back to Raj's office, and she only lifted her hand to me when she picked up the telephone from the desk. She looked — devastated. And angry, too, perhaps. I could not imagine what she had found at the hippie's shack!

She spoke to someone at the other end of the line. "This is Mrs. Roger Collier," she said crisply. "Dr. Collier is playing golf. Will you please locate him and get him to the telephone. He may still be close at hand. I'll wait until you determine that."

She sat down in the desk chair and rested her head on her hand. She could speak briskly, but she looked beaten.

I pretended to read my book.

"It's been rough, Lissa," she said.

"You don't have to talk to me about it."

She smiled at me — wearily. What *could* have happened in a short half hour?

We had waited for five minutes, about, when Sally stiffened. "Raj?" she asked sharply.

His voice said something, but she broke in. "That doesn't matter," she said. "You are

102

badly needed. Yes, I do mean badly. I think we have an o.d. down in one of the river shacks. I don't want to be asked to pronounce . . ."

Again Raj broke in.

"I think I do know the signs, Raj. Froth at the nose and mouth, congestion of the internal organs — lung edema. They tried to tell me it was a drowning, and the lungs do sound that way.

"No! I don't carry a stethoscope! But you go there, Raj. And right away, before those kids do something crazy . . .

"Of course they do crazy things. The authorities won't like a funeral pyre, you know, down there at the government sand dredge.

"Yes, it's the shanty painted lavender, with hex signs. I told them you'd come. But get at it *now*, will you? Yes, I'm sorry about the game . . ."

She put the phone down, pushed it back on the desk. "I'm sorry, Lissa," she said softly.

"Will the doctor go?"

"Yes. He'll go."

"Does o.d. mean . . . ?"

"Overdose. Of heroin. And the police are needed, but Raj has to call them rather than me."

I could see that. But I made no comment. I decided I was ready to walk home, and she agreed, going with me to the door. "Take it easy," she told me. "I'm glad you were the one here."

If she was glad . . .

That evening I had a bone for Puddles, and I took him out on the lawn to enjoy it fully. I was pulling a weed here and there but mainly just sitting on the grass watching the busy little golden dog, when I heard voices on the far side of the thick hedge.

It was Mrs. Collier, Senior — Mary Bridell — and her son Raj.

If they stayed long or said much, I would make my presence known.

But not much was said, not really, and it took less than five minutes to say it.

I heard Mary Bridell ask her son, "What went on today down at your office?"

He said he'd played golf in the morning and had held his usual afternoon office hours. Nothing much had come up.

She protested. The evening news on the radio had said . . .

"Oh, Mother, dear Mother, can you actually listen to that news fellow?"

"I can when he says that Dr. Roger Collier pronounced a man dead of an overdose of heroin down in a commune dwelling at the river."

"Yes. I called the police, of course."

"You didn't play golf down on that river-bank."

I heard Raj laugh. "No. Sally interrupted me in the middle of one of my best slices. She was minding the office, and this character came after the doctor. She went to the shack. Jehoshaphat, Ma, you should see one of those places!"

"Thank you."

"No beds, just a mattress, or maybe just old quilts on the floor. A table, a broken chair or two, boxes, a few dishes. Those kids call that *living!*"

"And one of them was dead."

"Yes. From an overdose of heroin. Sally saw the possibilities. She knew he was dead, and while the police might have called me in anyway, she made me go there and pro-nounce the fellow dead and *then* call the po-lice. So my part shows up as clean as snow, and my testimony at the inquest won't even mention golf — or Sally. How about that for wifely devotion?"

I was ready to stand up, to call Puddles, to proclaim my presence . . .

"Oh, Roger, Roger," I heard Mary Bridell say. "That girl you married. She'll make a man of you yet, if you don't watch out."

They moved away before I had a chance to say I'd overheard. Overheard what? That a mother wanted the cord to remain uncut? That, and the proclamation of the astounding miracle of birth? Not to be relinquished, not to be shared.

Chapter Three

It was the end of June; I had lived in Two Bridges for two months, a little more, and I felt that I was really becoming a part of the community. I knew my way about the place; I had become familiar with its resources and its lacks. I had learned something about keeping a house, training a puppy, and was able to live a life completely, not only as an observer, a listener. I was participating. I received in turn pleasure, and some hurt. I was free to make my own observations, to form my own opinions and to speak them.

No longer was I restricted by a manager, a public relations fellow, and an agent. Nor was I protected by those good people.

I had made friends, some of whom I liked better than others. There were the Langans, those very rich, very provincial people who had decided to take over the restrictions and the protection I had so recently escaped. They, singly or as a family, stood ready to advise me on all matters. I couldn't so much as buy a housecoat without Mrs. Langan popping up at my elbow in the shop to advise me not to buy the silky batiste one with the pretty ribbons at the throat, but to take one of the checked gingham, no-iron ones. The latter was cheaper, would require less care — and was completely without charm.

"I'll take the yellow one," I could tell the clerk, and smile an apology to Mrs. Langan. "I like pretty things," I told her.

I hoped she was not rebuffed, but I was choosing my friends rather carefully, and to lose the Langans would not disturb me.

"And it would also be fairly impossible," David Masters assured me.

"Do they bother you?"

"Not anymore," he said. "When I first came here, I felt I had to endure such people. But I've grown up —"

"And become successful, so you can be independent."

"Well, you came here a successful person. So you have a head start."

I considered David one of my friends, and I liked being able to claim him as one. Another was the Bishop who continued to watch over me in a benevolent fashion. When he had to go away for a few days — some sort of church meeting which he spoke of in just those terms — he tenderly brought me his jar of *rumtopf,* with a written-out direction of how to care for it in his absence. If I added fruit — "Not the seedy berry type, Lissa!" he admonished me. "If you put in cherries, pit them. And add an equal amount of sugar! And stir the thing! Every morning, remember. That is most important!"

He put the jar on my kitchen counter. Even when closed, it perfumed the whole house.

"I am leaving this with you," the big man told me, "because you are the only one of my friends I can trust."

To stir the mixture every day? Not to drink the brandy already in the jar? I didn't think so, entirely. His gift was to prove to me that I could do for others. And I could!

Mary Bridell had become my friend. Except when she was out of town on a short trip, she would seek me out at least once each day. She could tell if I was tired, if I had not slept the night before; she could tell if something was bothering me or pleasing me. She didn't ask for details, just — "You've lost your sleep. Better take a nap this afternoon!" I would, I did, and I always felt better. Mary Bridell might have spoiled her son, and know it, but her big heart had room for compassion and friendly interest toward me and probably others.

Sally, of course, had become my friend. At

first, she had been wary. And so had I. But we soon recognized an empathy between us. She had her reserves; so did I. We could chatter girl-talk, and yet respect each other as individuals. We could depend on each other, for understanding and loyalty. Those things were most important.

In this new life of mine — after living my first adult years as a public figure, always conscious of publicity and audience reaction — I was now ready to relax in my new environment. I could do as I pleased, dress and speak and live that way. I decided I could think as I chose, too, and speak my thoughts, not to disturb anyone else.

This was a mistake. Almost at once I found that I could not observe and enjoy without needing to take sides. If I didn't like the color of the new sidewalk waste bins on the main street, I could not just laugh and say so at some small party. I found people ready to agree with me; just as many ready to dispute my taste. But what difference did my opinion make? For that matter, what difference did it make if the trash cans were tan or bright green?

It did make a difference. Life in Two Bridges revolved around the town's civic pride and development. All right then! I would take sides. I would say that I did not care for the tan waste bins, they were not prominent enough, they would not attract litterbearers to drop their candy wrappers or plastic cups into them instead of the gutter. Bright green, or even red, would be better.

And I believed I could state my stand — on that and other subjects. Should guitar music be a part of church service? A guitar played well, I thought, might be an improvement on a wheezy organ, or a good one carelessly played. The Bishop and I delighted in this discussion.

"What about Christmas Eve, Lissa?"

"Well — no. The *Gloria* should be done by an organ. Of course, the best possible church music is produced by a chorus of men — young seminarians, or a really rousing choir."

"You're a dreamer."

"I know. And it's fun."

I didn't think dogs should run loose, for their own protection, and I said that.

But should I speak my opinion of what sort of doctor Raj Collier was? No. I should say only that "he's very attentive to me." Which was true. Besides, I was not ready to say, after two months, what sort of doctor he was. And not saying presented its own problems.

Of which I had plenty — ones that I was

prepared to face, many more that bobbed up unexpectedly.

Adjusting to my new way of life could be difficult. Living alone, as I did, might give privacy to my moments of failure and frustration. Living alone could take me by the throat and make me figure out how to reach a vinegar bottle pushed to the back of the bottom shelf of a low cupboard, or how to zip a dress up the back. I would never, probably, be able to lift my right arm up and back. That arm was often actively painful and it still was weak. I had to devise ways to do almost everything with only one strong arm and hand.

Since this was difficult, frustrating, and sometimes impossible, the temptation was great to go live in a hotel and eat food prepared for me, have a maid spread up the bed, and dust under it. Or I could send for the woman who had served me well as dresser and companion when I was on tour. She would come, she could come, and live with me, help me dress, do the pesky zippers, fasten the bras behind my back . . . And I would not learn to be independent.

In one very low time I even went out to the nursing home at the edge of town. I had heard that it was a pleasant retirement home as well, and perhaps I could live in such a

place, be cared for, with a nurse available —
and Dr. Collier still could take care of me.
This would be easier.

The place was pleasant; it had a large en-
trance hall and an attractive living room.
There was a piano, a TV set and elderly
people looking at me curiously. I was shown
about. Single rooms were available, but no
suites. I could have my own furniture — but
of course there were rules and regulations as
to hours, noise, and so on. I left, promising
the matron to return and play for the guests
when I was able.

I went home to Puddles and my yard, my
nasturtiums, and the bottle of vinegar still in
the back corner of the low cupboard.

I decided that frustration was a necessary
part of the recovery I would need to make.
So I lay flat on my stomach and used a pair
of serrated kitchen shears to coax the vinegar bottle within reach.

"You nut. You could have bought another
bottle or borrowed vinegar from us," Sally
told me when I boasted of my triumph.

"And what would that have done for my
character?"

"You be careful and don't hurt yourself or
get into predicaments."

"Oh, I've done that so much I have a
name for them. Inextricable predicaments."

Sally laughed, but her eyes were concerned.

"I'll be careful," I promised hastily.

"You do wonderfully."

I knew better. I knew how often I lost patience, and sometimes hope.

Often — too often — it did not seem that my arm was recovering as quickly as it should — or even as well as it should. To move the fingers had, on accomplishment, been a thrilling achievement. But what good was movement if no skill or dexterity followed? I wanted to be able to do more than squeeze a rubber ball. I wanted the arm to be well, and not hurt anymore. Was it too much to ask that I be able to sleep again on my right side?

"That will come, Lissa."

But *when?* I was bored, tired, disgusted with exercises. I wanted to *use* my right hand! To hold a fork, or a glass of water — and not spill food all over the place. What satisfaction was there in being able to hold an apple, bite into it, and eat it? I agreed to try to crochet or knit, just to force my hand and fingers into use. I did try, and the results were a sorry mess. I found myself weeping in frustration, then laughing at my tears. What difference did it make if I could knit? I had learned how to knit when I was twelve. But for many years I had not found it desirable to knit. Why should it be important now?

Oh, I knew the answer. If I could hold even a large wooden needle and make some sort of recognizable rug or scarf, soon I could hold a pencil and write with my right hand, or eat dinner out in company neatly, acceptably. Yes, I wanted to be able to do those things, so I crocheted a lopsided mat and knitted a scarf that was ridiculous. It wouldn't even unravel!

Sally and I collapsed into hysterical giggles over that sorry scarf. "I'll give it to you for Christmas!" I promised her.

"Oh, by Christmas you'll make a good one."

"Promise?"

"You're the one who has to promise."

And I was the one. I knew that I had to go daily for therapy at the doctor's office — for massage, for whirlpool action to keep the muscles alive and in tone, for exercises carefully devised and supervised. I must do all these things regularly; I must do enough, but not too much.

These things were boring; they often were painful.

And sometimes they were fun. Sometimes I didn't mind them. Sally, often enough, was the one who made the difference. She often "happened" to be in the office when I went there. If she were not, she often left me an interesting article to read, or some small task which I could do for her.

There was therapy in cleaning instruments, in folding strips of gauze. She started by showing me how, and then, when I knew how, such tasks became my duty. "Oh, thanks, Lissa. You're a great help." She would discard a sloppy sponge, she would ask me to do a pair of forceps over if a dull spot showed. I learned to accept these reproofs, and I tried very hard to please Sally, not to have to do any job over.

I can realize now how much time and real wish to help me went into her part of my therapy. Of course Raj knew what was going on and he approved, but it was Sally who made my dreary therapy tasks interesting and productive.

There were many things about Sally Collier that took learning about, and which developed into my genuine liking for her. This state took awhile — and when I did tell myself that I liked her, I was surprised to know that, at first, I had not been prepared to like her at all.

But why?

She was my age; she was lovely to look at. David Masters loved her, and had for ten years. Couldn't I *like* her? But at first, when David told me about Sally — that she was the nicest girl in town — when I started to discover things about Raj, I had decided that I did not really like a woman who could stay married to a man she could not possibly admire. And I condemned her for doing it.

I recognized the Bridell money, the Collier money; I recognized Raj's physical attractiveness, the impact which the man made upon all women.

David said it was the physical which held Sally.

I didn't like that explanation if it were true. A woman had to admire a man if she were to love him. It was only after I had known Raj and Sally for two months that I began to ask questions about admiration.

I would lie awake at night and think about these things. A bright yard light at my front walk, another over the kitchen door, made even the inside of my house bright, without disturbing shadows. I could look out into the blowing shrubbery, the tops of the tall trees — and think. Were there many sides to admiration?

Just as there were many ways to develop a musical theme, could not a woman, in physical love with a man, find other appealing things about him?

Raj's even temper, his gaiety, his strong, firm hands — I thought about him, and thinking, I came to know Sally, to like her and understand her.

Of course I had come to know Raj, too. I suspected that he had qualities which Sally knew and that David Masters did not. I said this defensively to myself. But it was true!

I knew for myself that Raj would work hard, and that he helped many, many people. Still, I listened when any of my new friends would advise me to take my arm elsewhere.

Why did they do that? I asked Bish one afternoon when he fetched me in his jeep to help him make peach preserves.

"I don't know how to make any kind of preserves," I warned him. "I can't even peel your peaches for you."

"You're a pleasure to look at."

"Bishop, really!"

He grinned at me wickedly and lifted the car up the steep drive to his barn — his home.

It was cool in his kitchen. The wide doors were open at both ends of the house and a good breeze blew through, coming from the river and the trees below his hill. I pushed my sunglasses to the top of my head and watched Bish as he set out his pans and his jars, opened a sack of sugar. He split a golden peach and offered me half. The seed had come out, leaving the red heart glowing and as sweet as honey.

I asked again what I could do to help.

"Oh, you can stir and count peach kernels . . ."

"Do they need to be counted?"

"Of course. One wants a few; one doesn't want too many." He dipped a wire basket of peaches into very hot water, then sat down and began to slip the skin from the fruit. "Does one?" he asked, after about ten minutes.

"Does one what?" I asked. I was making a mess of trying to get the peel from a slippery peach.

"Hold with your right hand, peel with your left."

"But . . ."

"I know what you are supposed to do. When I retired, I put aside all such things."

He had not, but I helped him with his pose.

I told him he might be misjudged, and this led of course to my consideration of Raj Collier, why he was criticized, why he might just as easily be admired.

He asked when I had done all this thinking.

So I told him about the nights when I

119

couldn't sleep. "There must be reasons for a woman like Sally to live with Raj for ten years, help him. And don't mention sex."

He turned his round baby-pink face to me. "Me?" he asked in so much innocence that I laughed aloud.

"I know Raj does things he shouldn't," I said. "But perhaps there are other things to balance . . ." I looked up anxiously.

"I am sorry you don't sleep," said the Bishop, getting up to put his peaches into an enameled pan, then to measure sugar carefully. I pushed the five peach pits toward him, and he smiled at me when he came for them.

"I don't worry about not sleeping," I told him.

"Perhaps you keep yourself awake with your thinking."

"I've always used such nights — I used to develop themes or to shape phrases. You know? Little protractions, or shortening of notes within measures?"

The Bishop came back to his stool at the table. "You put that much thought to Raj Collier?" he asked.

"No. To Sarah. I find that I like her, and I want to understand her."

"As you do your music," murmured the Bishop.

"Well, it's a little the same," I agreed. "Lightness in a quick passage, how much *rubato* to give to the slow ones."

"That's for Mozart," said the Bishop.

"It's for Sally Collier, too. How far can I venture into her life, how much of myself does she want to share?"

"I see," said the Bishop.

I got up, went to the stove and stirred the fruit and sugar with the long wooden spoon.

"I am going to add cinnamon to some of the jam," the Bishop told me. "You can call it my *rubato*. Peach jam tends to be too sweet and bland."

I laughed. "Why not a little lemon peel?"

"Good girl!" cried the Bishop. "Do you think about such things at night, too?"

"No. Just Sally . . ."

"And Mozart."

"Not too much Mozart lately, I'm afraid."

"But your past thinking did you a lot of good. I'm glad to know about it. I have been wondering how so young a woman could have given the reading of depth you did to Scriabin and Schumann."

I was inordinately pleased. "You've heard me!" I cried.

"Records," said the Bishop. "Long before I knew you in person, I prized my album of Alicia Bartels at Carnegie Hall."

I stood thoughtful — and sad. "Records," I repeated.

The Bishop glanced at me. "Not all of us," he said crisply, "leave such a testament of our life's work!"

"I know," I conceded. "It's just —"

"You're too young to have a past," he agreed. "But there is another side to the coin, Lissa. You're plenty young to hope for a future."

I stirred the peaches again, then went to sit at the table.

"Making records was work," I told my friend. "I never liked doing them as well as a concert performance."

"You didn't put on a long white dress, for one thing."

I laughed. "It wasn't that. Records can be played back. Ignoring a review or two, you can tell yourself that you did the concert well. But when you hear the playback of a record — I never was satisfied. Not once."

"I understand Toscanini had the same trouble, and that Barbra Streisand does."

"I should think everyone would. You have things you want to put into your music — maybe it's just one note — and if that note doesn't come through, you're not speaking to the listener as you hoped to speak. I think it was a matter of empathy, Bish, as much as sympathy I strove for."

"But the *feeling* was there. It came through. You still feel deeply, and it shows."

"Well — Doesn't everyone *feel?*"

"Everyone is not as honest a person as you are, Lissa."

"Why not?"

The Bishop laughed sadly. "Oh, my dear . . . It does sound the easiest thing in the world, doesn't it? But no, everyone does not feel. I suppose, with footlights and all, you didn't have to look too closely at your audience. Besides, you were busy with your *rubatos*. But in my life, to stand in the pulpit, to look down at the rows of blank, closed faces — Good God, some of them felt so little that they weren't even *bored!* Try speaking to that crowd sometime!"

I laughed. "I've played to the wrong audience a time or two," I admitted.

"And you wondered about yourself instead of the people. I have. What was wrong with my message. Did I choose the wrong words? The wrong topic?"

I nodded.

"And that night you did some of your thinking, didn't you? You should have said, 'The hell with them!' "

I laughed. "I could have said it then. But I can't here, with Sally."

The Bishop went to look at his preserves, to let the amber liquid sheet from the spoon. "Almost done," he announced.

"Do you know?" he asked me. "Half the time when I felt my failure as a preacher, half the time, that was my fault. But then, Lissa, I did have to conclude that there are pews and pews full of people who don't *feel*. And if they do have stirrings and can't sleep at night, they're not like you. They don't lie awake and figure things out. They take a red pill or a green one. They leave the worry about friends to people like you."

"I don't *worry*, Bishop."

"No, you just think yourself into a white stew. And I'll now stick my neck out and give you a bit of advice about your present thinking. And it will be good advice, too. Not like some of the stuff I hand out." He stopped what he was doing and turned to face me. He had tied a large piece of muslin — maybe it was a flour sack — about his waist — a comfortable waist, though the Bishop was not a fat man. He was wearing a spotless white T-shirt. Tennis shoes.

"Perhaps you don't want advice?" he asked me.

"I want anything — and anything at all — that will give me hope of progress in the use of my hand and arm!"

He looked sorry, and turned back to the stove. "Did the doctors warn you that progress would be slow?"

"Oh, yes, they did. But see here. I do try using my hand. I can pick up the peach, but I am not sure at all that I can hold it. I can hold a comb, and by ducking my head, I can scramble things up in my hair . . ."

The Bishop laughed. "I wouldn't quarrel with the chance of scrambling," he assured me. His head was as bald as an egg.

I nodded. "I try to move my fingers," I said. "I want, of course, to move them into some semblance — oh, not to play again the magnificent chords of the *Second Hungarian* — I renounced hope of that when I began to be thankful that I had kept my hand and arm. But I would like to think that my fingers could one day attain the rumbling roll of *The Firebird*'s opening." I made feeble wiggles of my fingers against the table edge, and smiled up at the Bishop, who was watching me. "Or I would love to do the sparkling notes of the Mozart *Rondo*."

"And you do not want those notes to be less than sparkling."

"Oh, I stand ready to begin as a child begins, the fingers clumsy and weak . . ."

"You don't think stirring the jam is such a beginning?"

"I try to believe that. But the truth is, I don't *want* to stir jam!" I sat silent, thinking of the things I did want. To practice for hours and hours, all the old hated exercises. I wanted to walk out on the concert stage again, to hear the roll and roar of applause. I wanted to have a big orchestra around me, I wanted to bow to Bernstein, to Suskind, to —

The Bishop began to fill his jars. I reached for another peach. "You are very patient with me," I said faintly, hoping that he would recognize my apology for what it was.

"You're discouraged," he said mildly.

"Yes," I acknowledged. "Yes." Then I lifted my head, ready to make the plunge. "Do you think," I cried tensely, leaning toward him, "that I am following the right course? That what I am doing *is* the right thing?"

"What you are doing . . ." repeated the Bishop thoughtfully, putting the cap on his jar.

I sat back. "Oh, you know . . . making beds, sweeping the front stoop, stirring your blasted jam — all the therapy stuff I go through."

"Are you worried about its being the right thing, Lissa?"

"Sometimes, yes, I am. Especially when

people ask me about Raj, when they suggest that I am not doing the right thing."

He dipped a teaspoon into his jam, and came to me, offering the taste. I looked up into his face and accepted the spoonful.

"Just like a baby robin," he said, satisfied.

"It's delicious."

"That's the five peach pits. Now — you get busy with the next batch, and I'll give you the advice I offered fifteen minutes ago."

"I'm listening," I said meekly.

"Well, I should hope so!"

I did listen, and I decided to take his advice. I said nothing to anyone about my plans, except I had to tell the office that I needed to take a short trip. They were the ones to tell others that I had business to attend to. I hired a car and driver — such things were available in our neighborhood. I made various appointments and reservations, and I went to the city. I registered at the hotel, I had my hair cut, and I saw the specialist at the big medical center. I asked him about my progress, I asked him if my course of therapy seemed to be the right one. What sort of job was Dr. Collier doing for me? Was he a good doctor, to be trusted . . . ?

And here, as I later learned was natural, I met the blank wall which professionals can set up about the personal aspects of their colleagues. My man, the specialist, looked again at Dr. Collier's record, his medical school record — and then he looked at my arm. He kept me at the hospital for two days while he made every test.

Finally I sat down across the desk from him in his office. He was a big, rangy man; his homely face and Dr. Kohl's recommendation inspired confidence. He smiled at me. "I consider that you are doing very well, Miss Bartels," he said warmly. "These things go slowly; you've certainly been told that they do — but I see marked progress in the past three months. You can use your fingers more; you have an improved posture even when you are tired or off guard. I would say that your course of therapy has shown good results, and therefore it probably is the right one.

"Now . . ." He tipped back in his chair. "If — I am judging from a few things you said when you came to me this time — if you do not *like* Dr. Collier or trust him . . ."

"Oh, I do *like* him!" I said hastily. "He is a very friendly, kind man. And if he has done me the good I should expect, why shouldn't I trust him?"

Fortified with this reassurance, I returned to Two Bridges. Bish brought Puddles back to me, and I made my report on the trip. I found ways of saying certain things to other people . . .

Sally asked: "Did you have a good trip, Lissa?"

I smiled at her. "I had a fine trip. I brought you a can of white asparagus."

Mrs. Langan —

"While I was in the city, I saw my specialist," I told her. "He says I am making very good progress. He thinks Dr. Collier is doing all the right things."

She smiled at me. "Well, that's fine, dear. But — you go to the office so often — Do try to avoid gossip about you and Raj, dear. He has a certain reputation, you know. With the pretty young women, I mean."

I knew what she meant. But I had never known Raj to make a gesture of that nature, or to say one word. If I trusted him as a doctor on my case, I would trust him in anything, in any aspect.

I told Mrs. Langan as much, and she smiled at me again. "Well, one has to begin by trusting one's doctor," she agreed. "I'm glad you are home again. Tee has bought a houseboat, did you know? Would you enjoy spending the weekend on it with him and me and Mr. Langan?"

I declined, saying that I planned just to be

happy in my return to Two Bridges, to my home and my little dog.

"And your doctor," she added silkily.

I decided that, in the future, I would not be even courteous to Mrs. Langan!

But she was not easily discouraged or rebuffed. And when she or some of my other friends would again suggest that I should change doctors, I listened politely and thanked them for their interest. In some cases, it was interest, and honestly kind. Coach Shannon, father of Jimmie next door, was one of these, and when I told him the doctor's report, he was honestly glad.

Thinking about this matter, I began to see that some of my friends' advice had roots in personal reasons for pique. In my first weeks of living in Two Bridges, I had detected the rivalry there was between the Langan and the Bridell-Collier families. The Langans wanted to be the richest people in town. But the Bridells probably had just as much money.

I asked David Masters if, perhaps, Tee Langan had once been in love with Sally.

He smiled at me. "I could agree that Tee's mother thought it would be a good match. Sally had breeding and taste, neither of which is to be found in the Langan jewel box."

"I see."

"I doubt if Sally ever gave Tee a second

glance, even when they were high school age. But there also was a daughter, Lissa."

Yes, there was. Diane. "Raj!" I cried in surprise.

"Raj indeed."

"Did her mother try . . . ?"

"In that case, Diane was the active one, with Mamma beaming along behind."

"But she could have been no competition for Sally."

"It wasn't that," said David, puffing on his pipe, watching the smoke drift off into the summer air. "Sometimes before Raj recognized Sally's superb qualities, I believe Diane and her mother decided that the Bridell and the Langan families should be joined. But Raj — Now this may be the only complimentary thing I'll ever say about the fellow — but he did have the ability, even as young as he was, to be perfectly lovely —" David's gray eyes slid to my face — "to be perfectly lovely to silly women and neatly step out of their reach."

I nodded emphatically. "He still does that," I agreed. "I've seen him do that at the office and at a party. And the women do get crushes. There was one woman who left notes in the office: *I love you, Dr. Collier.* Mrs. Ward would gather them up and stack them on his desk. Nobody said a word. I think the woman phoned him, too. I'd have thought he would refuse to give her appointments, but he didn't. He showed extremely cool patience with her."

David nodded. "That's why he gets my one and only compliment."

"I blame the women," I told him.

"You may."

"Oh, *David!* You talk as if Raj cultivated his charm . . ."

"Doesn't he?"

"It couldn't be called a bedside manner?"

He exploded into laughter. And I felt my cheeks getting pink. I didn't want to be thought naive.

He emptied his pipe. "Let's play some more tennis," he suggested.

One couldn't call it *tennis*. David would lob balls to me, I'd try to hit them. It was good exercise, and sometimes it was fun. "I have one more thing to say about Raj," I told him.

He sat back on the steps and twirled his racquet between his knees. "One more?"

"I think one will do it. It's on your side of the argument, too." I saw his eyes brighten. "It's this," I said quickly. "Sometimes I have thought Raj was a little smug about the way the women act."

"But he always expects them to be charmed?"

"Oh, yes," I agreed. "He does expect it. Even with the very old women. I've been told that he is extremely popular out at the nursing home."

"Which all adds up to his being a spoiled man, doesn't it, Lissa?"

"I suppose it does," I agreed. "But a person might understand that he isn't that way deliberately. I mean, the women . . ."

"And I'm just jealous," David agreed. "Now, will you please play some tennis?"

Even while we were still chasing balls around my lawn, with Puddles getting into the act and having a wonderful time, I was debating whether I should tell David how hard Raj worked as a doctor. He couldn't know that. If David ever got sick, he attended to the matter while he was in the city. I was sure he had never been in Raj's office.

But I did know what the doctor did, and it might be only fair . . .

Now Raj Collier was not a handsome man in the sense that David Masters was handsome, or even Tee Langan. Raj had thick brown hair which sometimes got a bit long and shaggy. His eyes were rimmed with thick, dark lashes; his nose was too big, as was his mouth. It was a mobile face that quickly showed his emotions, if he permitted that. His body was lean, strong, quick-moving. He dressed well in casual clothes, tweed jackets or suits. He looked well enough in his white jacket — but it was the inner man who exerted the charm, the appeal.

Just as it was the inner man who could work hard for long hours. He did take days off — several at a time, and as often as once a month. But when he was working —

He would be in his office as early as seven in the morning, alone, of course. He would, first thing, dial his answering service. Say, on a typical day — I had got this information by my persistent questioning and interest.

"Why does the doctor come in so early? What does he do, if no patients are there?"

First, then, he would call his answering service. And, on my typical day, there would have been two calls. A man with an earache had called at 2 A.M. He had refused to consider going to the hospital twenty-five miles away. The second call had come from a woman who didn't say what was wrong.

Raj would call the earache patient and would get no answer. The woman, he knew, could wait. But so the day would have begun — a day that would contain nothing very dramatic, though everything he did would have a touch of drama.

At seven-thirty Raj would get a cup of coffee from the percolator which Ward had prepared the night before and put on a timer. He would light a cigarette and read yesterday's mail. Then he would sign a heap of insurance forms. Maybe he would have another cup of coffee at noon, but this might be his only food until he finally would sit down to dinner often as late as ten-thirty at night.

He sometimes would see forty patients a day.

At about eight-fifteen, he would call the woman. "Hello, Kathleen," he would say kindly. "Dr. Collier here. What happened last night? You seemed to be upset. Well, is your stomach upset now? Oh? Your hands and feet feel numb." Kathleen would be a young woman who had lost her first baby by a miscarriage just a week before. Raj might think her symptoms were an emotional reaction, but she would deny that she was upset. He'd tell her kindly to be very careful about what she ate, to stay with the bland diet he had given her. Then, if things did not improve, she was to come to the office to see him.

This would take as much as ten minutes. Next he would take up a card and call a stomach specialist in the city. He'd ask about the doctor's wife and daughter by name; in turn, he would report that Sally was just fine. He probably had never seen this specialist, but he consulted with him regularly and sometimes sent patients to him. Their rapport was excellent. He would use this method of personal warmth, which I felt sure was natural to him, with all the doctors he consulted. He kept family data on their cards in his files.

This done, he would again call the earache man, who answered this time. Raj would tell him to come in. "Don't wash, Jack. You can wash afterward. Come right over."

Jack would come right over. It would be eight-forty by then. He'd say that he'd had the earache for a week, but it had got bad, real bad, in the night. Jack was a short man, overweight, in his early twenties.

Raj asks him if his throat is sore. Does he cough? Jack says yes to both things. Raj listens to his heart and lungs. He gives him a nose spray, a pill to dry up his cold, and enough penicillin to last five days. Jack is to stay in.

Jack doesn't ask what is wrong with him, but he does suggest that Raj put him on a diet so he can lose weight.

"Not now," says Raj.

At a minute or two after nine, Mrs. Ward will arrive. Raj has been aware that patients have been coming into the waiting room; he can hear them talking.

He will talk to Ward for a little, then tell her to send in the first appointment. He sees patients from nine to twelve each morning. Office hours are one to two, and six to eight, each day. He charges from seven to ten dollars for an office visit, fifteen to twenty-five for a house call. He points out that if he had a hospital, the mornings would be devoted to hospital work. He then could hold his office hours in the afternoon and not have to make so many house calls.

His first patient may have an infected foot, which he treats for a reduced fee because she is on Medicaid. If he had a clinic, he would not have to see welfare patients, giving him more time for his private practice. But he is kind to these poor people, and sees a lot of them.

The next woman who comes in kisses him on the cheek, and he pats her shoulder. She has a sore arm; he examines her and tells her she has a shoulder sprain. He prescribes a rubbing ointment, a heating pad, and rest.

She also has trouble sleeping; this can be terrible, she assures him. Raj says that he knows it is terrible. "My way is to count respirations," he tells her. "One-two-three-four. But if you start thinking about what Jane What's-her-name said in the beauty parlor, you start back at one. I give you my personal guarantee you'll never reach fifty."

The woman laughs and leaves.

It would now be nine-thirty, and eight teen-agers come in. The town council has hired these underprivileged boys to clean litter and brush from the riverbanks and the wooded ravines. Dr. Collier has been asked to give them physical examinations and immunize them against poison ivy and sumac. They have come in for their weekly shots. During the examinations Raj has discovered that three of the boys are drug users, and one has bad kidneys. He has been treating them all. The total fee from Two Bridges is ten dollars per patient and four dollars for medicine.

Raj is injecting each patient on his backside when the phone rings. The caller is a chronic complainer whom the doctor knows well.

"Myrtle, dear," he says, "I have told you that the best treatment for sciatica is bed rest. Yes, it is like a tired toothache in your legs. I *am* telling you what to do. Please do what I ask . . ." He lays the phone down, the woman's voice can be heard; she is talking fast and loud. Raj makes a note on his desk memo and picks up the phone. "Don't yell, Myrtle," he says gently. "Yes, and if it gets too bad, it will mean surgery. But just now — I have people here, sweetheart. I hope you'll get better. If I had something else to suggest, I'd mention it. Good-by, dear."

One of the boys says his throat hurts . . . Raj puts him on the table and looks down his throat. Yes, there are white patches. "The beginning of a fine strep," he tells Mrs. Ward. He has her call the drugstore for a prescription of penicillin, and he sends the boy home to bed. He tells his friends in the group to check on Nemo.

The boys all leave, and Mrs. Ward brings in the mail. She has opened one letter and hands it to the doctor, smiling. In it is a check from a lawyer, not David. It is in payment for two examinations Raj has made for medicolegal cases won two years ago, but the bill has gone unpaid. One of the patients recently returned to Raj, who refused to accept his case, another medicolegal matter, until the lawyer paid the long overdue bill.

By noon Raj has seen the last patient, and Sally brings him coffee and a sandwich. She suggests going home for a proper lunch. Raj shakes his head and smiles at his wife. Then he goes out to the car, which is a good one.

As he drives away, he snaps on the recorder, which plays a taped medical lecture on long-bone-end injuries in teen-age boys. Sally has installed this device. The lectures have been taped and distributed to physicians. She has installed another recorder in Raj's bathroom at home so that he can make some effort to keep up on medical affairs. She herself listens to the tapes.

The two house calls are to elderly bed-ridden women. One is the wife of a doctor who has retired and bought a cottage beside the river. Raj could turn this visit and other charges over to Medicare. He prefers to extend professional courtesy, and makes no charge. "If another doctor trusts you enough to let you care for his wife," I heard him explain to Ward and Sally, "what bigger return can this pill roller expect?"

Office hours begin at one, and Raj is back by one-thirty. His first patient is a man with emphysema who lectures the doctor for smoking a cigarette. Raj laughs and says he stopped smoking a year ago and gained forty pounds. "The girls didn't like me any-more," he tells the old fellow, "so I had to start again. But don't let me catch you with one!"

Office hours are supposed to end at two, but Raj often sees patients until four-thirty.

A lifeguard from the town's beach can come in with a cut toe, the pin in a man's hip may have loosened, a girl could have stomach cramps, and a man could come in with a facial blemish which may or may not be a benign growth. Raj removes it and helps his lab technician prepare the tissue for sending to a commercial laboratory in the city.

When through — at four-thirty — he probably sees a drug detail man, a salesman, who distributes samples and talks about old drugs and new ones.

This man gone, Raj goes over the day's patients with Ward. He has made notes which need interpreting; she will type these records the next day and add charges to the bills.

Then Mrs. Ward goes home, and after, perhaps, another house call, or even a brief rest, Raj will resume his office hours. Without Ward there, now he will not examine a woman alone. She must bring her husband or another woman. Quite often Sally will help him with the evening office hours, and it is Sally who tells, amused, about the woman who screamed when Raj was positioning her for a fluoroscopic examination. "There the poor man stood, heavy X-ray gloves on his hands, suspected of making a pass at the lady."

His first patient on the night I am telling

about would have a hard knot in his stomach. His work is down on the docks, where he does heavy lifting. But Raj finds no rupture and says the man can return to his work the next day. The patient frowns, takes seven dollar bills out of his wallet, throws them on the desk and departs.

The telephone rings. Raj answers and listens. "How much did you pay your neighbor for her advice?" he asks. "Well, that's about what it's worth." He hangs up.

A patient comes in with a strep throat. A man with cysts on his groin, a man needing a hay fever shot, a woman who is sick all over. "She starts with her hair and goes down to her toes with her complaints," Raj tells about this woman. A woman with a child who is running a fever of 104°, a man for a hormone shot. "Psychological," Raj explains. "He gets one every time he wants to make love." A man needing a physical examination for an insurance policy, a diabetic whose urine has changed color.

It is nine-thirty. A woman in her fifties comes in with a minor lung disorder. She becomes short of breath. Raj checks her heart and blood pressure; her breathing grows heavier. All the classic signs of heart failure are there, and the woman seems to know it. Raj puts his arm around her and has her lie down on the table. "I'm here," he says. "Don't be frightened."

He tells her that he is going to call her son to take her to the nearest hospital. After he has telephoned, she is still breathing hard and he holds her hand. "It will be all right," he says. She looks up at him. "I know," she says. "I am not afraid."

A few minutes after ten, and the office will be empty. Raj has seen forty-three patients during the long day; his total fees are two hundred and eighty-eight dollars. Some pay cash, others are billed. A few never pay. Raj does not sue these. He wants no part of small claims court.

Sally, he has told me, will have a Scotch and soda, a large steak, salad and fruit waiting for him. He has seen Sally in the office; he sees her now before he goes to bed.

"Poor Sally," I said once to Raj. "You work a long day, you don't say ten words to her. You're not with her for ten minutes . . ."

Raj shrugged and smiled at me.

I said the same things to Sally. Her reply came quickly and sharply. "I am doing what I chose to do when I married Raj!" she said.

"He was still in school then?"

"Yes. Going through a hard grind. I know. I watched him make it."

She wanted no pity, no criticism.

Was Raj a good doctor? A bad doctor? I don't know. And I couldn't ask Sally. He would leave on his trips, and he was badly missed. He probably would break down if it were not for those trips. Wherever he goes, whatever he does, I thought about those things, and decided that I could trust Raj Collier as much as I've ever been able to trust anyone other than myself.

Raj had his faults, and many of them. Certainly all that were attributed to him. I had myself seen him respond to a woman's crush on him, if only briefly. I found myself unable to understand and I, too, deplored this sort of development.

I found that my whole analysis of Raj as a doctor and as a man was a matter of good against not-so-good, as I came to know him, as I came to know Sally, and to like her as I had never liked another woman. I did wonder why, with a super-god man like David Masters available, Sally should have married Raj Collier. That was harder to understand than the reason for her staying with him.

David, whom I saw much less of than I did of Raj, was the better man, the super-man. I only wished I had, or could ever hope to have, anyone as solid and as devoted as he was to Sally.

In this manner, I assessed these new friends, and I could have told myself that I was mistaken, that I didn't know the whole story. But I found that those who did know it felt the same way. Denny, David himself — neighbors who might speak of the Colliers.

Even little Jimmie Shannon next door. He was to have a birthday party and issued the invitations himself, coming to each guest in the company of his father. I happily accepted my invitation.

"Okay," said Jimmie. "Now I got to go ask Mrs. Sally."

"And the doctor?" I asked.

I caught the strange look on Mike's face — a look which instantly vanished. "Jimmie made up his own list," he said. "Believe it or not, there are some kids on it."

"Jimmie behind?"

"Yes," agreed Jimmie next door. "But I won't ask Dr. Collier." He shook his head emphatically.

"Oh," I protested. "Just because he gives you shots . . ."

Jimmie shook his head. "But I like Mrs. Sally," he said warmly, his smile wide.

"Who else is coming?" I wanted to avoid taking any sides.

"You, and — oh, a lot of people. Mr. Masters . . ."

"You like him?" I asked.

"Yeah. I like him a lot. He has a keen car. I like it better than Dr. Collier's. Don't you like it better?"

"Well, it's not red . . ."

"No, but it's better. I'm pretty sure Mrs. Sally likes it better, too."

"Yes. Once I saw her riding in it."

"But she's got to ride mostly in Dr. Collier's car, I guess," said Jimmie philosophically. "Mrs. Sally does things she's supposed to do."

I laughed and glanced again at Mike. "He's right," he told me. "We set Sally up as a model of what a young wife should be. A bit hard for you dames to follow . . ."

"Leave me out," I told him. "I'm not a young wife."

"That can change. You and Sally have become close friends, haven't you?"

"I hope so. And I'm with Jimmie. I like her a lot."

"She needs friends, too. Be nice to her."

I often met up with this protective attitude in others. David, of course. Bish . . .

"Raj has gone on one of his trips, Lissa. Keep an eye on Sally, will you? Ask her to do things for you. And even find some things, maybe, to do for her."

"That last is harder," I warned him.

He knew that it was, just as he knew that I would try. I asked Sally if she would have time to take me to see a fabulous spring some thirty miles from Two Bridges. She had her own car.

"Are you feeling sorry for Sally?" she asked, her chin up.

"I've no reason to feel sorry for you."

"Nobody has," she agreed.

Which was as far as she would ever go. She certainly made no defense of Raj. He could stand alone. And she would. It was clear that she definitely expected to live with her choice of life, and do the job as well as she could, too. When Raj went away, she stayed close to the office, doing the many things she could do there, my therapy for one big item.

We did not again mention the trip to the spring. I took the warning she had twice given me. I would watch, think, and make no move of any kind.

As a reward, when I asked Sally if she'd want to do some hard labor and help me stack my folders of music scores on the shelves I had bought and installed in Mrs. Bell's house, she agreed quickly.

"Oh, I'd love to!" she told me.

And we spent a happy afternoon and evening taking the folders out of the packing box, arranging them neatly on the shelves which reached from floor to ceiling. She even fastened the labels on those shelves. "What an array!" she cried when we had finished.

"More than ten years of my life," I agreed.

"And you played them all . . ."

"From Czerny to Bach."

She stood gazing at me. "I know you must regret . . ."

"I regret the plane accident," I said.

"I didn't mean that. But ten years and more ago, you decided to become a concert pianist. You gained much, you sacrificed some things, I suspect. Would you do it over?"

I felt that she was talking not entirely about me. "It was the thing I wanted to do at the time," I said slowly. "There were periods before the accident when I thought I should make a change in my life, that I was losing too much — friends, a family — things like that . . ."

"But you didn't give it up."

"No. I didn't. Not until I had to."

She nodded and rubbed her hands together. "Well!" she said. "That's settled between us, isn't it?"

Chapter Four

It was like trying to solve a whodunit, I decided, this searching into what had become the mystery story of Raj and Sally Collier. I couldn't peek at the last pages; I had to detect the clues that were given me, and set the trail.

My thinking — I called it "reasoning" at the time — whatever it was — took off along strange bypaths and had to be retraced. One of these . . . Of course I came to the eventual determination that an inferiority complex had nothing to do with Sally. She had no reason, need, or excuse to feel inferior to Raj. By birth and breeding, there was a good chance that she shone more brilliantly than he did. Her family, the Bradfords, was a firmly established one. As for intellect, Sally would shine right up there with Raj. Everyone conceded this. Her school records had been fine; she herself would have graced a profession had she not chosen to marry and be Raj's wife.

I agreed heartily to this claim. Sally's performance in Raj's office during the weeks I had been going there indicated that she had talents. Oh, of course she was not a doctor. Raj knew more medicine than she did; she herself constantly told people that.

"No, I can't prescribe for your cold, Mrs. Janoes. I can give you the vitamin shots which he has ordered, but you will have to wait until the doctor gets back for any new prescriptions. Yes, he does know more medicine than I do."

Of course that was true. Just as a plumber knows more about pipes than does his wife. Or so I reasoned.

I used much the same sort of hyperlogical reasoning to reach the conclusion that sex was indeed the real secret of this marriage which I was studying; perhaps it was the only secret. David Masters had decided that long before me. He had told me, but I wanted to draw my own conclusions, and I did. Sex and sex attraction had to be the reason for Sally, no meek and mild girl, to go along with all the ups and downs of her marriage to Raj.

Her husband was a ruggedly attractive, lovable, and promiscuous animal. Sally had married him because she loved him, and unlike the other women who fell in love with him, she was his wife. She had the advantage.

I had come to this stage in my thinking —

naive as it was, perhaps — when I reached another "stage" in my development as a part of the whodunit that made up my life in Two Bridges.

I was in the office almost every day, and I had become thoroughly familiar with the routine of that office. Within a month, I would, occasionally, answer a telephone. I would, of course, amuse a child if the child made the advances. This performance developed into "Lissa, will you keep an eye on Johnny while his mother is in the examining room?"

Keeping an eye on Johnny could involve a good bit more than my eye and Johnny. He might slip out the door and need to be chased down the hill; he might need to go to the bathroom, which would involve belt, buttons — and a peeking eye to see that he didn't clog the plumbing with paper towels, or punch all the soap out of the dispenser.

It took a little time and experience, but I learned.

Another thing I did was to talk to the old people who came in, or, really, to let them talk to me. There was one old man in particular; he had a skin disease and needed treatment once a week. I heard every detail of his life — his small farm, his three marriages.

"A man can't be nice to a woman; they

151

take advantage. Keep 'em busy, that's the way!"

I decided that he had a point there. Oh, I learned all sort of things! About lice, for instance. That there were three kinds: head, body, and crab. That lice and the scrubbiest of the communes dwelt together. That doctors . . .

"The doctor isn't here," I might have to tell a thin young woman, her skirts to the floor, her feet bare and crusty-dirty, her hair a revolting mess.

"But he gives me medicine . . ."

"I can't give you medicine."

"Sure you can. I know the name. It's called Kwell."

I shook my head. "I'm really not an employee of the office," I explained.

"But it's just back in the cupboard. Look, Red, you ever have lice?"

She leaned across the desk toward me. I pulled back a little, and she stood erect. "I guess you haven't," she agreed. "But let me tell you, the damn things itch! And if you had any sort of feeling . . ."

Fortunately, Mrs. Ward came in just then and rescued me. She told the girl — she called her Jinks — "The doctor will have to give you the prescription. Yes, for Kwell. Come back, or call, this afternoon. He'll take care of you. Meanwhile, why don't you take a bath?"

The girl said something extremely rude.

"With your clothes on and your mouth open," Ward called after her.

Laughing, she turned back to me.

"I think she's tragic," I said faintly.

"Well, she is, of course. She'd tell you that she's changing the world. That one day we'll all live as she does. . . ."

"And have . . . ?" I gasped.

So I did a little, and I learned a lot. Even during my treatments, I could not help but see and hear things.

Gracious goodness, yes! All kinds of things. Once there was a death while I was in the whirlpool, but I didn't know about it until later. A time or two before an ambulance had come and taken a patient on to some hospital; this old man had a heart collapse. Cardiac arrest, Raj called it. He died, the ambulance came . . .

I knew that births took place in the office. I had heard Raj explain to someone that a country doctor could do much worse than perform an office delivery. "I have instruments here, if I need them. Things can be sterile; I won't need to hurry off because I have patients waiting on me. Two hours after delivery, mother and child can be taken home by ambulance . . ."

This all sounded reasonable. Ward told me that she guessed they'd done as many as fifty office deliveries since Raj had come to Two Bridges, with no deaths and almost no complications.

This was all to the good. I got a real thrill out of hearing a newborn baby cry, and, like the new mother, I looked upon the doctor as a god — at least.

But my investigation could not remain upon this peak. If I stayed around the place, and I did — for an hour or more each day — longer when I found myself useful — I must come to realize that, as his detractors claimed, Raj did do some shady business. Or he could be careless in a way to overbalance the good doctoring which he did.

Many patients paid for each visit to the office, or for the medicine which the doctor dispensed. They paid, they were given a receipt. Others were billed, and they, too, got a receipt upon payment in person or by check through the mail.

But there were those . . .

Payments were made to Mrs. Ward at the desk. If there was any question about the bill, she had the answers. Sometimes when Ward was busy, Sally would sit at the desk, and there came the time when I would sit there, answer the telephone, make notes of appointments, consult the day's list and send the proper patient back to the examining room. I became proud of my business-like voice and manner when I did these simple things. So I knew the routine, even if I only heard it while beside the whirlpool bath in the therapy room, or lying on the table while the diathermy apparatus did its mysterious work.

Raj would know I was there; Sally and Ward did, of course. And on that particular afternoon they would know that I had heard the unholy row that went on.

I was on the table, getting drowsy, thinking about the sunshine outside, the walk home. Perhaps I would go around past the market and get Puddles some liver, which he dearly loved . . .

The door was open; people moved about. Patients came in, saw the doctor — once he had stuck his head around the door and asked me, "How're you doing?"

So everyone involved knew that I overheard when Judy made her terrific row in the office. I was glad I was not sitting at the desk, helpless against the large, determined woman. She identified herself by name. I knew who she was. My cleaning woman was a friend of hers, and once when my girl wanted to go to some sort of church meeting, she asked me if I would let Judy take her place. Cecil would vouch for Judy's honesty, and so on. I had found Judy vigorous and talkative — a good worker.

That afternoon the waiting room was full, I knew. There would be plenty of available and willing ears. I heard the front door slam open, and I heard the woman's strident voice say several things before I really began to listen. She asked Mrs. Ward if she knew who she was. Hardly pausing, she told who she was. My interest pricked. I knew, myself, who Judy Chilton was.

A large woman, with a perfectly egg-shaped head and round, well-fleshed arms. She usually wore the white or gray uniform which such household workers-by-the-day did wear in Two Bridges. I'd seen her on the street a couple of times after the one day she had spent in my home. She always greeted me with pleasant courtesy and a gold-toothed smile. I would judge she was around fifty years old.

So I pictured her leaning across the desk in the entry hall, telling Mrs. Ward what her trouble was. She was demanding to talk to Dr. Collier. She didn't care *how* busy he was! She had a few things to say, and she meant to say them to him! Her voice rose to such a pitch that I was sure Raj could hear her wherever he was in the not-too-large building. Smiling, I pictured him locking himself in someplace.

For Judy was raging mad. So far as I could tell, she had paid a bill of thirty-five dollars for some sort of minor surgery which Raj had performed on a girl named Sandra, whom Judy called her adopted child. "Her name ain't rightly Chilton, but she goes by that name. Sandra Chilton."

In a pause Mrs. Ward must have said something.

"Damn right, I paid it!" shouted Judy. "You told me to, and I did; the insurance company was supposed to pay me back. Well, they paid, but they didn't pay me! They sent the check to Doc Collier, and what does he do? Naw, I ain't sayin' he put it in his pocket, Miz Ward. That boy's been raised better'n that! But he did just about as bad. I guess you were off, and Miss Sally wasn't tendin' to the books, the way she does sometimes. So Doc, he comes out here and he credits that payment — that money he should'a give to me! — he goes and credits it to the delinquent account of my stepson and his no-good wife. It should be right there in the book, Miz Ward . . ."

Mrs. Ward said something, and Judy

broke in, roaring. "Damn right, you'll look it up! Damn right, you'll correct things. But you ain't gonna do it later. You gonna do it now!"

And then she went over the whole thing again.

It was stealing, she declared. She wanted to talk to the doctor and tell him it was stealing. Chilton — her husband — had gone off and left her six years ago. And Judy was not about to hand thirty-five dollars over to Chilton's no-good son and his wife, who didn't do nuthin' but lie around and drink wine.

I couldn't believe my ears, and I began to wish Sally were in the office; she could get things straightened out, I felt sure.

Now Judy was threatening Mrs. Ward, and Raj, as well as her stepson and the insurance company. She declared that she had a brother who worked for a mighty smart lawyer in Kansas City; she would get him to sue Doc Collier.

Judy herself worked for Mr. Langan — she diverged to remind Mrs. Ward how she had been hurt when working in the Langan home, and she had a paper saying that Mr. Leroy Langan would always take care of Judy. He'd sure help her get the money that was rightly hers!

She shouted, she repeated herself, and repeated again. She could be heard out on the street, I felt sure. She got more and more excited, her language got more and more extreme. "Sandra, yes!" she screamed. "I pay her bills! But not the Chilton outfit. No, sirree! By God . . . Who in hell did Doc think he was? Damned thieves here, every one of them. Crap, that's all it is," she shouted. "A lot of crap!" Then there was a pause. "I believe I'll have a heart attack," I heard her say in a gasping voice.

I believed she could.

And in the pause, I heard Mrs. Ward say firmly, clearly, that the matter would be cleared up and corrected.

I supposed Judy left. I thought the poor woman had a case. I wondered at Raj's touching the books. Sally kept an eye on them, I knew. Maybe there wasn't any truth in the whole thing.

Mrs. Ward did not mention the matter to me when she came to get me up. Raj did not, of course. If he thought anything at all about my overhearing the scene, he probably asked himself what a pianist could know about a doctor and his office affairs.

He'd been careless; he had made a mistake. And it would irritate Sally. Though anyone could be careless . . .

But the other things — they angered and frightened Sally — and me.

I had been told that Raj did some shady medicine. I'd been asked if I knew it. I always found some sort of reply. "He's been lovely to me. The specialist is pleased with what he does for me."

But day in and day out in the office, I did see things and hear them for myself.

Of course I saw only the preliminaries, but I got to know when an abortion was in the works. Nobody spoke of these matters, naturally, but I came to know, to recognize a certain nervous air of conspiracy.

Perhaps an agitated middle-aged couple would come and talk to the doctor. In a day or two they would return with a white-faced young girl . . .

Sometimes a young girl would come alone or with an equally white-faced young man. Sometimes the patient would be an older woman, quiet and determined.

Always there would be payment in advance for "minor surgery."

"I want to pay for the minor surgery the doctor plans to do."

I didn't know how much was paid. The surgery was to be done on Sunday, when the examination rooms would be free. Mrs. Ward surely knew what was transpiring, but a good nurse sees nothing, hears nothing. Once the surgery was planned for Mrs. Ward's afternoon off. I came in as usual, and Raj hustled me through.

Sally was never present. That was invariable. On Sunday she would be in church. On Ward's free afternoon, she customarily did come to the office, but once, or twice perhaps, she had driven Mary Bridell to the city. She didn't arrange things so. Raj took the opportunity if it came.

At these times, I'd feel strange. The break in routine was disturbing. But I really only suspected what was going on. I didn't *know* a thing! Raj did do minor surgery in the office. He was good about accommodating his time to another's convenience. . . .

But sometimes the smoke of gossip would make itself noticeable to me. I would smell that smoke and begin to hear a word or two, see knowing looks . . . Something would be said about the "so-and-so" girl or the eminently respectable wife of a young businessman.

I could have talked to Bish or to David; I suspect that they each made opportunities for me to talk to them. They could have realized that a woman like me, coming from what some would call my sophisticated background, could not understand the elaborately braided events of smalltown life.

There was the day when I saw my first walking stick. I was on my way home from the office, and I was standing there staring at the trunk of the huge oak tree at the edge of my property. I must have made a strange picture to any passerby in my blue denim jacket and skirt, my blue denim shoes, leaning this way and that, looking, looking at the bark of that tree . . .

"Something wrong, Lissa?"

It was David Masters, pulled up in his low-slung car. I flipped my fingers at him, but I did not turn around. "The bark moved," I told him, gazing hard at the spot.

He stepped out of the car and came up behind me. I pointed and he bent over. He is a very tall man, thin and graceful.

"Walking stick," he said, straightening.

"What?"

He took a pencil out of his coat pocket and touched the tree trunk. "See?" he said. "Feelers."

I could not believe or understand . . .

"An insect," he said, moving his pencil gently down along the bark. There was a shiny line, another.

I looked up at him and back at the tree. "It's gone!" I cried.

"No, it isn't. See, it's here . . ."

"But — it moved."

"Few people ever see a walking stick move."

"Will he move again?"

"Perhaps as soon as we leave him alone."

"He looked like the tree bark."

"I know. You have sharp eyes."

"A bug," I marveled. And David laughed.

"Well," I conceded, "that's one more thing I've learned about since coming to Two Bridges."

David walked up the driveway with me. His eyes were amused. "You've learned other things?" he asked.

"Oh, yes. Yes. But sometimes the learning has not been so easy."

"And you've been thinking?"

I nodded. "Thinking," I agreed.

"Not too much?" Now his gray eyes were keen.

I shrugged. "I hope not. Though how much is too?" I rummaged in my pocket for the house key. We could hear Puddles getting excited on the other side of the door.

David spent a pleasant hour with us, but I did not talk to him about Judy, or abortions, or —

I knew that drugs — pharmaceuticals — were dispensed through Raj's office. I saw the cartons arrive, I saw them unpacked.

Mrs. Ward, sometimes the lab technician, often Raj, would check these boxes, unpack them, checking the contents and putting them on the shelves. Two of the cabinets had locks, and I guessed they contained narcotics, but I didn't know.

Once when Sally had helped with the task of unpacking the shipment, I heard her say something impatient about their not needing to go into competition with the drugstores. She realized that it would take a varied inventory to keep up with all of Raj's prescriptions, but if he would tell them what he might be using . . .

Raj retorted that he saw no big deal in being able to hand out antibiotics and cough medicine.

Sally repeated, "Antibiotics and cough medicine," below her breath.

"And painkillers for arthritics," Raj added, going back to his office.

There were a lot of boxes; the boxes could contain a lot of different medicines — different colors and sizes of pills — different bottles. Even empty, smaller bottles, and cartons of small, plastic pill bottles. They were not all for antibiotics, nor even painkillers as such.

There were other drugs dispensed. I didn't know, and didn't want to know, what drugs. I never did think Raj trafficked in hard drugs. But he was overly generous with his painkillers. The patients would come for these medicines; they would give money — more money than they gave for cough medicine — and they were more urgent in their need. These patients almost never saw the doctor. Mrs. Ward would look at her record, she would unlock a cabinet and measure out the red pills, the white ones and often enough not a word would be exchanged more than the initial "I gotta have my perscription filled; I'm clear out."

I saw these things. I didn't *know* that anything irregular was going on. But there was a feeling, a furtiveness here, too. Mrs. Ward doing her duties of obeying the doctor. Sally occasionally voicing a protest, and Raj blandly sure that everything was being done according to the necessities of practicing "in the backwoods."

I could have talked to David or Bish about these things, but what would I have said, specifically?

And then there was the excitement — what I came to think of as the gunshot development. It was then that I began to think of myself as a private investigator, assembling evidence . . . of what, I still had no concept.

I could not, at this present time, go back and decide just how I knew that a gunshot was involved.

I had gone to the office early that morning. Mrs. Ward and Raj were to start me on some new exercises with pulleys. I'd do the necessary work under supervision, then bake the newly used muscles under heat.

The exercises hurt, and I was inclined to be weepy. "Like the weather," said Raj, putting his arm comfortingly about my shoulders as he went out to answer the telephone.

He came back quickly and spoke to Ward. "Put Lissa in the oven," he said, "then get a room ready. There's been an accident. I'll need surgical dressings, probes, and stuff."

Maybe he said that a man had been shot.

Maybe Ward said something about having enough to do without people getting shot. I don't remember.

It was right to bring a shot man to the doctor's office. I expected the ambulance to swush up, as it did often enough. But not that morning. I had barely got settled in the chair, my book at the right angle, the heat lamps set, properly directed, when I heard the bustle at the back door of the building. The therapy room door was open. I saw three men come shuffling down the hall, supporting a fourth man, almost carrying him. He groaned and cursed alternately, and Raj's voice told him sharply to be quiet.

"You'll fix him up, Doc?" asked one of the man's friends.

"I told you to bring him in. I'll know more when I examine him."

I heard him tell Ward to "cut his pants off." So the injury was to a leg, I decided. I heard Raj tell the three men to wait out in the car, but to keep quiet there, too. Why? I asked myself. The men didn't question his order, but came along the hall again. One of them saw me there, and he went back to Raj.

I heard Raj say, "Forget it! She's okay."

He was talking about me. The man had evidently been embarrassed to find me where I was, a witness to whatever was going on in the office that morning. This started up all my thinking again.

It was the anxiety of all the participants that the affair be conducted secretly, quietly, which attracted my attention and subsequently my interest. If the injured man had been brought in, as other accident cases often were brought in, I don't believe I would have given the matter any more than passing interest. There were patients out in the waiting room, as always at that hour of the day, but they, too, resignedly, expected emergencies to occur; they expected the doctor to take care of them.

But this hush-hush, their shock . . . no, not shock. The *embarrassment* at finding me in the therapy room — that sparked my attention. Who was the man hurt? I asked. Someone prominent, I decided. How was he hurt? In a hunting accident? No, there would have been no need to try for secrecy — unless one of his friends had shot him.

Perhaps he had been shot in a place where he had had no legitimate business to be. "Caught with another man's wife," was the phrase which most quickly came to my mind. And I laughed at my own absurdity, yet I knew some concern, too. Should the injured man have been where he was, and where he had been shot? Who was he? Did I know him? I sincerely hoped not.

And just as certainly I would not speak of what had gone on in the doctor's office that morning. I didn't say anything to Ward when she came to fetch me, to help me arrange my clothing, put on a raincoat, tie a plastic hood over my hair, and start for home. Nor did she tell me anything.

Others were not so discreet. Before evening I heard people talking and asking questions of each other. No one came out directly and asked me if I had been in the office when . . . ? But they talked around me, hoping that I would fill in the story which they had acquired or devised.

Tee Langan was the one who informed me that it was against the law for a doctor not to report a gunshot wound. Did I know that?

"Tee," I told him patiently, "all I know about doctors is that, for the last fifteen months, I have seen too much of them. And my knowledge is entirely centered around my right shoulder and arm."

He said something consoling, and probably really kind, about my having had to go through too much. Then he resumed his lecture. He was a lecturing sort of young man. Doctors, he informed me, had so much more responsibility than the mere healing of the sick.

I tried to divert him by saying the task was not so "mere."

"I know that," he agreed earnestly. "But don't you think that moral consciousness is as important to a doctor as his knowledge of drugs and surgical techniques?"

"Moral conscience is important to piano players and businessmen, too," I told him.

And for all I knew, Raj had reported the gunshot to the police.

There was no account of the accident in

the local paper that evening, though I had known it to do selective reporting before. A certain name was being mentioned around town; an argument over a poker game was hinted at; another story said it was a bridge game . . .

But everyone was talking. Clare stopped by for a time that evening; I was laboriously picking up twigs and small branches from the wet grass.

"Denny is supposed to do that, isn't he?" she asked.

"I'm supposed to use my back and arms, too," I told her.

"How is your arm doing?"

"Oh — it's better. I'm told."

"Do you still go to Raj's office every day?"

"Almost every day."

"Did you hear anything down there about Mr. Ferguson being shot?"

"Mr. Ferguson?"

"Yes. He has something to do with the University. I know gossip flourishes in the doctor's office. . . ."

"Nobody mentioned Mr. Ferguson to me."

She accepted my word, which had been truthful. Had I been playing the rules of gossip I would have told her what I knew. But I didn't play the rules, nor want to.

She was right about one thing: almost anything could be a matter of gossip in a doctor's office. I was in a spot, or I could be put into one, because it was common knowledge that I went to the office so regularly.

"What's wrong with Mrs. Beauty-parlor-owner?" people would ask me.

"Is Mr. Banker sick?"

"Does the Shannon child really have to have shots every other day?" Jimmie next door? Did he? Didn't he? Should I ask his parents?

No!

These questions were all alike. Gossipy pumping for the information I could be expected to have, and probably was too dumb to appreciate as significant.

If they could get so excited over Mrs. Beauty-parlor's frequent visits to the office — she was on a strict diet, I just happened to know, and came in for vitamin shots — why shouldn't the town get excited over somebody's being shot?

Our local paper didn't mention the event the next day either, or the next. And of course I did some heavy and heavier thinking about the whole matter. I went back to what I had seen and heard in the office that morning; I reconsidered all the things that had been suggested and said to me since.

And I came to the realization that some-thing was very wrong.

Indeed I was not at all happy about my conclusions. I told myself to stop worrying, or thinking, about affairs beyond my control or even interest.

But I was still doing some thinking — I had almost decided to ask Ward some ques-tions, which would have been pure folly — when Denny came to weed the flower beds. He worked all afternoon, and about four o'clock I took him a cold bottle of Coke and suggested that he should rest a little.

"It is a very hot afternoon," I said, having spent most of mine in the coolness of my house.

Denny sat down on the edge of the stoop, stretched his legs before him, and drank his Coke in thirsty gulps. "I guess you've heard about that man who got shot early this week," he said to me.

"Was there a man shot?" I asked, sitting down beside him. Puddles was exploring the hedge.

"Yeah, there was," said Denny. "On one of the boats. A card game, or drinking — maybe girls. Dames, anyway. And anyway, he got shot in his leg, and Doc fixed him up.

Clare says Doc is in trouble because he should have called in the police. She works for Mr. Masters, you know, and she learns all these legal things."

"I hope she is wrong about Dr. Collier's being in trouble."

"Yeah. Me, too. And I guess she is, because nothing's been said about there being an arrest."

"Maybe Dr. Collier reported the injury," I suggested.

"Oh, no, I don't think so, Miss Lissa."

"Maybe there wasn't any gunshot injury." I watched him.

He laughed and drained the Coke bottle. "There was one," he assured me. "And I don't blame the man, and even Doc, for keeping quiet. I'd do the same in their place."

"Do you gamble, Denny?"

"Who, me? On my income?" He laughed, then his pleasant face quieted. "I was thinking," he told me. "Not about myself, but if Clare would ever get into some scandal or something that talk would hurt, I'd want the whole thing hushed up. Wouldn't you?"

"Would Clare — ever — ?"

Denny sat up straight. "Oh, no, ma'am," he said quickly. "But sometimes things happen when you least expect them, and the way this town builds up a story . . ."

"I see what you mean," I murmured.

"Have the police questioned Dr. Collier?" I asked after a long pause.

"I don't know. I guess they might have. Sure, with all the talk going around, the law would have heard some of it. Wouldn't they?"

"I would think so, Denny."

"Yeah." He leaned forward to rub Puddles' ears. "But I guess they couldn't, or wouldn't, do much of anything about it. Raj is the only doctor here in town, and besides, he's a Bridell."

"That covers a lot," I agreed.

"Well, you know what I mean. It happens in a town like Two Bridges. But maybe it happens in other places, too. Your name stands for things, whether it's Kennedy or Roosevelt or Rockefeller."

"But that can be good."

"I know." He began to pull little weeds from the flower bed near the step.

"I see Clare now and then," I told him. "She seems to be a very nice girl."

"Yeah," said Denny. "She is."

"You sound pretty downcast about it."

He looked up at me and tossed his hair back from his face. "My trouble is, other men think she's nice, too."

I picked up the Coke bottle. "What other men, Denny?"

"Oh, a lot," he assured me.

"But Clare . . ."

"Naw, she doesn't play the field. Like she could, you know? But she gets crushes. Not on me, I'm sorry to say. I'd grab *that!* But she's pretty gone on Raj Collier. And then there's Mike Singley . . ."

"But a lot of girls get crushes on doctors and basketball stars, Denny."

"I know they do. The trouble comes, Miss Lissa, when the doctor or the basketball Big Man notices the girl. And Mike sure notices Clare."

"Won't he be back in college soon?"

"Yeah, sure. He has a scholarship, and in a year or two, he'll be eligible for the professional draft. He'll make that. He's good. These guys get paid enough to get married, and a lot of 'em do. And the thing that bugs me is, if Clare and Mike should get married, this whole town would go crackers. They're that crazy about their basketball players."

I was sorry for Denny. And his Mike Singley didn't seem such a great prize to me. But then, I wasn't Clare.

As for Raj — I believed she did have a crush on him. A lot of women and girls did — all ages. I'd seen Clare talking to him, and

I'd seen her once in his car. "He gave her a lift," I told myself at the time.

Oh, dear. I didn't want Clare to be foolish. I didn't want to have any more things to think about.

Sally thought Clare was a nice girl, just as I did. She talked some about the commune down the hill below our houses. "Why should a nice girl like Clare choose to live in such a place?" she would ask. "Those free-living girls think they are independent, but when they get into trouble, they come to Raj —" She broke off.

I knew they did come to Raj. Maybe, as talk claimed, to get drugs. I wasn't at all sure that was a possibility. But they did come to the office, wanting to be rescued from the old, classic "trouble" which young girls can get into. My grandmother had used that term.

By then, I knew that Raj took care of such girls. I heard Sally protest to him about it, and there was at least one time when she happened to be in the office — as she frequently was, and almost always was when Raj was away — I felt sure she had turned down a girl who came in wanting an abortion. The girl protested. The doctor, she said, had promised her . . . She had the money . . .

Sally said she was sorry.

"I'll come back," the girl promised. She did not happen to be one of the young, frightened creatures.

"I don't think you should come back," Sally told her, pleasantly firm. "The doctor won't do what you want."

Raj found out about this — I decided that the girl had told him. I was in the office when Sally sent her away. I was there on the next afternoon when Raj came roaring in, shouting his protest to his wife.

She replied to him . . .

I was shocked at their quarrel — at its violence, its force, its cruelty, one of them to the other.

Raj told his wife to stay out of his office! He said he meant what he said!

Sally — against his thunderous shouting, her voice was like thin icicles clashing together. "I won't stay out," she told him. "I will do everything I can to protect you. There is no need for the scandal you are building up to."

I lay there trembling, wishing I could trust myself to get down from the high table to find my clothes and creep away. Tears burned against my eyelids. I was so sorry for Sally!

I admired her so much, and she was right.

There was no need for Raj to do illegal things. He was a good doctor with an established practice. Why, then, must he risk everything . . . ?

I was angry at him, and distressed for Sally. What must it be like to love and need to defend an unscrupulous, deceitful — though certainly an enormously charming — man?

I hoped that I would never fall in love and be exposed to so deep a hurt.

Chapter Five

Sally had spoken warningly to Raj of the scandal which he courted. But even I, new in the town and not knowledgeable at all in the matter of doctors and their ethical practices and commitments, knew that scandal was a constant fact with Raj, and about him, whether his wife knew it or not.

David Masters said he thought she did know it. "Women are capable of a protective blindness and deafness," he told me.

It wasn't that I'd knowingly handed on to David my concern about the young Colliers. But he was a skilled lawyer; he knew exactly how to get a thing out of me. Bish was pretty good at this, too. Only with Bish it was more a matter of his knowing a thing before I did and getting me to acknowledge, and then to discuss with him, what he already knew. He said this was good for my soul, and I supposed he knew about that.

With David — he came to Two Bridges almost every weekend. Sometimes he had business in the general neighborhood and would be there during the week. When he came to see me, as he often did if we didn't meet elsewhere, he was clever at detecting some concern fogging my thoughts, to make me seem inattentive to more immediate things about me.

This particular evening he had brought a bucketful of grass plugs to plant and try to make grow in a bare place back at the edge of my lawn. The trees made thick shade there, and I was sure the grass never would grow.

"We'll try zoysia," said David. "And if that doesn't work, I'll bring Bermuda from the city."

"I don't mind the bare spot," I told him.

"But of course you do. It's downright treasonous to claim otherwise!"

"Could Denny do that?" I asked, watching David grub away, raking, smoothing, pulling up this bit of growth and that. I'd never before seen him get so begrimed.

"Denny could do it," he agreed. "I want the stuff started right." He went off for the hose, and came back again. As usual, Puddles must have a tussle with the hose before one could get down to using it. The puppy would bite at the stream of water, bark at it . . .

"The reason," said David, laughing and adjusting the nozzle to a fine spray, "that I think Sally may not realize the constant threat of scandal for Raj, is that people like the girl, they want to protect her."

"From what?" I asked stupidly.

"From talk, dear. From *talk* — a cruel weapon if carelessly or maliciously used."

"Can they do that?" I asked. "It seems to me that everyone in this town and around it gossips and builds up a story — any story —"

"I know they do. But not with Sally. You don't repeat to her these things you hear, do you?"

"Well, I don't seem to have the gift for gossip. I ask dumb questions —"

"And you set your pretty head into a turmoil of questioning and worry."

Yes, I did that.

"But you don't come out and say to Sally, 'Did you know that Raj can be asked to do an illegal abortion? For a price?' "

I laughed unhappily. "Of course I don't. But she's in the office . . ."

"She's there, she suspects what Raj is up to, but she doesn't know that there is talk about those things — yet. You see, Redhead, no scandal has yet reached the courts. In the way of complaint, lawsuit, or arrest."

"Oh, dear," I said.

David glanced up at me.

"The truth is . . ." I began. "I've always thought . . ."

He nodded. "You've always thought that doctors, through their choice of that profession, through the training and example which had taught them, you thought that they were all noble and dedicated people."

"But aren't they?" I asked, troubled.

"Oh, yes. Some of them are, Lissa. They really are. For the reasons I mentioned. They are good straight guys to begin with, their medical training either instills that dedication in them or the example set by such dedicated doctors converts them. Then, there are some men — women, too, I suppose — who cleverly decide that they can make a better-than-good living by practicing medicine that way." He pushed three plugs of grass into the damp earth. His knees and hands were covered with mud.

"Some . . ." he said slowly, and then did not continue for a long minute. "Well," he said then, briskly, "we have rascals in all professions! Take the man who collects my trash . . ."

I laughed, and that ended the discussion of Raj and the medical profession in general.

Of course I continued to hear talk that bothered me, and I saw what I saw when in the office. I decided that Raj probably was the rascal David implied him to be, and I was sure that he was a ladies' man. All ladies, but particularly for and with Sally.

They could disagree, and did, but generally Raj's attitude was beautiful and kind to her and about her, with her. He frankly admired her intellect. "She's a better doctor than I am," he would say proudly, and mean it.

He was, as well, gallant to girls like Clare, warm and comforting to women like me — women of all ages, of all appearances. We wanted to think he meant his gallantry and his warmness, and by and large I believe he did mean it.

I could not argue the fact that there was all sorts of gossip about the man; it floated in the air like pollen, and settled in every sort of place. Not only did this talk center upon the way Raj practiced medicine, but it dealt in detail with the many paths he walked.

I deplored the stories, I deplored the happenings which originated them, because I considered it a great waste of Raj's genuine abilities. He could have been a very good doctor, and filled a particular need.

Though he did fill a *need,* I supposed. There were these people who wanted his sort of doctoring, who wanted service in all shades of gray as well as shining white. The thing was, I felt sure that Raj could have stayed on the bright side, the good side, and filled a need enough. A need that was felt right in his own home town, in the small town of Two Bridges. He might have lost some patients who sought irregularities, but he would have gained others which he did not have under the system he was maintaining.

I learned to know about a woman who would not send her early-teen daughter to the office for a flu shot until she had determined that Sally was there.

That sort of situation was bad.

Could something be done about it?

The town as a whole knew about what went on with Raj and his medical practice; they must have known those things before I ever heard of Two Bridges or came there to live. He had been practicing medicine there for about seven years. And so far as income and popularity went, he would be considered successful.

David said there were rascals in all professions, and situations like that of Raj happened elsewhere. It happened in politics, in the church . . .

In my own professional field, I had known an impresario who had made money by the way he presented a bad soprano. Publicity, gossip column build-up, TV build-up, even the lighting and setting of an appearance — the massive orchestra to accompany her. But sex symbol or whatever, she still was a bad soprano, and if the public had protested and had stayed away from her concerts, it would have quickly ended the matter.

If people who knew what Raj was, or even suspected, would not come to his office, would not call him . . .

But they did come, they did call.

So — who was at fault?

The days went by, of course, the weeks, and then the weeks became months. We were into the midst of summer, the hot days, the hot nights, too, sometimes, though usually the many trees and the river could cool the evening air.

And then the time came, the time when the terrible things happened, and I was in on it all, though out of it, too. It is now difficult to unscramble all the events, to line them up, ready to be told about in sensible sequence. At the time, it was impossible to consider them at all in a reasoning manner — or a reasonable one.

I remember that Sally even apologized to me later for my involvement in the affair. I was a patient. I should have been able to come to the office, have my treatment, and depart in peace, relaxed and helped.

Which was true, of course. Only —

Once before, I had felt the same sort of helpless participation in tragic events.

I had, on that occasion, attended a football game. I was a guest, a celebrity in the bright, noisy, crowded stadium. Television cameras, a brief interview had featured my being there. I sat in a box, a chrysanthemum bright on my shoulder, a blanket warm across my knees, and I had enjoyed the game. The gay scene, the music, the colors and sounds can now come back to me vividly.

Then, even as we watched eagerly to see if a first down actually had been attained, one of the players on the field collapsed, and there, before our eyes, the young man died of a heart attack. Minutes — even seconds — before I had cheered the tremendous efforts which perhaps had caused the attack, his brutal forward push against brutal defense. I had cheered him on, and when he collapsed, when he died, I felt guilty and helpless as well.

That day in the crowded stadium, and on the hot summer night as a new resident of Two Bridges, I *was* a part of the things that happened. I knew they could happen, I had known they could — and yet I myself had condoned the chance of their happening by being a passive onlooker.

That evening, Sally had invited me to have supper with her. It would be supper, she told me, light and informally served. Mary Bridell, her mother-in-law, was in the city for a church meeting. Raj had gone fishing. I knew that he had gone; he had told me that for a few days I would be "at the mercy of Ward. Sally will see that she does right by you."

Two days before I had seen his departure, the gear assembled in the driveway, then stowed into the trunk of his car. I had smiled at the man's boyish gaiety; I had seen his casual dress, his hair blowing in the breeze, the sleeves of his yellow shirt rolled up.

It was when I went down to the office for my therapy, with Sally supervising as promised, that she invited me for supper. I was happy to accept. The Collier home was an exciting place to be, with its boxwood hedge, fifty years old, reaching to the second-story windows. Sally had our supper served, not in the formal dining room with its sparkling Georgian silver and lace-tipped linens, but on a low table in the library where the couches and easy chairs were covered in russet suede, and there were paintings of country scenes upon the walls. It is a gracious home, and whatever has happened I have never lost that feeling of elegant hospitality which marked my first sight of it.

I don't exactly remember what we ate that evening. A cold salad, I think, and hot rolls as light as feathers.

We sat relaxed, looking out through the long windows. Through them one could see the corner of my house, and the curve of the street down to the river. We talked about all sorts of town affairs.

Laughing gently, idly touching upon familiar things the new little shop that was going to offer "unusuals." I had been there, and told Sally about it. We mentioned a patient who came to the office and always left her eye glasses at the desk. "She expects someone to get rough." We talked about the Langans and the trip they were taking, and which I had been invited to share.

"Mr. Langan says I must go to Arizona with them next winter," I said. "It will help my arthritis."

"Don't go," Sally advised. "I don't believe, in your case, you'll have arthritis in Two Bridges."

"I suppose they meant to be kind," I mused.

"That isn't usually their motive. Which

sounds catty, and is. But those people — everything they do is calculated. And their trips — Oh, my!"

"Have you gone on any?"

"No, but friends have. They stay at the best hotels — that gives them an address and stationery — but when just the three of them go, they engage a double room, with a rollaway brought in for Tee."

"But he's . . ."

"He's thirty-five," Sally agreed. "They could afford a suite, they have to pay for a third occupant — their excuse is that Tee should be near his parents in case of sudden illness."

"Do they . . . ?"

"No, they don't." She laughed and shook her head. "They'd be funny if they were not so dull."

"They are dull, aren't they?" I asked.

"Very. But they approve of you. Beatrice is dropping hints that Tee probably will marry you."

I stared at her in disbelief. "That's no compliment!" I assured her.

"No. I felt the same ten years ago. Poor Tee. His choice of girls don't co-operate very well."

We watched the evening joggers go down along the street. The men wore shorts and thick gray sweat shirts. The women and girls wore an assortment of play suits, their hair usually tied with a scarf. Three happy dogs accompanied the group.

"Should we be doing that, too?" Sally asked me.

"It might be fun. And Puddles would love it."

Sally laughed. "He certainly would."

We talked about the banker and his wife whose young daughter had lost her tooth retainer.

"She went to the drive-in restaurant after a movie," Sally told me. "I'm conservative. I think eleven o'clock, when the movie ended, is late enough for a fourteen-year-old. But anyway, she came home after midnight, and her parents relaxed, fell asleep. Then she wakened them to tell them she thought she had taken off the retainer and had left it at Johnny's.

"Her dad groaned, got up, called out at the pizza place, but they couldn't find the retainer and said they'd probably cleaned it up with the plates and napkins and stuff. Yes, they put that sort of thing into the garbage pails. So there went Molly and Jo Edward out to rummage through the garbage at one-thirty in the morning."

"Did they find the thing?"

"No. Which didn't make anyone any happier. It reminds me of the time Mary Bridell lost her diamond ring. She decided she'd pulled it off with her gardening gloves, which were torn and which she had thrown into the garbage can. She came to this decision and ran down the street waving at the trash-truck driver. He told her he couldn't unload there on the street, but she was most welcome to ride to the dump with him."

"She didn't!"

"Oh, yes, she did. Dignity, wide-brimmed gardening hat and all. What's more, after they'd found the glove, *and* the ring, she rode back to town in the empty truck, smiling and waving to her friends as she passed them."

The picture was completely ridiculous, and we laughed merrily as we accepted our silver compotes of lemon sherbet and black cherries. Sally returned to the matter of fourteen-year-old girls going to drive-in theaters with boys. "Then they go on to eating places like Johnny's," she said, "and even worse places, drinking smuggled-in beer, and there's horseplay that leads to problems. Kids eighteen years old, and certainly the younger girls, can't handle such things. They drink, they drive their cars — often enough their fathers' cars — they believe in top speed, and on these hills and curves, accidents just have to happen!"

We finished the meal, and we talked about the needlepoint Sally liked to do; she had made some beautiful things. I said I wished I could learn, but of course with my almost useless hand . . .

Sally thought I could do it; she thought I should try. Could I close my fingers tightly enough to hold the needle? No! Not with my left hand! It was through doing such things that my fingers would regain their supple strength.

I tried to laugh. I promised to keep trying. "But remember the knitting!" I warned. "Are you going to want to accept the first fruits of my needlepoint?"

"I'll love it. I —" She looked up at the houseman who had come to the door. He was bringing her the telephone; there was a call.

She glanced at me and lifted the instrument.

"There's been an accident," she whispered to me. "A bad one."

"But," she said aloud, "Dr. Collier is out of town.

"No, I don't know where to reach him. Not exactly. He's fishing, and he often goes to several places.

"Not for a day or two, I'm afraid."

I was folding away the needlepoint. Sally would do something.

"Yes," she was saying into the telephone. "I will open the office and do such first aid as I can."

She apologized to me as she went out to the car.

"I wish I could help . . ."

She smiled at me. "When you get home, you can call Mrs. Ward and ask her to come in. Tell her there are young people hurt."

She drove away, and I walked home, remembering that we had been talking about such things.

I couldn't find Mrs. Ward. She wasn't at home. I called a neighbor. Ward had gone to the city, she thought. "Her boss is away, and she's taking a day or two for herself."

That was probable. That day only Sally had been in the office.

I took Puddles for a short run, then I decided to go down to the office myself, thinking that, without Mrs. Ward, perhaps I could be of some help.

And that office! As I was coming down the hill, I saw the cluster of young people — boys and girls in their teens. One girl was sitting on the sidewalk, her head down to her knees; she looked utterly disconsolate. The boys leaned against things. I had noticed before that the young people did a lot of leaning and lying about. There were several young people inside the office, including my Denny, whose clothes were smeared with blood. He held a towel to his face. I tried to ask him what had happened, but he just stared at me and went outside. I got only a word or two of explanation from anybody; the kids were all frightened as children get frightened, bewildered that some game or toy could suddenly turn out to be dangerous.

Among all this, Sally alone was calm and efficient. She had put on a white gown. She smiled at me and asked if I would "stay with the telephone." I told her about Ward, and she nodded. "That figures," she said.

She had tucked her hair back and up. I was to send the ones who were hurt back to the examining rooms; she'd take them in turn. The others should be kept outside. "Lock the door if you need to."

A policeman came down the hall, and she spoke earnestly to him.

"Find Dr. Collier," she begged. "He's somewhere along the lake or the rivers. Try calling the resorts, and you might trace his car license number. Use your car radio. Don't tie up this phone. If he can be located, suggest that he be flown here. *We have problems!*"

Indeed we did. I helped where I could. I fetched bandages for Sally, and did a little first aid myself. I washed one boy's face, and I gradually learned what had happened. The overloaded car had gone over a guardrail down into a ravine. The first injured were brought in by a car that had been following.

"Chasing you?" I asked, opening a roll of cotton.

"Well, something like that."

An ambulance was on the way, and it soon came, bringing in a dreadfully injured girl. Her name was Bonnie . . .

There was blood, and more blood. Her arm, the ambulance men told us, had been torn almost completely off. They'd done what they could with tourniquets and pressure . . .

The stretcher came in between the rows of frightened young people. Even Denny's black eyes looked pale.

The policemen were scared. We were all scared. Maybe even Sally, though she didn't show it. She took over at once, directing the stretcher back to the treatment room where she had spread sheets on the table. She supervised moving the girl, and stepped to the side of the table.

"She works like a man," said the policemen in awe. "Like a doctor."

I couldn't do much to help, except hand things and scoop up the clothing, the towels and things that had been packed around Bonnie's arm. I carried the whole mess back to the incinerator.

"All I can do," Sally said to me, "is to get her ready to send her on to a hospital. Keep the ambulance here, Lissa."

I told the driver, who nodded. He was making coffee. "I expect that'll be clear to the city," he said gloomily.

"If Raj only had his hospital!" I cried.

"He'd still be off — fishing," said Sally woodenly. Her beautiful face was wooden — or like stone. She looked stern and sad and angry, all at once. Hoping against hope that Raj would be brought in, she worked over the injured girl. Treating her for shock and tying off blood vessels, she told me, "I'll give her antitetanus — she may already have that. And of course the shock is bad . . ."

Watching her, my own shoulder and arm throbbed in pain, but Bonnie was unconscious. Had I looked so? White, the skin almost blue, beaded with moisture. Sally had me tuck blankets about the girl. She sent one of the policemen for bags of ice, which she packed around the injured shoulder. The parents were notified.

Bonnie's face — she was sun-tanned, which made her pallor very strange, there were freckles across her cheeks and nose. Her hair was a rich brown, and thick. Sally had fastened it back out of the way with a strip of gauze so that she could daub red stuff on the girl's forehead and temple.

Bonnie knew nothing of this. "I should be giving her blood," Sally murmured. She did get plasma, and the driver helped rig the rack and the bottle. Bonnie lay rigid, her head back, her features sharpened. In life — in activity — she would show that her mouth was large and generous. She had been wearing a brown pullover, brown slacks tucked into boots . . .

Sally had focused all the light in the room upon the table; beyond it the shadows gathered furry in the corners of the room. The faces of those who worked — Sally's, the ambulance man's, the policeman's, and my own frightened one, I suppose — surrounded the helpless girl. We looked strange, too. Our eyes were bigger than normal; our mouths were held into tense lines; shadows darkened our cheeks.

Finally, after not too long a time, Sally stripped off her gloves; she talked to the policeman. The arm would have to come off, she said. Had he heard anything at all about Dr. Collier? I was aware that there were more people in the building — though not many. Someone asked if Sally could do something about the arm, and I at least was remembering the foot accident which Sally had taken care of. I conjured up that scene — the fisherwoman instead of the slender young girl — I remembered, over and over, my own accident, and how I must have looked and been — the scene of the crash, and the scene in the emergency room of the hospital, with doctors and nurses to do for me. I'd been in a big hospital with lots of help available. But this girl, Bonnie . . .

"A doctor has no right to leave his patients!" I blurted, half sobbing. "No matter how rich or young he is!"

My outburst had startled all in the room. I looked up contritely at Sally. She brushed her bare arm across her face. "You pass a law to keep him on the job," she said grimly.

Though of course there was no such law.

Raj still had not been found when we watched the ambulance take Bonnie away. Her parents went with her — the siren echoed back and forth from hillside to hillside. When it was gone, I began to tremble, and tears ran down my cheeks. Sally brought a white apron and tied it around me. "Your dress is a wreck," she told me. "And save the weeping until we've patched up all the other idiots." She spoke sternly, and I was angered by her tone. But I did help her, fetching the things she needed, spreading newspapers on which she cast the bloody wads of cotton . . .

As I moved about, I heard the policeman getting names; by then the news had spread, and there were a lot of people out in the street; some had come into the waiting room and hall. These were parents, two men from the highway patrol, a few who were just being grimly curious. By then Sally was working on the cut across Denny's forehead; it looked deep, and the boy was protesting fiercely at her roughness when the police came into the room.

"Is that boy Dennis Marion?" the state policeman asked.

Sally said that he was. She restrained Denny's convulsive effort to get off the treatment table. She asked me for adhesive, and I gave her the roll.

Thus occupied, it took both Sally and me a moment to realize that the policeman was arresting Denny. The boy knew, but I was slower even than Sally. Then —

"You can't do that!" I cried loudly. "You

can't arrest him! Unless you arrest all the others. Will you go down the highway and arrest the girl in that ambulance? You —"

Nobody paid any attention to me. Denny had been driving his father's car . . .

"His father's car." The words echoed in my mind, spoken in Sally's voice earlier that same evening. Liquor had been found in the wrecked car — beer and wine. Questioned, Denny admitted that he'd had a "beer or two." He was a minor. Eighteen. Bonnie was even younger.

When Sally had finished dressing the deep wound, the officers took the boy away.

I was shocked. "What will they do to him?" I asked in a thin voice.

Sally shrugged and sighed. "In this town, who knows?" she asked wearily. "Don't you want to go home, Lissa?"

"No. I'll help you clean up this awful mess."

It was a mess. The treatment room, the examining rooms, the waiting room. Coffee cups, Coke bottles from the machine — gauze and cotton — soiled sheets.

Sally worked steadily, saying something about records. We should have kept records. Would I . . . ?

She stopped what she was doing and turned to face me, her eyes enormous. "In

200

this town," she said again. "If they'll let a doctor like Raj function . . ." She broke off and turned away.

"I'm bitter," she admitted.

Why not? I asked. Why shouldn't she be bitter?

Chapter Six

I was frequently to ask, why not, indeed. Before the ambulance with Bonnie could have reached the city, the Highway Patrol located Raj's car. I was sitting at the desk, trying to make the notes which Sally wanted. She would call out names and items to me. "Can you spell Merthiolate, Lissa? Oh, don't worry. Write it your way, and I'll type the record later. I especially want to get the numbers — location of wounds — and all about Bonnie . . ." Her voice drifted away as she went into the lab or the supply closet.

The phone rang, and I took the message. Dr. Collier had been located at the Four Winds resort . . .

This was a very plush hotel on the big lake. I had heard the Langans tell about it gushingly. David made fun of it; he called it Hillbilly Elegance.

"Could we talk to Dr. Collier?" I asked.

He was not "available." Would I want to talk to the young lady who was with him?

Young lady? What young lady?

"Is he returning?" I asked faintly. I was

making notes, and I saw with horror that I'd written "with a young lady" down on the pad. Sally saw it, too. She had come out to the office and was leaning over me. I put the phone down. "He'll be here in an hour," I said faintly.

I tore the sheet off the memo pad. "I wonder if he did any fishing," I asked naively — stupidly.

Sally took the note from me. "I am sure he will bring some fish," she said crisply.

"I wonder why he couldn't come to the phone?" I said aloud, still stupid.

"He didn't want to," said Sally. "He thought I was on this end of the line."

He would be back in an hour and we still had much to do. For one thing, we still had a boy sitting morosely in the waiting room, moaning now and then from the mighty headache he said he had. He had a great knot on his forehead, so I believed in the headache. He was waiting for his parents, who lived out in the country and seemed to be in no hurry to fetch their son.

Sally and I finished the notes, and we once more faced the litter of newspapers, bandages, tape cartons and dirty towels. "We need a firehose," said Sally. She had put fresh sheets on all the tables. There was a big pan full of instruments to be cleaned, sterilized, and put back into the proper cabinet shelves and drawers.

We could leave it all for the night, we told each other, and go home to bed. Our clothes were a mess.

"But something else could come up," Sally reminded herself — and me.

"*Tonight?*" I cried, my voice squeaking.

She smiled at me and hugged me gently. "I'm sending you home," she said.

I assured her that I would not go, but we were still talking about it when Raj came into the office — white shirt, dark trousers, his usual friendly smile. He looked around and whistled.

"You should have seen it an hour ago," I told him.

"Raj . . ." Sally began.

"I know about the accident," he said quickly. "The Patrol escorted me home."

We didn't ask about "the young woman," but we thought about her, all three of us. He toured the office, looking at things. He asked questions. Sally answered in the same manner as Ward would have done — technically, briefly. He read the notes which I had made and smiled at me. The names were all there — the names of the parents, the injuries, their extent and treatment. He gave the papers back to Sally. "Very good, Dr. Collier," he said to her, and he would have kissed her, but she stepped aside; she went out to Ward's desk and uncovered the typewriter.

"What now?" Raj asked her. "Do you know it is nearly midnight?"

"I must make some proper reports," said Sally. "We'll need them. I do think you should take Lissa home. She's beat."

"Where's Ward? Didn't you have any help at all?"

"I had Lissa."

"She didn't have any help," I said gruffly. I was trying to decide where to put the shoe and the bloody sock we had taken from the boy whose leg had been cut.

Raj tried to laugh Sally out of her determination to make out accident report forms at that hour, but he got nowhere.

"We'll need them," said Sally, "in a half dozen ways." And finally she said, "Tonight is going to bring us into court, Doctor."

Raj stared at her, then, saying something below his breath, he touched my elbow. "Come along, Lissa," he said. "I'll get my stubborn wife after I've taken you home."

I glanced at Sally; she nodded, and I went with Raj. I was suddenly very tired. I wanted to weep; I wanted a hot bath; I wanted to get into bed and sleep. Forget . . .

I did weep, even before Raj had unlocked my front door, thanked me and gone back to his car. I let Puddles run for ten minutes, then I filled the tub with hot, foamy water, and I felt as if I could go to sleep right there. But once in bed, I did not sleep. I went over and over the events of the long evening.

I again sat in the Colliers' gracious home and ate black cherries and sherbet from a crystal dish. I saw Sally work over that young girl's mutilated arm. I heard again the sounds of the evening. And over and over I thought about Raj. And Sally.

Perhaps because I had been there, Raj had offered no apology to Sally; he had tried to praise her. In her turn, there had been no recriminations.

But by now they were home. Before I got into bed, I had seen lights in the upper rooms of the big house. What had the husband and wife talked about? Was the "young lady" mentioned? Did Sally protest to Raj? Did he attempt to justify his absence?

I thought not.

I thought with them there would be the same feeling of emptiness, of emotions exhausted. And I felt tears again on my cheeks. The whole experience had left me very sad.

Raj had scoffed at the idea, but Sally was

right. We did have a court case develop from that terrible night. We? Yes, we.

Bish was angered by the event itself. That a group of young people should be so wildly irresponsible as to wreck a car, injure nine people, cause a young girl to lose her arm, that Raj had turned up missing, and that I should have been involved in it all.

"Sally was angry, too," I pointed out to him. "Sorry."

"I can see all sorts of differences between you two girls, Lissa. The big one being that Sally married Raj Collier, for better, for worse. For *his* irresponsibility, and her need to fill in for him. But you . . . If you are drawn into that court case . . ."

Publicity. Yes. Feature stories. My own injury rehashed, recounted.

"I won't be, will I?" I begged, feeling cold and frightened.

"I'll do all I can!" the good man assured me. "I'll talk to Masters."

I suppose he did, because David was as mad as Bish about the whole development. And he told me all about the involvement with the court, angry about that, too.

He appeared on my doorstep early on Saturday morning — red denim slacks, cotton-knit pullover. "How about a game of golf?" he asked me.

I stared at him, unbelieving. "But it's rain-ing!" I pointed out.

"I know it's raining. Best kind of weather for your kind of golf."

"You're crazy."

"But harmless. And I have an umbrella."

He did have an umbrella, a huge one, and I put on a thin silk raincoat. He wanted to take Puddles but decided that we'd better not, what with club rules and all. "There may be other nuts out there," David told me seriously.

There were not. We could walk the whole nine holes and see only a groundskeeper, picking up twigs and branches. The man eyed us suspiciously, but spoke courteously to "Mr. Masters."

He stood watching us until we were out of sight behind what the English call a coppice. We were busily talking, as we had talked busily since leaving the car.

David knew that I had shared that awful night with Sally, and he expressed his anger that she should have let me do it. I told him that I had gone to the office on my own — there was no one else to help, so I stayed, though she had repeatedly tried to send me home. And, anyway, I didn't want to talk about the affair.

"But you think about it."

"Yes. I think about it all the time. Talking about it only sharpens each thing I saw and heard and did."

I had accepted a date with Tee Langan and had asked to be taken home early because he tried to pump me. Where had Raj been . . . ? Things like that. Everybody did talk about it. Even Jimmie behind and Jimmie next door, too.

"What did they do with Bonnie Politte's arm?" asked one of the children. "Put it in the garbage bag?"

I was horrified . . .

Even Mrs. Ward at the office and of course any other patients I saw there would ask about that night, or talk about it among themselves. I wanted to forget the whole shocking thing. I even considered leaving town for a time, or abandoning my therapy and staying in the house.

And now to have David seem ready to make me talk . . .

"Please," I begged him. "I was glad to see you this morning; I like walking in the rain and getting my shoes all soggy. But I won't talk about that night!"

"An excellent idea!" said David readily. He put his hand under my arm to help me cross a little stream of water. "But I think talking to me might be a necessary thing, Lissa."

"Why you?" I asked crossly, pulling away from him. "I believe I want to go home."

"No, you don't," he said firmly. "I'll take you back to the car, if you insist. But I'll still try to make you see . . ."

"Oh, everybody tries to make me see that I should talk about that terrible night. 'Get it off my chest,' is what they say. Even Bish. And now you . . ."

"The accident made you angry; the efforts to talk about it make you angry," he said.

"Yes!" I agreed. "It was terrible that such a thing could happen!"

"That young people could be so reckless, and so dreadfully hurt. That Sally Collier had to do what Raj should have been doing with his office nurse's help. That you should have been exposed to the horror. You were angry and hurt. You were frightened that night, and you've been frightened since by all the things that are being said."

I didn't speak. But he was right. I had been angry and hurt, and frightened.

"But you didn't believe the things that were said, did you?" he asked, his voice cool.

"I have to believe about the accident. I was *there!* But the rest . . ."

"You mean the things that are being said about Collier? And the girl who was with

210

him at Four Winds?"

I would not answer him.

We walked the length of that fairway in silence. Then —

"The girl was Clare, Lissa."

I whirled to stare at him; his eyes were steady, and in panic I looked away again. *Clare!* David's secretary. Clare, who had dark hair something like Sally's. Clare, who lived in the commune, who was "crazy about" a basketball player named Mike. Clare, whom Denny wanted for his girl, and —

Had he known that she'd gone off with Raj? Was that why he'd packed his father's car with kids and beer, and had driven so recklessly . . . ?

And I was angry and frightened all over again.

"I won't believe it!" I protested. "Clare is not that kind of girl! Raj is fifteen years older than she is. Besides, she has a crush on Mike Singley. He plays basketball; and then there's Denny, who cuts my grass . . ."

David was watching me. And I broke off and just stared at him. His pullover shirt was white with little-men figures in red woven into it. I gulped and started to walk again.

David stayed at my shoulder, and soon he put his hand through my arm. Somehow, the warmth of his touch was comforting. "All women are what you call 'that kind,' Lissa," he said gently. "For men like Raj, they are. He looks at them, considers them, all in the same way. Clare, Sally, even you."

I whirled on him, completely shocked. "That isn't true!" I cried. "If I have to be one of your *women*, I *know* it isn't true!"

He smiled down at me wearily. "Not you, maybe," he said quietly. "I hope things will stay that way, but don't put it to the test, dear. Remember, he was 'that kind' for Sally. And it seems certain that he was for Clare."

He didn't like saying such things, he didn't like having to believe them. I remembered the anger which he had brought to my house that morning.

"I'm sorry," I said contritely. "I am sorry that all this — this — about Clare, you know — I am sorry that it upset you so much. And of course it did. It upsets me, too. Terribly."

"I know it upsets you," he agreed. "But that, really, is not why I am angry. I am sympathetic with Clare. Did you know that the girls in the commune have been against her in what she did, falling for a known Don Juan like Raj, and going off with him?"

"They don't call that free love?"

"I don't believe they do. He's too establishment, perhaps. Anyway, Clare's made a thorny bed for herself, and I am sorry. I deeply deplore the gossip there is, and will be, about her. She's been a fool, and I am sorry for her. Being a fool is always hard to get over."

We walked along. I was deeply thinking.

"Did — do — people know?" I asked anxiously.

"Oh, yes. I am surprised that you didn't."

"I wouldn't talk about the accident," I reminded him, and myself. I looked up at him. "But why, David?" I asked him. "Why should Raj . . . ?"

"Because of Sarah, you mean?"

"Of course that's what I mean. She's beautiful, and clever. Why should he ever look at another woman?"

"Now you're getting back into the male personality again, Lissa," he said, laughing. "You could just as easily have stayed with Clare and asked why she did as she did."

"You mean women are fools, too."

"They can be. But let's consider Raj, and why he makes a fool of himself. He's married to Sarah, whom I admire very much. As you do. As most people do.

"All right. Then, why does Raj seek his pleasures elsewhere? And there is an answer to your question. Yes, there is, Redhead.

Listen. You're around the Colliers a great deal, aren't you? In the office every day; you're friends with Sally. All right! Then you are aware that Sally disapproves of certain things Raj does, and she speaks up about it."

"Not to others, David."

"But she does speak to Raj . . ."

"I suppose . . . Yes, she does. I've heard her — well — protest." I was thinking of the drug dispensing and the abortions.

"So she disapproves. Though she knows, as we all know, that Raj Collier has to have approval to remain alive as Raj Collier. He is a spoiled man, and a rich man's spoiled son. If Sally won't give him the approval he needs . . ."

"He goes elsewhere, and that makes you angry."

"It did, the first six or eight times, Lissa. Now I am used to it. I expect it."

"But you were angry over this."

"Oh, yes. Mad as hops. And I'll tell you why. Over and above the fact that Clare has cheapened herself. She's put herself on the open market for any and every man. But let's go back to the car. I'll buy you a hamburger and a milk shake, and I'll tell you why I am angry."

Ever since, a milk shake, sipped slowly,

can bring back to me that rainy day when we sat in David's car, and he told me . . .

"Circuit Judge Russell Evans," he told me, his jaw muscles tight, "had the opportunity to make at least a token protest against these overindulged young punks who, at the age of eighteen, drink in drive-ins with fifteen- and sixteen-year-old girls, and then, in a drunken state, drive the family Pontiac, or Buick, or whatever, at speeds over a hundred miles an hour on our hilly roads, with the resultant loss of an arm to one of the girls.

"But he muffed it entirely, to the sorrow of this whole community. Because what penalty did the culprit, Dennis Marion, receive? Why, he must work for six months in a doctor's office!"

I sat up straight.

David's eyes sparked. "A fearsome penalty, isn't it?" he asked dryly. "Most young people Denny's age think it is a privilege to work in a hospital — in the city, the candy-stripers have prestige! To have a job in the doctor's office here would be considered a fine thing. The work would be interesting, the contacts pleasant, and the kid would be doing a helpful service. Most boys would seize the opportunity. Don't you agree?"

I considered the matter. Yes, even Denny,

I thought, would have liked a job in Raj's office.

"But your judge thought it was a penalty?" I asked.

"He did. You see, Lissa, Denny, as the driver of the car, was originally charged by the Prosecuting Attorney — his name is Akers — Fulton Akers. He charged Denny with felonious wounding, which indicates somewhat the personal feeling he had in the matter. He had, it seems, himself investigated the case.

"But later, and not very wisely, I think, Akers recommended a reduced charge of careless and imprudent driving, which the judge accepted as the charge. I won't go into the differences between a felony charge and this misdemeanor one. Though I will mention my suspicions that the felony charge would have made it more difficult, and perhaps impossible, for the girl's parents to collect from the Marions' insurance company."

I didn't know until later what I thought about this. I didn't know anything about Denny's parents, beyond little things he had told me. His mother baked her own bread . . . His father felt his son must earn any car he would own . . . There were a couple of other children in the family, younger than Denny. I'd found the boy pleasant, though sometimes unreliable. I waited for David to continue. His face still looked stern.

"Under the reduced charge," he told me, "Judge Evans could have sentenced Denny to anything from one day to one year in jail. He could have fined him from one dollar to a thousand . . ."

"I'd hate . . ." I began.

"You'd hate to have a young boy go to jail," David agreed. "And yet you have had an injury similar to Bonnie's."

"I know. I thought of it that terrible night when she was hurt. I wished we had a hospital and competent surgeons."

"Bonnie's arm was lost on impact," David told me. "I inquired about that. Nothing could have saved it, once she was thrown through the windshield. As for the jail bit, even a day in the poky would have given your boy a chance to reflect on his sins and the fact that his intolerable actions had caused a young girl to be deformed for life. A year would have been incomparably better."

"For Denny," I murmured.

"For any kid who did, or might do, what he did, Lissa. Because by that sentence, Judge Evans would have served notice on other drunken, spoiled boys, and their parents, that these youngsters could not drink and drive and scar their girl friends for life with impunity in this county of the State of Missouri."

"Bonnie wasn't Denny's girl friend."

"She evidently was for that night."

I nodded.

"And our judge has in effect given the green light to such reprehensible actions against society by imposing a penalty which most young people would consider a reward. For the next months Denny will work in a comfortable office and do interesting things — things that will make him feel noble and of service."

"Instead of cutting my grass."

David glanced at me, and for the first time a smile trembled on his lips. "I'll find you another Denny," he promised. "I imagine this one may even feel abused, because the judge did suspend a six months' sentence on condition that the boy does not drink again for two years. Which is pretty silly, because Missouri law already states that he shall not."

"But he did."

"Yes, he did, and Bonnie was hurt, his father's car is a total wreck, and I'm mad because Judge Evans gave that young rascal an honor when the least society demanded was a stern warning that maiming on our highways will not be tolerated and condoned. And I know I am already sounding like a trial lawyer making a summation, so I'll let myself say that Justice wept yesterday in that courtroom."

"I am shocked, too," I told him. "It does seem that this whole affair has given me a great many shocks. Of course Denny's sentence — But you're right. Working with those nice people, helping in that nice office, doing things for the patients . . ."

"Like you."

"Like me. When I was in that big hospital back East, the young people who pushed my wheelchair and delivered flowers and things — they did love doing the things they did. To do such work, even on a small scale, shouldn't be a punishment, and I guess I'm pretty mad about that, too. Because it won't be a punishment. I am certain of that."

"I am sorry — and mad, too, yes — that you were mixed up in this dreadful thing, Lissa. I cannot understand . . ."

I put my hand on his arm, and he looked down at me. "I am the only one to be blamed for my being there, David," I told him. "Don't even feel angry about it, because while I was subjected to one shock after another that night, it was a great experience. I went to the office of my own accord, I stayed there on that basis, glad to be able to help a little and to see people helped. Sally was wonderful, you know."

"Didn't you blame Raj for not being there?" He was studying my face, which tells what I am thinking or feeling before my words do.

"Of course I blamed him!" I cried. "It was terrible for Sally to have to do what he should have been there to do. I have been feeling that he might have saved Bonnie's arm."

"No. They tell me it could not have been saved."

"But Sally still did so much! Bonnie could have bled to death . . ."

"And then," he said dryly, "Denny could have been held for manslaughter."

I rubbed my hands with the paper napkin. "David . . ." I said in a small, squeaky voice, "would you be willing not to talk about it anymore? I just don't think I want to . . ."

"Sure," he agreed. "I didn't mean to carve your wounds any deeper. I thought if you knew how things were, you could stop fretting about the affair. I suspected you were wondering if there were ways you could have helped more, or could help now."

I wouldn't comment on that, but he was right; he knew me too well. He touched the horn as a signal, and our trays were taken away. He said he wished these places served up hot, wet towels, and I laughed at the idea.

"We'd have to go to Japan for that," I told him.

"Why, Miss Bartels, I would love to go to Japan with you!" he said, starting the car. "Do you want to go home now and pack?"

I settled down into the car seat, happy to be smiling. David was a kind man, and he knew how to comfort me without so many words. I did like him. A woman could trust him, and like him. Even love him . . .

All the next week David was back in the city, and I was tempted to write him a letter to tell him how Denny was making out in the doctor's office. I never had mastered writing decently with my left hand, and I was only painfully learning to do it again with my right. David wouldn't have minded such a letter, but I decided to wait and tell him in person. When I saw lights in his house down on the riverbank, I would phone him. He would come up, and I would tell him that Raj was taking the Judge's penalty to Denny just about as seriously as David could wish.

Raj said that he knew Denny was coming

to work in the office as punishment, and he laid down strict rules of behavior for the boy. He was to be on time, he was to wear the white garments which Raj would provide, he was to keep his hair trimmed and his manner quiet, respectful. He was to speak only as required for the performance of his duties. And at no time was he to be caught visiting with the patients. His friends were not to come around, nor could he use the telephone.

I heard about these rules and wondered if Raj would stick around to enforce them. He did. For some time he worked hard and steadily; he was being the good doctor I knew he could be, working long hours, seeming to have no other interests.

As for Denny, Raj set every grubby task to the boy; he must wash an old man's lousy head, he must remove a smelly dressing from an old injury . . . Mrs. Ward told me some of what was going on. I saw the rest for myself. Denny must clean up after a nauseated child — first the child, then the floor, the table, even the wall.

Raj exposed the lad to the shock of injuries. He took Denny with him to "help," and to watch, when a man was injured in a tractor accident, stepping across the power take-off, getting his coverall leg caught, drawing his foot and leg into the gears.

I was in the office when that injured man was brought back there. I saw the exact shade of green which tinged Denny's young face.

These experiences were bad. No hospital aid is exposed to such things, but Raj exposed Denny.

The worst thing he did — at least that I knew about — was to make the boy stand by and take orders while Raj attended to a man who came to the office one morning, a well-dressed gentleman in his fifties, pastor of one of the town's churches. While waiting to see Raj, he became very ill. I heard Ward tell the doctor that the "Reverend" was having a heart attack.

"Take over here," Raj told the nurse. "Come with me, Denny."

They went out to the waiting room. Denny helped lay the man on the couch and then transfer him to the table in the examining room. He knew the patient, and the whole thing frightened him terribly. But Raj spared him nothing of the man's extreme illness, his terror, and finally his collapse.

This tore Denny to pieces, and I was horrified. When Sally heard of the measures Raj was taking, she protested sharply to him.

"*We* have to take it," Raj reminded her.

"You did, the night Bonnie was hurt."

"Yes, I did. But we are older, we have had training — we are not exposed to it raw, without any compensating knowledge of what is happening. What you are doing amounts to holding that boy's hand over fire. And you will accomplish one of two things. You will turn him into a sadist, ready to inflict raw hurt on others, or you will make a nervous wreck of him. The night after Mr. English died, Denny's mother told me that the boy sobbed and cried the whole night long."

I saw enough of this, and I was ready to tell David what I saw. When, on Friday evening, I saw his car go down the hill, and I knew he was back, I waited an hour, then I walked down to his house.

I knew David's home well, but I had never been in it. The house was a large one, with a great wide deck cantilevered out over the river. On the ground floor was David's office and a space for his car and small speedboat. The lawn sloped steeply down to the riverbank. There was a great amount of glass. The house was built of cedar left in its natural state, with a huge chimney forming the center core of it all. There were bright deck chairs set on an expanse of concrete outside the office windows and door, and I found

David sitting in one of these. He looked up in amazement when I came down the drive and around the corner of the house.

"Lissa!" he cried, jumping up. "Of all things! I am delighted! Will you come inside?"

I selected one of the chairs and sat down.

"Playing it discreet, eh?" David teased me. "Well, I believe you still have a reputation to maintain. Could it stand a drink?"

I let him get me one, and when he returned, I told him all about Denny and what Raj was doing to the boy.

He listened quietly, shaking his head a time or two.

"I don't think I can make you understand how awful it's been for the boy," I said earnestly. "Several times I've thought . . ."

"He could be punishing Sally," said David in his quiet, reflective manner. "Yes, he could be. Well, there go all my thoughts that Denny was being rewarded, don't they?"

"I'd like to think Raj, too, had been protesting the judge's sentence, David."

He pursed his lips and considered what I'd said, then he looked up at me. "I'd like to think that, too," he decided.

I set my glass on the little table and leaned toward him. "I hoped you could figure out a way to help," I said.

"Help," he repeated. "Denny . . ."

"And me. And — well, anybody that needs help, David. The whole situation seems to be wrong."

"Yes, it is wrong," he agreed. "And maybe I can help. Let me think for a minute. You go on looking beautiful in your green dress . . ."

I laughed. I knew that I was not beautiful. My face is too pixyish and childish, my hair is too red and has to be shag-cut, short, to make it easy for me to comb. The green dress was a simple linen shift, and I never can make a scarf look right; I don't think that evening was any exception.

"You should be sitting in my chair," David told me, "and get my view."

"Do your thinking," I told him, "while I figure the possibilities."

He smiled at me and sat gazing down at the river for as much as ten minutes. I watched him and felt my tension relax. Would David like to know that he had this effect on me? Probably not. I could tell Bish such things, but David was younger, and relaxation would not be . . .

"I think I can help," he said, breaking into my thoughts. "I believe I can go to Judge Evans and get him to send Denny to work weekends in the hospital at Burton. Or Menard — that's a larger town and the hospital would have more for an aid to do."

"Can you arrange that?" I asked, no longer concerned with maintaining David's ego.

"I think so," he told me. "In the past, I've done a favor or two for Evans. And the thing would work as the Judge meant it to work. It will be punishment, because Denny's father will have to drive him over and back — his old man will be as mad as hell. Menard is sixty miles from here, and even if the Judge confines the service to weekends — as probably would be the way he'd do it — both father and son will suffer from the ruling. Since I personally feel that the father was about as much to blame as Denny was for the accident . . . Yep! That will work out."

And so it was arranged. Denny had to take care of my grass on weekdays, an arrangement which ended when school began. I missed his cheerful presence and the tidbits of gossip he brought me. "You're just going to have to work harder yourself at newsgathering," Sally teased me, "in order to keep up on what is happening."

"But the hospital work does seem to be a better arrangement," I conceded.

"It certainly is better. Raj never does anything by halves, and he was punishing that boy too viciously. I believe David was the one to get things changed."

"David is wonderful," I agreed. "Don't you think so, Sally?" I hoped I sounded innocent, but I probably didn't make it.

"I've always thought David was wonderful," she told me. "I've known him for ten years, you know."

And for as much as two months, things went along smoothly in this pattern. Summer slipped away, and autumn came to the mountains. Sleeveless dresses were exchanged for sweaters and skirts, suits, even topcoats. I became involved in many things. The town began to give a series of really large parties, some so large that the hotel must be used. These affairs followed a pattern, I discovered. One was invited for cocktails and dinner. One dressed according to his wish — some simply, some elaborately. The same people attended each large party, the same food was served. There would be an hour of rather heavy drinking and tiring standing about which preceded the setting out of the buffet which offered various salads and relishes. I became a connoisseur of melon balls and watermelon pickle. I could recognize the thin, crisp sort which I liked. There would be a beef roast, sometimes prime rib, more often what was called a steamboat round, but usually very good; the hotel did this roast especially well. Sometimes there would be ham; often there would be chicken or shrimp, both fried in crisp batter. There would be vegetables, potatoes cooked in various ways. Hot rolls would be served at the small tables, and coffee. Desserts were never elaborate and often were ignored entirely. I tired during the cocktail hour standabout, and I disliked having to try to juggle and fill and carry a plate to the table about as much as I disliked having someone offer to do the task for me. I didn't like the noise which accompanied a large party. One cannot gather a hundred or more people into a single room and not have deafening noise! But some parties were more fun than others. Some hostesses found new ways to do the same old things, or chose the guests and determined the seating arrangements for interest and compatibility. And of course there was the hostess who got warm at her own party and discarded first her shoes and then her panty hose . . .

I still went to Dr. Collier's office every day for therapy. And I still helped there, doing more things, feeling that I was being useful. This was good for my morale.

But the best thing I did, much better than the parties, and even better than feeling that I could be of service — I was beginning to play the piano again. I cannot begin to tell what this meant to me! Bish said I did not need to tell. It glowed in my face, in the way I walked and talked. "There is a lilt!" he insisted.

When I first came to Two Bridges, Mary Bridell had told me I could use her piano "When you're ready, dear."

I knew that I could use it. I knew that I needed to make no arrangements — I could go up to the big house, go into the front parlor, sit down . . .

I wanted to do it. I wanted to touch my fingertips to the keys and make a sound. And yet I feared doing it. I was timid. At night, I would tell myself, "Tomorrow I will try. I won't be able to *play*, of course, but I'll go up."

And the next day I would find reasons not to go, to delay going. It was raining. I must take a book back to the library. I must go to the bank . . .

But, after all this, the day did eventually come. I went up to the big house. I told the maid that I wanted to try the piano, and she smiled, then led the way to the shadowy parlor where Mary's light mahogany square stood waiting for me.

"Would you like a lamp, Miss Bartels?"

"No, thank you. I won't be here long. I won't really play."

"Yes, ma'am." And she withdrew.

I walked across the carpet to the piano. I touched the golden, silky wood. I slid between the keyboard and the bench. You would not believe what it was like, the first time, to sit on that hard piano bench, facing again the keyboard of a great piano. It looked huge . . .

I don't remember back to my childhood and the first time I ever sat at a large piano. Probably then I was not awed. But that day in Mary Bridell's front parlor — there were chrysanthemums in a green glass bowl, and the house smelled faintly, pleasantly of wood smoke, of leather, and the sharply fragrant chrysanthemums in the green bowl.

I sat there for a long minute before I lifted my hands and touched the keys ever so lightly. You must understand that, while the injury had been to my right shoulder, I could not play only with the left hand because of the pull on the right shoulder muscles. They needed to be restored and retrained. Now I thought, careful to maintain a balance, perhaps I could learn again to play. I was frightened of failure as a child never is, but I was also anxious to make a sound, to learn to put sounds together.

I touched the keys. I dropped one finger, and another, and I played! I *played!*

Oh, not well! Not quickly, and not at all firmly. But I could sit erect before the piano, I could hold both forearms up, and my muscles would do the things I told them to do. That first morning I played nothing but a few feeble scales. I came back in the afternoon, no longer frightened. That evening I was invited to eat black-eyed peas at the commune, and I played little tunes on their awful piano. I went back to Mary's the next day, and the next.

I played the simplest things. The minuets — Paderewski, and of course Beethoven. And I was delighted. No great concerto had ever pleased me as much.

Mary Bridell, Sally, even Raj complimented me.

"It isn't good," I assured them. "But it is a beginning."

And they were pleased for me.

I spent those two months repeating the attempts and slowly advancing. I was overly careful not to tire myself. I mastered the minuets and a few other simple things. I took the motifs from which Bach had developed his fugues — sometimes one measure only — and I labored as he must have done with counterpoint, and counterpoint again.

At the end of that time, persuaded that I would be able to play again for my own pleasure — it was like learning to speak again, Raj told me, after a throat operation or a stroke. It should be enough that I could play at all!

And it *was!* But I soon wanted my own piano. So I arranged to go to the city. I hired a car and a driver. Bish would have taken me, or Sally. I could have asked David, even. But I wanted to do this on my own. When I decided I was ready to have a car, I'd get all the help available. But a piano . . .

It was to be the first piano I had ever owned. Would you believe that? Of course there had been the one in my grandmother's home. There had been pianos at the schools. And then, when I began to be known, the piano companies vied with each other to supply me with an instrument.

But now . . .

I was fussy about tone, of course. I was embarrassed that I could not thunder out chords and run flashy arpeggios to try the pianos. But the tone must be right. Finally I decided on a small grand. And it was to be sent to my home. When it arrived, I displayed it proudly to my friends.

"Don't tire your arm," Raj cautioned me again. "I notice there is a key. I could lock you away if you overdo."

I promised to be careful, and I was, because to be able to play at all was excitement enough. I would get stronger and better . . .

Chapter Seven

And then, with the hills beginning to blaze with color and Bish able to show me wild geese flying across the pale sky, I began to hear bits and pieces of gossip. My cleaning woman said a word or two; at a Friday night dinner party I caught a phrase, "You can't be lucky all the time!"

And the Langans again tried to move in on my life. They had heard about the piano. They had heard I was able to play again, and Tee took it upon himself . . .

"At the risk of sounding possessive," he said in his pompous manner of passing out orders, "I would suggest the work I hear you do down at Raj Collier's office might not be such a good idea, Lissa."

He had come to my house uninvited. I was not very glad to see him, but of course I invited him in, and after a few minutes I offered him a drink. He would take one, his parents being absent. When they were around, he was a teetotaler. I don't know why that fact upset me. Well, it was hypocritical, of course. But why should Tee

Langan's being hypocritical make any difference to me?

I brought him his drink, with a little soda in a glass for me. It looked like what was in his glass and would seem hospitable.

"I enjoy helping a little when I go down to the office," I told Tee.

"Just how much do you do?"

"Many days I do nothing. But sometimes, when they are busy — Sally comes in regularly, you know; Mrs. Ward and Raj can get tied up — I answer the phone or make out receipts when a patient wants to pay for a visit. It helps, but it isn't important. Why shouldn't I help?"

"Are you alone there with Collier?"

"Not often. Maybe a time or two, when Mrs. Ward will leave early. Why shouldn't I be alone with him? She is, a lot of times."

"You are not Mrs. Ward."

"Well, now that's a self-evident fact." I was getting impatient with Tee.

"You've been here in town for months. You must know Raj's reputation."

"So far as I am concerned, so far as first-hand knowledge goes, he is an excellent doctor; he has done well with my arm."

"And you're grateful."

I jumped to my feet. "I think I don't want to continue this conversation, Tee. I'm tired. Would you . . . ?"

He rose to leave, assuring me that he was fond of me and only had been trying to protect my name. . . .

He made a poor thing of his attempted apology. The Langans could not really believe in any error they might have committed. And Tee, trying to say he was sorry, that he had only wanted to help me, got himself in more deeply than ever. He mentioned the chance that, if I had to undress for my treatments . . .

"Oh, I do," I said, beginning to enjoy his bumbling efforts. "At least my blouse or my dress."

"All right! If someone came to the office, saw you alone with Raj — People *talk,* Lissa! They really *do!*"

"Yes," I said. "It would seem so. And thank you very much, Tee. . . ."

He patted my shoulder, a gesture which always makes me flinch. "Just be careful," he urged. "Raj has got himself into the gossip columns pretty strongly these days. I mean the town is really talking!"

He was right. When I became aware of such talk, there must be a great deal going on that I didn't hear. My acquaintance was limited; there were not a lot of people I could go to. Tee and the Langans would have been a rich source of information, but that was out. Sally, too, for different reasons. Denny was occupied elsewhere, and I always deplored my few efforts to pump the boy. Bish would have delighted in an inquiry, but he wouldn't actually have told me much.

I assured myself that I needed to know not only what was being said, but what had happened. So I would ask David. He might not know. He might not tell me if he did know. But I could ask him, and I did, the next chance I had. Which could come soon because David seemed to be in town all of that particular week. He would stop at my house, or I could call him and invite him — perhaps marinate some steaks, and invite him to dinner.

Within a day or so, he did stop, whooshing his car into my driveway, beating a tattoo on my door knocker. He said he had come to see Puddles, who was delighted. I invited him in and told him that I had been hoping to see him.

"Something happened?" he asked, going over to the shelves where I kept my scores. He took down one folder, then another. He examined them while I talked.

While I told him as much as I knew. "Something is going on, David," I said. "I wouldn't ask Tee Langan — but I hoped you would know. What's Raj supposed to have done now? If asked, I would say that he has been working very hard, and steadily, for the past couple of months. He . . ."

David put the folders back in place, turned and came over to me; he put his big, clean hand across my mouth. "Shut up, will you, Lissa," he said pleasantly. "All this, about needing to take off your blouse when you get treatments in Collier's office — and telling me how hard he works, and the rest . . ."

"But . . ."

He nodded. "Would you button yourself firmly into your blouse and come down to *my* office? I have something to show you. You can bring Puddles if you like."

"He'd like it," I said readily. "And I have him pretty well house-trained here. But he thinks other people's carpets are just new fields to conquer."

David laughed, and we went out to his car, hearing Puddles' frantic barking as we drove away. "I've never come back, but he keeps trying," I told David.

David's house — as we drove down the hill and then up again toward it . . . "It's a tree house," I declared. "It really is, David."

He slowed the car and stopped. "From

here, it does look that way," he agreed.

"I chose to come to Two Bridges," I told him, "because of all the trees."

"May I give my house your name?" he asked, sitting back, relaxed, gazing up at his home, its windows and walls glinting in the afternoon sun.

It was built upon the highest bit of land above the river, the ground broke away below it, to give him a magnificent view of the river, downstream to the old covered bridge, upstream to where the river curved and seemed to leave us. The house itself soared into the sky, rising above the treetops and foliage that was cool and green in the summer, but on that afternoon showed every shade of scarlet and gold. As we drove on and turned into the drive, I felt as if I were suspended in a forest-like bower, and was floating in space. I told David I felt this way.

He nodded. "Like floating in a cloud," he agreed. "On a foggy day I think we do float a little. Come inside — you will see what I mean."

I did see. From every window there was a miraculous view of the river valley. Every room was on a different level, or seemed to be. From David's office and carport on the lowest level — the housekeeper had rooms there, too — next above were the living and dining rooms. The master bedroom was on the third level, with two guests rooms on the fourth. And down again to the office at ground level, the largest room in that house, though the core of it was the living room, the ceiling of which soared . . . "How high?" I asked David, looking up and up.

"Thirty feet," he told me.

And that thirty feet became the height of the house itself. Honey-gold cedar sheathed the walls and ceiling of the living room, while the floor was of strip oak. The color of the wood and its texture created a spacious, flowing feeling which was at the same time rich and warm. The focal point of this living room was the fireplace, with the wall opposite a huge expanse of windows which brought the trees and the view into the room. The furniture arrangement centered about the fireplace. The wide couches and the deep caramel leather chairs were pulled together by a large, off-white, sheepskin rug.

The dining room was more intimate because of its lower ceiling; but it, too, was surrounded by windows, the glass left bare to allow the view to be seen to advantage at all times.

The whole house — its fine architectural lines, the simplicity of the furnishings, and the extensive use of wood combined to create a house that blended with the country-side.

"It is beautiful!" I told David.

"And it lives well the year round," he said. "Now, let's go down to the office again . . ."

"Do we have to?"

"I told you that I had something to show you."

His office was a place of business; there the glass windows and sliding doors could be covered with drawn, dark green curtains. David seated me in the tufted swivel chair beside his desk and said that he had a tape he wanted to play for me.

I watched him as he inserted the cassette and touched buttons; outside the window a red-berried branch of hawthorn blew in a single gust of wind.

"I made this," he said, "the day when Clare returned to the office following her weekend at Four Winds. She came here, and I made this record which I shall play now for you."

"To show me how wise I am?" I asked, feeling strange. "Or how silly?"

"Listen," he told me, sitting back in his own chair at the desk, which was wide and neatly stacked with weighted papers. I was admiring again the clean, firm lines of his face. His intent gray eyes, his lean cheeks and firm lips — even his hairline was crisp and clean-cut against his forehead and temples.

"She came here that day . . ." David said. Then her voice came in clearly. She was asking if she could keep her job. I remembered, of course, that this would have been immediately after Denny's accident, and Bonnie's.

"I didn't know if you'd want me to work here anymore," said Clare's voice. "After all that has happened."

Then David's quiet voice. "Why not?"

There was a pause. "Yeah," said Clare, "why not? Sure, why not? Don't you listen to what people are saying, don't you know what happened?"

There was another pause. "I went to Four Winds with Dr. Collier," she said, speaking fast. "He asked me to go for the weekend — and I went. I've never seen places like that, Mr. Masters. And any girl wants to see them. So I went. We rode horseback, we danced to a good orchestra, and we ate fabulous food. We went out on the lake in a ritzy speedboat — we swam, and sat around with almost no clothes on, and drank things. And" — her voice sharpened — "we had a suite at the main lodge. Complete with a wide bed. One bed. I was in that bed, and Raj was taking a shower when the police came to get him, to tell him that there had been this awful accident, and he was needed at home. He told me he'd have to go — he left me some money and the keys to his car.

"Now," she continued, speaking more quietly, "I could have stayed there at Four Winds, especially for the rest of that night. Then I could have driven back to Two Bridges alone. Unchanged, so far as anyone knew. I could have gone on as if nothing had happened, living in the commune, working for you when you happen to be here."

"Why didn't you?" said David's quiet, reasonable voice.

Clare had been shocked. "Why didn't I?" she cried, her voice shrill. "Look, Mr. Masters — a lot has *happened* to me! I wasn't a nice girl any longer. I had taken Raj's money, and — and . . ."

"I understand all that," said David again. "But I still would urge you to proceed as if nothing were changed, work here, dress as you have always done, live as you have always done. Look, Clare. Men get drunk and they make spectacles of themselves. Men of eminence and standing, men who are well-thought-of, go on benders and are even found in the gutter. Their friends know this, but these men manage to resume their lives and their business. They go on."

"But a girl . . . Could I do that?"

"You could try."

The tape ended there; David rewound it with the usual whirring whisper. He turned in his chair to look at me. I was sitting a-quiver with many emotions.

"She has been trying," he told me. "She has valiantly been trying to pick up the pieces and go on. It can't have been easy. But she is becoming a very good secretary. I would recommend her for a full-time job anywhere she might decide to go. But now . . ." He turned away to gaze out at the hawthorn tree. "I don't know," he said slowly, "what Two Bridges will let her do."

I gulped. "The gossip is . . ." I began, coughed, and tried again. "*Is* she pregnant?" I asked.

"And that's what the town is gossiping about, I suppose."

"Well, of course it is. Gossip is this town's life blood."

"It's every town's life blood, Lissa. You know that, if you'll stop to think. New York, Hollywood — Two Bridges. Individuals, people, newspapers, magazines — all need gossip to live."

I sat unhappily and stared at my knees.

"Lissa?" he asked.

"I don't want —" I began. "Please, David, I don't want you to be cynical in the face of this tragedy."

"I am not cynical, Lissa. I am angry, and sad. Aren't you angry?"

"That she went off with Raj and got pregnant? Yes. I am angry and frightened because Raj would hurt Sally so. That's a part of your anger, too, isn't it, David?"

"Yes. Oh, yes. But that is a part of an old and continuing rage, Lissa. Just now . . ." He whirled around. "No!" he shouted. "The pregnancy is not why I am angry! She took that risk, and girls these days know they take that risk. But I am angry at the real tragedy of this whole affair, and that, Lissa, is that Clare has left town again. Last night she and Mike Singley were married in St. Louis. He's a basketball player, and she has dated him some."

I waved my hand to silence him. "I know who Mike is," I said crossly. I had not heard . . . "He's tall, conceited — a showoff — I suppose she married him because she is pregnant."

"Yes," said David. I glanced at him. He was really sad about what Clare had done. "He'll give her no life worth having," he said. "He knows the child isn't his. I can't let myself imagine what Clare's life is going to be. She shouldn't have taken this step. The other one, the going off with Raj, was a somewhat natural thing. Her pregnancy certainly was natural. But to marry this boy . . ."

I leaned forward in the tufted chair. "Would you have married her, David?" I asked.

My question startled him. Color flared quickly into his face, and he looked at me in astonishment. "Why, Lissa — I don't know!" he said. "The idea had not occurred to me. I liked her idea of rebuilding her life. I stood ready to help her in that. But — well, yes, if she found that she could not have done without marriage, perhaps I would have married her. I didn't love her. I don't. But I could have given her my name. And a name for the child."

"And now you are angry because Mike stepped in and gave her that."

He sat gazing at me. "Yes," he said slowly, "I suppose that is why I am angry."

"If it's any comfort to you," I said, standing up, "I believe Raj is furious, too. I don't know why. But he's been in a towering rage for days, slamming things and snapping everyone's head off. I thought it was because he had learned that Clare was pregnant, and he couldn't do anything about it."

David was on his feet, and he stood looking down at me. "You're a smart girl, Lissa," he told me. "Compassionate, warmhearted — and smart."

"Take me home, will you?" I said, embarrassed. "I don't think my head will hold any more. I must sort out what I already know."

David didn't argue with me. He took me to the car, and we started down the hill, neither of us saying very much of anything. As we passed the commune at the foot of my hill, I put my hand on his arm. He nodded and slowed the car.

"It looks as if they are moving," I said in surprise. All sorts of furniture and gear were set out on the sidewalk. There were several cars in the street, and young people — two boys were endeavoring to load the old piano into a pickup truck. Since my efforts with Mary Bridell's square, since I'd bought my own instrument, I had often gone down to the commune and played on the old wreck. The girls had loved it. Now one of them came across to David's car. She wore a long, full-skirted coat over her short shift dress, her fingers combed through her blowing long hair as she came toward us. "We're moving," she announced.

"But why . . . ?" I asked.

"Oh; you've heard about Clare, I suppose."

"Yes . . ."

"Her getting married was what tore the whole thing to pieces, you know. We took a vote and decided to disband. I guess she felt she had to get married. But she could have stayed here and had the baby. We wish she had. She was the one who held us together. But now — it seems as if we can't beat the establishment, so we are selling or giving away our stuff."

"I'm sorry," I said. And I was sorry! "Where . . . ?"

"A couple of us are going home. I am. I'll try that again. Two of the girls have a room . . ."

David and I drove on up the hill, not speaking until he unlocked my front door. "I have a couple of steaks," I said faintly.

"Good. I'll stay. I'm feeling lonely, too."

Chapter Eight

And then several months passed, not always quietly, but with nothing startling happening. I went to a basketball game with Peggy Shannon, who endeavored to explain the game to me. We both were thinking of Clare but would not speak of her. Later that winter I was to go to a game with Tee Langan where I saw Mike Singley play, and he was good.

In late October, I took Puddles up to Bish and told him that I was going East for a week or two.

"Don't stay," said Bish, smiling at me.

"Well, of course not!" I answered.

But when I reached New York and saw my friends, they urged me to stay. And I realized that I could pleasantly take up a life of going to the theater, of travel, and benefit balls — recitals.

But I shook my head. And I said to these gay and talented people, also, that I could not stay. It was not that I loved the town of Two Bridges more, not that I loved the people more. But theirs had become the lives I shared, and that I would share.

Of course, while in New York, I went to see Dr. Kohl, the specialist who had sent me to the Ozarks. He said that I was making fine progress, that I must have found a good doctor. And I said, with sincerity, that he was a very good doctor. Raj was.

"How are the mountains?" Dr. Kohl asked.

"Very good," I assured him. "I like them. They are sleeping mountains, as you know, humped round and comfortable in their sleep. I prefer them to the grandeur of the Alps or the Sawtooth, which stand arrogantly on end and shout their magnificence."

He laughed. "You've certainly become a convert," he assured me. "How long will you be here?"

"A week longer, perhaps. My agent and my friends are giving me a royal time."

They did give me one, but I was glad to be back in Two Bridges. I reported to Bish and to David what Dr. Kohl had said. "Raj is a good doctor," I told them. "Sometimes."

I said that I planned to buy a little car, that Dr. Kohl had said I could safely drive one, but he advised me not to go where the pressure would be great — into the city, or out on the big freeways.

Bish offered to help me in the purchase,

and David warned me not to let our good friend sell me his jeep.

It was good to be at home again. I quickly took up the routine of my life. I learned to drive my car, but I still walked around town and out into the country. I worked in my house and in my yard; the roses were put to bed for the winter, the lawn kept tidy. I practiced daily at the piano, listening to Raj's warning not to overdo, not to tire the new muscles. One Sunday I played the organ for church service, and felt inordinately proud of myself.

I resumed my regular course of therapy for my arm, shoulder and back. And I found myself working again in Raj's office. I answered the phone; I sometimes served as receptionist, hearing a crisp professionalism come into my voice as I would send patients back to the doctor, or tell newcomers to sit down, the doctor would be with them. I made appointments, I called patients when some emergency would cause appointments to be canceled. Sometimes I even transcribed records. If I could play the piano, I could type. Raj said I was being useful to the point that he would need to adjust my medical fees.

I liked being useful. I liked helping. I found myself watching Raj with new interest, remembering what Dr. Kohl had said about him. And I thought a great deal about the possibility of a man's being both a bad and a good doctor.

From that point I began to wonder if Raj was unique. Was it possible that other doctors were the same sort? Allowing for variation in sorts of "badness"? It would be very human; few people's characters were all white or all black. The hitch in my argument, of course, was that I felt pretty sure that when a man took on doctoring as his profession, he must surely be ready to pledge that he would not be entirely human.

All these things kept me busy. My happiness was assured by my association with Bish, my close friendship with him and Sally. And David.

I felt that I had become a real part of the town. As Christmas drew near, I felt this ever more plainly. There were local charities, there were the neighbor children. I was expected to attend all sorts of school and church programs. A hard rain washed out one corner of my lawn, and I found any number of neighbors ready to advise me, to assist me with the problem — Denny, the trash collector, the mail carrier, all offered advice.

And I gave some parties of my own.

Mrs. Langan had pointed out to me that I must do this because I was indebted to so many people. I tried to say that I was planning some sort of entertainment in return, but she swept right on. I must use the hotel, she said. My house would not accommodate a hundred people.

"I don't plan to invite a hundred," I said meekly.

She didn't hear me. She was recounting the menu — exactly the same menu that featured every large party.

"I won't do it," I told Sally Collier. "I have decided not to attend one more cocktail-buffet dinner party. I am sick of melon balls and roast beef and ham! And how would it look if I didn't attend my own party?"

She laughed at me and pointed out that, by not giving a party, I would get few invitations and so might escape the vicious circle.

"I've thought of that. It's the way the Colliers do, isn't it?"

"Oh, don't ever use the Colliers as an example."

We had started to walk home from the office, and had stopped to watch a string of barges going upriver. We leaned on the stone wall and occasionally answered the wave of a mittened hand. We had decided that river work must be cold in the winter.

The men wore heavy coats, caps that protected their ears, yellow leather mittens . . .

"I'd like to entertain as Bish does," I said thoughtfully. "A few people at a time. Maybe a series of small dinners or Sunday luncheons. I'd need help, of course."

"I'd help you."

"I meant manual help. Labor. Like cook, waitress . . ."

"I can get that for you, too. But I'd like to help you plan your parties, Lissa, and I'll do it if you promise not to invite Raj and me."

"Oh . . ."

She glanced at me, and I said no more. We started up the hill again. We did not need to discuss the situation any further.

But the parties were planned and given, and successfully, too, I felt. Mary Bridell came to one of them. Bish and David did. Of course the Langans; that was to the largest catch-all affair. Sally told me of a couple I could hire, a wonderful cook and her husband, who served as butler and wine waiter. My own cleaning woman, Cecil, would help in the kitchen and clean up before and after.

"Do I have to have the parties all the same?" I asked Sally.

"No. I don't see why you should. In fact, it would be more fun, more interesting . . ."

So we planned four dinners — one of

twelve people; two of eight, which was my choice of a proper-sized group; and one lovely, intimate affair of only five. I didn't worry if the guests were not evenly mated; I was always sure that any extras were men. Never an extra woman!

Sally and I had a picnic planning four different menus and four different settings. If the guests compared notes — and I was sure they did — I hoped no one felt discriminated against. I don't believe they did. When I invited what I called the barbecue crowd — the Shannons and other young people with whom I had picnicked and backyarded all summer — I used my very prettiest china and crystal, tall red candles in low white holders, a centerpiece of gardenias and red camellias which Mike said "really smelled." They did, too, and the ladies wore the single flowers home in triumph. For these jolly folk, I started with onion soup, followed by turkey roll baked in a flaky crust, vegetables — oh, lima beans, I think, and squash — ending with vanilla ice cream aglow with cherry sauce. "We had the best," Peggy Shannon assured me afterward, just as Sally had predicted.

For the next group, I used a dark green and white table, and the guests were what we called the intellectuals. The Rector and his wife, several people from the University . . . I started on stuffed eggs with mustard, assuring Sally that this was a classic Continental hors d'oeuvre.

"Tell them!" she urged. "We call them deviled eggs in these parts."

The eggs were popular, and the stuffed breast of veal widely acclaimed. One of the professors identified the crisp German torte — I'd had one sent from a bakery in the city.

The third dinner was the largest one, and the one which the Langans attended. For this I had an all-white table, except for the exceptionally pink centerpiece of carnations misty with baby's breath. I can still see Mrs. Langan's fork exploring the mushroom and artichoke appetizer. She accompanied the shrimp Newburg entree with a running account of how she made patty shells. None of the Langans ate the braised celery and zucchini, but Tee asked for another serving of the chocolate and nut roll.

"So it passed," I told Sally. Our early morning meetings had become great fun on the day after each party.

I saved the best for the last. This was the small party. Bish and David were both there. The centerpiece was in the European fashion of all sorts of flowers — pale yellow roses, daisies, freesia, carnations and iris.

The appetizer featured Brie and beluga caviar on toast strips; there was squab and French peas with lemon butter, and a sort of pêche Melba for dessert. For each dinner, I offered only a couple of cocktails before dinner, and selected wines with the meal. Mary Bridell told me afterward that some people thought I could have offered highballs as well as cocktails. She had come to the intellectuals' party. "Did you enjoy the dinner?" I asked her. Sally hung on her answer.

"Very much," said Raj's mother. "It's only all the drinking beforehand that helps us endure the heavy buffets given here in Two Bridges."

I looked in triumph at Sally.

"Lissa says it is the first party series she's ever given," she told Mary.

"I've been to some wonderful parties," I assured Raj's mother. "But before — in my life before the accident — the affairs were arranged by my agent, or manager, and we had to select the guests, and arrange the tables, for their publicity value."

"You could have taken pictures of these parties," Sally assured me. "And you did it all yourself ."

"Oh, come on now."

"Yes, you did, too, Lissa. The guests, the

arrangements, all of it. Did *you* have a good time?"

"I enjoyed every minute of the dinners."

I had. I was enjoying everything just then. This was, I decided, a lovely time of year. The mountains were beautiful on a clear day or in the morning mists, and certainly by moonlight. We had snow, and for Christmas dinner at his house, Bish fetched me in a sleigh, bells ringing, the horse stomping. Jimmie next door was enchanted, begged to go with us, and we took him. David complained bitterly that we should not have been allowed to travel in style. I liked that day, and the gay people. I was very happy.

Realizing my state of euphoria, I discovered that I was doing no worrying or thinking about Raj. He was working steadily, and took only short, occasional weekend trips to ski or to see a hockey game in the city. The longest trip he took was to New Orleans for the New Year's football game. I was really pleased to know that Sally had gone there with him. I wondered if David knew that she had.

Raj was showing the very best side of himself, which could be very good. I was in the office the afternoon when one of the rivermen was brought in with a broken upper arm. Knowing that I was touched by all broken and injured bones, Raj explained to me what he was doing for the man. He let me watch him apply the splint. He was using plaster over foam, he told me. This was more effective than the use of the fiber base. A patient could wear a cast comfortably for four weeks, and he'd known of one case where it had been worn for six months without discomfort. He used the foam for knee casts, and one such as he was doing on the upper arm; it allowed a slight movement of the shoulder and elbow joint which would speed activity and full strength. This certainly appealed to me, and I admired Raj for knowing about such things.

But, in contrast, were times when Raj could prove to me that he was a bad doctor. I discovered that he drank; that he sometimes drank too heavily. During that winter I decided, against my will, that he was drinking while at the office. This I felt was unwise. When I had to decide that he was habitually drinking too much, I felt as if the bottom had dropped out of things.

He had been drinking a great deal too much on the night when Clare Singley's baby was born.

This happened in mid-March, which can often be, I am told, a bad time in the hills.

After Christmas, we had had a couple of heavy snows, and ice in February, all of which, with March, began to melt during a series of warm, springlike days. Snowflowers bobbed up in unexpected places, and everyone decided that winter was over, though even I was skeptical about that.

Then it began to rain very hard, and after about four days of this, it was accompanied by warnings of flash floods, dripping shrubbery, and soaked lawns. Puddles hated all this. When I would let him out, he would roll his eyes imploringly to me.

"It's terrible," I told the little dog.

The wind came up and howled around the house and down the chimney, tossed the trees about; branches whipped off and fell across the overhead wires, playing hob with everything called civilized. The electric power went off, and sometimes on again, erratically. I built a fire in the library, planning to toast bread over the coals. Sometimes the furnace worked, sometimes it did not.

Sally came down the hill, hooded and booted, to see if I was all right. "It's a terrible night," she told me. I helped her unbundle, and hung the heavy waterproof coat in the bathroom.

"Do you often have weather like this?" I asked.

"Often enough. Raj was called out in this one."

"Oh, no!"

"Yes, he was, Lissa. Out to the Singley farm."

"But that's . . ."

"Yes. It's up the mountain, up the road to Bish's place. I told him I was coming down here. Is your phone alive?"

I lifted it and nodded when I heard the dial tone. The lights came on, and we went into the kitchen to prepare some supper. Raj would come there from the Singley call. Mary Bridell had gone to Arizona three weeks before, and Sally said she hoped she would stay there "until we dry out."

We carried trays back to the fire, and had half finished our supper when we saw car lights sweep into the drive.

Then Raj was stomping on the doorstep, and we let him in; his thick hair gleamed with raindrops.

"Whoosh!" he cried. "What a night! Do you have anything to drink, Lissa?"

"Raj . . ." Sally began, and he turned on her swiftly.

"If you'd been where I've been, you'd want a drink, too," he said roughly.

Discreetly I went to the kitchen to prepare a tray of hot food for Raj. I added a bowl of

262

soup to the scallops and salad which Sally and I had been enjoying. I slipped a mince pie into the oven to warm, poured coffee, and gingerly, as always, I carried the tray back to the library.

Raj had made his drink, and he was telling Sally about his trip out to the Singley farm. "You wouldn't believe how that road up to the house was rutted," he said. He ate some of the soup. "The girl was in labor, all right. But I told Singley to take her to the city."

"Can he make it that far, Raj?" Sally asked anxiously.

"If he reaches the main highway he can. Of course there's Menard, or even Burton, on the way. Both towns have hospitals. As I certainly do not."

"And you feel she needs a hospital?"

Raj didn't reply.

"In this weather, Raj . . ." said Sally anxiously. The wind was still throwing water against the window. It sounded like surf.

"I got out to their place and back," Raj pointed out gruffly. "They should make it to the main highway, and on."

I went to fetch the wedges of hot mince pie. Sally followed to fetch the coffeepot. "He probably knows what he's talking about," she reassured me. She was wearing a long-sleeved dress of scarlet wool jersey, with a black and white scarf folded into the throat. Her black hair caught beautiful lights and shadows from the fire.

The Singleys did not make it to the city, or even to Burton and the small hospital there. The low water bridges were all flooded, and in one place there was a bad washout of the road itself. An accident had limited highway traffic to one lane.

Some of this news came over the radio, and I was not surprised when Sally called me very early the next morning to tell me that the Singleys were bringing Clare to the office; the father-in-law expected Raj to be there to take care of her. "His expression was, Lissa, 'Doc will take care of her, or else.'"

I gasped. "Was his manner threatening?"

"Yes, I'm afraid it was. Even over the telephone which I had answered. He's a rough type of man, I'm afraid. He added that 'Doc' couldn't very well refuse to accept this patient. And he couldn't, of course."

She didn't add, "under the circumstances," as she probably was thinking, as I was thinking.

"Is it still raining?" I asked meekly.

"Yes, but not so hard. The fog is thick,

and there are many roads washed out or closed by flash floods. Some accidents."

I finished dressing, wrapped up and took Puddles for a short walk. I had just turned back toward the house when I saw Mrs. Ward's car coming down the street. She waved to me, slowed, rolled down a window. "Seems the stork doesn't know it's Sunday," she said. "Doctor has a hot delivery."

I nodded. "Did he send for you?"

"Why else would I be out in this quack-quack weather?" She drove on.

Back in the house, I made the bed and cleaned up the kitchen, thinking hard. Of the burdened girl down at the office, of Raj and Mrs. Ward. Of Sally. Raj wouldn't suggest that she help. But I could. I moved about more briskly then. I assembled some food, and got into rain gear. Then I backed my car out of the garage. I could be of some help. I could make coffee and fetch things — talk to the family — even to Clare. I thought.

Anyway, I would go down to the office. Raj might send me home again.

But he did not; he and Mrs. Ward were busy. Raj had had no breakfast. A ham sandwich and coffee would be fine, he told me. Would I bring it in when it was ready?

None of the Singleys had stayed with

Clare; she said she was glad to see me. She looked terrible. I combed and braided her long black hair. And I was very frightened.

While I was doing this, Sally came in. I considered going home, but I did not. And the Singleys called to see how things were going. I said the doctor was busy — No, the child had not yet been born. I put the phone down, feeling cold, though the office was well heated. I could hear the voices from the treatment room; sometimes Clare would cry out . . .

Sally called at noon, and I told her that I was shocked at what childbirth could be. "I expect you have a right to be shocked," she said. "Why don't you come home, Lissa?"

"I — I'd rather stay. Will you walk Puddles for me?"

"Of course."

"Sometimes there are things I can do here."

"Like answering when I call. Yes. Do you need anything?"

"Maybe some canned soup and some milk. If you're coming down again."

"I may."

The weather was getting worse again. There was thunder and lightning, and the wind was blowing a gale. The river's surface whipped into little whitecaps. I lit the fire in the waiting room, and shivered in its warmth. Raj came out once and slumped into a deep chair, telling me that he was bushed. He'd been drinking — I could smell the liquor. I reread the page of the magazine I was holding. Now and then I would look briefly across at Raj, and I was frightened.

Mrs. Ward stayed with Clare. I took her coffee and food and returned to my chair in the waiting room, to *House Beautiful* and *Today's Health*. Raj had a short nap in the chair, then went to look at Clare and talk to Ward. Afterward he went into his office and closed the door.

I wanted, desperately, to talk to David; there must be something, I thought, that could be done beyond just sitting about and letting that girl suffer. Now she moaned almost steadily. But I would not call David from the office and I would not leave and risk the hilly drive to his home.

At three, Sally came back and talked to Raj and to Ward. Then she came out to me, bringing my coat and boots with her. "You're to go home, Lissa," she said firmly. "This thing can go on into the night. I hope you will agree to stay at home . . ."

I didn't argue. I well knew that I had no business hanging around the doctor's office when he was busy with a serious case. "I'm fond of Clare," I told Sally when I went out to my car. It was difficult to drive against the wind, but she followed me up the hill and waited until I was safely inside.

I left my raincoat hung over a chair by the door, and spent a restless hour or two, wanting to be back where I would know what was happening. I took poor Puddles out twice, anxious that I be ready to go if a suggestion might open the way . . . I told myself that someone besides the medical folk should stand by Clare. I was a friend, and I could substitute for family. . . .

"Oh, you want to be there for your own sake!" I said aloud at one time.

It was black dark when I saw car lights edging out of the Collier garage, turn and come back, ready to take a car to the street. I snatched my hooded coat and was down to the foot of my drive before Sally reached the corner. She was driving Mary Bridell's big car. I waved to her frantically, and she slowed, stopped, rolled down the window. "Oh, Lissa . . ." she protested.

I opened the door and got into the back seat. "I want to go," I said stubbornly.

"There won't be a thing you can do. I brought this heavy car — since we don't have an ambulance here in town. I think perhaps I can take Clare to the hospital."

"Will Raj . . . ?"

"If he's in no condition to drive," she said coldly, "I'll do it. I'll have to. Clare has been in labor now for twenty-six hours. But you shouldn't have come. How will you get home?"

"Raj's car will be there. And Ward's. If I were you, I'd take Ward along."

"I plan to."

"The radio says every river is in flood, Sally. If the big bridge is covered with water . . ." My voice shook. It wouldn't help much of anything if Sally and Ward, as well as Clare, should be drowned.

Sally saw that I was frightened. "I wouldn't do a thing without telling the Highway Patrol of our emergency," she assured me. "If we can't get out — we'll think of something." Then, as if speaking to herself, she said softly, "If we have only one storm a year, this would have to be the one!"

We reached the office; its lighted diamond-paned windows made it seem cozy, and it was warm inside. Ward came to meet us, looking very tired. She had taken off her perky white cap.

"How are things?" Sally asked, letting her coat fall away from her shoulders and arms. Her black hair was twisted up on her head.

"Things are going along, too long," said

Mrs. Ward softly. "I see you brought the cook back."

Sally smiled at me. "She thought Clare needed a friend."

"We all need a friend," said Ward grimly. She led the way back to the treatment room. Clare lay on her side on the table. There were great blue shadows below her eyes.

"She's stopped talking," Ward told us.

"Raj . . . ?" murmured Sally, taking Clare's pulse, then lifting the stethoscope from the hook. She glanced at Ward, who was shaking her head from side to side.

Sally used the stethoscope, gave it to Ward, and then she went down the hall to Raj's office.

"He says to try hot towels," she said when she came out. She carried a couple of bottles in her hands. "Will you put these out in the car, Lissa?" she asked. "Put on your coat. Pneumonia will only complicate things for us. Then call the Highway Patrol. Please? Ask about a chance of our getting through."

The Patrol told me that there was no chance for any car, heavy or light, to get to the highway before midnight. "And I wouldn't advise it then," the man added.

I went to tell Sally this, drawing her out into the hall. "I don't think Clare would hear us," she said. "She seems to be in shock."

"Is she bad, Sally?" I asked, dreading the answer.

"She is very bad, dear. Very, very bad."

And there we were. Clare on the table, wearing a white hospital gown, her black hair in a braid, her face the color of clay, smudged with shadows of pain and exhaustion. She no longer struggled, cried out, or begged piteously to be helped. Her eyes stared straight ahead. Mrs. Ward moved about, trying to keep the girl warm, bringing in the towels which she had wrung out of hot water. Without her cap, she still looked all nurse. Sally had put a white smock or apron on over her red jersey dress, and she alertly watched and directed what Ward was doing.

And then there was me, scared to death, my hands like ice in the warm room. I wore a tan woolen skirt, flat-heeled shoes, a tan blouse, and my red hair was probably standing on end. I went from corner to corner, determined not to be in the way, but hoping that I could do a few small things.

Raj was the fifth one of us, and I didn't know how he was looking. I hadn't seen him since early afternoon. Then he had worn a white coat over his brown cords and a creamy-colored pullover. Now —

I glanced at Sally and Ward. They had decided to turn Clare on her back, and were busy. I went quietly down the hall, opened the door of Raj's office. "Doctor?" I said quietly but clearly.

"Is that you, Lissa?" He was lying on the couch, and his voice was fuzzy.

I went into the room. The green shaded lamp on his desk was all the light there was. Raj looked up at me. "What you want?" he asked.

I rubbed my hands together. "It's Clare," I said. "She looks just awful, Raj. I came in — because surely you can do something for that girl! Surely you *want* to do something!"

He groaned. He pressed his fingertips to his temples, then he rolled off the couch, steadying himself as he stood erect. He came over to me, put his hands firmly on my upper arms and turned me about. He reached over my shoulder and opened the door and gently put me out into the hall. "Go home, Lissa," he said gruffly. "You're in way beyond your depth. Go home. You'll drown down here."

I heard the door close behind me. Slowly I went down the hall. In the little lounge, I made fresh coffee, and I opened cans of soup. I took bowls of this to Sally, then to

Ward. They thanked me and they ate, though I was pretty sure they didn't really taste the stuff they were eating.

I washed every dish in sight, and went out to sit by the fire in the waiting room.

I thought perhaps I should urge Sally to plead with Raj. There surely were things the doctor could do for Clare. He hadn't listened to me, but if Sally were to beg him. I felt sure he would do anything for Sally . . .

About eight o'clock — or was it nine? — Sally came out and told me that she and Ward had decided that they could not let labor continue. The hot towels had helped only a little.

"The baby can't stand this long trip, you see. Nor Clare."

"What will you do?" I asked.

She turned toward the hall. "Raj is going to have to operate," she said over her shoulder.

I followed her, and I heard her tell Raj that labor had gone on "Too long," she said. "Much too long."

"Just what do you suggest?" he asked, his tone cold and resentful.

"You know what I am suggesting," Sally answered, her own voice calm. "You know what is necessary."

I heard something slam, as if he had

thrown a book or a paperweight to the floor. Then he stormed at Sally. He was very angry at her for telling him what he should do. And, I thought, he was frightened as well. For which I could not blame him, though a doctor . . . His voice rose and roughened. "You know damn well," he roared, "I can't do a c.s. here!"

And then her voice, as cool as water. "Can't you?" she asked.

"You know I can't. I can't do that sort of surgery anywhere!" I wanted to weep, to cry out at the pain in his voice.

Sally neither wept nor raised her tone. "Can't you do it if you have to, Raj?" she asked.

"Not at any time," he answered quickly. "And now I'm drunk. You know I'm drunk."

"I know that you still will have to do this, Raj!"

He mumbled something, but then I heard him say, "Okay. Okay. I'll give it a try. But I'll need a drink."

I wanted to run. And I did run, as far as the treatment room. "Dr. Collier," I gasped to Ward. "He's going to operate."

She nodded. "I hope it works. Look, Lissa, you keep the hot coffee coming. Bring us a cup now — and then you stand by to run and fetch, will you?"

"I'll do anything I can . . ."

She gave me a big smile. "I know you will," she said heartily. "Now get that coffee."

Can I let myself remember? Can I describe the rest of that night? I was everywhere, in and out. I answered the telephone — the Singleys called again, and some woman wanting to know — she could see the office all lit up, she thought maybe Doc had forgotten and left the lights on. I answered her a bit sharply, then thanked her for her concern. "The doctor is busy," I said.

He was that. Very busy. Sick, clumsy, speaking roughly, he directed Ward and Sally — and me — in the changes that turned the treatment room into an operating room and the people in it — even poor Clare — into something like what they should be. Lights were moved about, extra ones were brought in. The table shone in a pool of brilliant light, with dark shadows into the corners and up at the ceiling. Strange shadows of people and the things they carried and used were cast upon the walls. Even I wore a mask, and Ward had twisted a towel around my head.

Clare, a mound of white sheets and towels, lay on the table, and her eyes stared blankly at the ceiling. I could not help but think of her, as she had used to be down at the commune, her bright slips of dresses, her bare feet, her flying hair. She had used to come up and sit on my doorstep and talk to me. And I had seen her coming out of David Masters' office, all trim and business-like, in panty hose, neat blouse and short skirt . . . A bright and pretty girl. Gay . . .

Ward explained some of the things she was doing to get the patient ready for surgery. She shaved that great, bulging belly, and painted it with some yellow-orange stuff. She folded towels across it. Sally scrubbed and scrubbed her hands and forearms at the basin in the lab, and stood by to watch Raj while he did the same thing. He looked terrible; a rim of white showed around the pupils of his eyes, and I thought he probably was as frightened as I was. I wanted time to stand still. I didn't want this awful thing to happen.

Sally, as she busied herself, told me there would certainly be things I could do, certain duties which would be allotted to me. She listed those things. There were basins, she said, pointing to four that were on a side table. "Basins, Lissa," she repeated firmly. "When we say to bring a basin, or put something in a basin . . ."

Then there were newspapers. I was to set a stack of them near the door, and "keep a clean one opened and spread on the floor."

"A cl-clean one?" I stuttered.

"Yes. You've helped me do this before. Remember when Bonnie was hurt? The night . . ." Her voice trailed away. I remembered the night, and the newspapers. "When they get cluttered, give us a new one," Sally resumed. "Then the sterilizers — we have two, and both are full. I plan to empty one. Here's a stack of dressings and towels. When this one is empty" — she put her hand on what looked like a drawer — "put these things into the sterilizer, close it and turn the knob to where it is now. Do you understand?"

I thought I did, and I nodded.

I stared at, but still would rather not look at, the instruments spread out on another small table — rows and rows of them — shining scissors and small knives and tongs. "So many?" I asked Sally in a faint voice.

"They're not what we really will need, and not half as many," she told me briskly. "We'll make do. And — Oh, yes, Lissa — Of course we don't have any baby blankets, but will you go to the cupboard and pick out about three of the softest towels? Bring them in here, don't use them for anything else, but have them ready for when we'll hand the baby to you."

I gulped. This prospect did terrify me. A *baby?* A real baby — in my unreliable arms? "Sally!" I gasped. She turned and threw me a beautiful smile. "You'll do it," she promised.

And now, at last, we were ready. *We!* Actually, we had moved very fast. Raj and Sally both put on rubber gloves. Ward sat on a high stool at the head of the table, ready to give poor Clare the anesthesia. She did this, I knew, for tonsil operations and bone setting. She knew how.

I trembled when I saw Raj pick up the first knife. "Well," he growled from behind his mask, "at least I'm here."

Sally's gray eyes lifted to his. "Yes," she said, her tone bitter. "Tonight you are here."

I was afraid to watch, but unwilling not to watch. I stood back against the wall — and did watch. Raj made the incision; I saw Sally's hands busy. Mrs. Ward said something, and I gaped at her.

Clare could *not* be dead! She could not *be!*

But Sally was saying sharply, "Get the baby! Raj! Get the baby!"

But he threw the knife away. It clattered to the floor. "I can't do it!" he cried. "Not this — not this —"

"You mean you won't," said Sally coldly.

"All right!" shouted Raj. "I won't. It's a damn grubby job . . . and . . ."

Sally leaned across the table to him, her face close to his. "It's your child," she said sharply. "You know that. It's more than this one child. It's all the children you could have fathered in *your* grubby life. *All* of them, Raj!"

He stood shaking his head. "I can't," he said again and again. He was sweating profusely. Drops of moisture fell upon the draped sheets, and his face was really green.

I spoke up. "He really can't do it, Sally," I told her.

Mrs. Ward echoed me.

I saw Sally's lips move. I knew that *I* was praying. She went around the table, and slowly she reached for a knife. She glanced at Raj. "Then help me," she said.

But Raj only watched her. I was the one to step forward and give her things. For hours my shoulders had been aching with a fire-hot pain, but there, helping Sally, realizing what she was hoping to do, I gave her things — sutures and clean towels — things like that. Ward was busy with folded gauze and instruments. I suppose she knew what she was doing, but I suspect that my "technique," and Sally's too, was pretty weird. I had had enough surgery under local and spinal anesthesia to guess that we did many wrong things. I would have said that it was not possible for me to be more frightened. But I was. Fear became panic, and terror became horror. This was indeed a "grubby" birth. The tremendous incision, the dark mass that Sally told me was the uterus, and the placenta — and finally — Oh, not *finally!* Very quickly indeed, there was the *child!* I looked at it in terror. But Sally was holding it.

"Lissa," she said, and I fetched the towels, the whole stack of them, but I did manage to get one opened, ready to enfold the baby. He was so dark, so little — his wrinkled face, his seeking mouth, his pitiful, weak cries. I wrapped him tenderly and held him.

Sally came around the table and lifted the tiny hand. "He has the long fingers of an aristocrat," she said. Her face was strange, her voice strange.

She turned away then, telling me that she would close the incision and "make things decent." She glanced at Ward. "Take care of the baby," she said.

I moved about, cleaning things up, and I followed Sally when she went out to the desk in the foyer. I had put her gown and cap into the hamper. "I'm going to take that baby," she told me, "and see if I can raise him like that aristocrat I mentioned." She looked for forms and began to fill them out. She had not once looked at Raj, nor spoken to him, since she had taken up the knife in the operating room.

But in a short time, he had recovered enough to come out, pick up the telephone and call the Singley family. "Clare," he said, "has died. At one forty-two. Her son is alive."

He then called the undertaker and talked. "Yes," he said, "we'll wait until you get here."

While he did these things, Sally moved to a chair near the waiting room fire; she sat in the deep chair and held the baby lovingly.

Chapter Nine

There was no use our waiting, said Raj, seeming to have recovered. Ward would clean things up and go home. He'd stay for the undertaker. Sally could . . .

Sally did. We wrapped up; the rain had stopped hours before, and we got into Mrs. Collier's big car. I held the baby on my lap, and Sally drove us home. I went inside with her, then insisted, firmly, that I certainly could walk down to my house. The lights were on. Besides, what other idiots would be out on such a wet night, at such an hour!

She watched me, I am sure, until I opened my door. Poor Puddles greeted me hysterically, and I let him out. Then we both went to bed. I was exhausted, and he seemed to be.

The next morning I did a little shopping for Sally and for the baby, who was looking much more human, and I got back with the diapers, shirts and baby gowns, powder and a blanket, in time to run into Mr. Singley and his wife, who had come, Sally told me, to claim the baby.

Mr. Singley was a tall rawboned farmer; his wife was short and stout. Fat. I didn't like them, and I could not see . . .

"They say they will name the baby Wayne," said Sally, taking my bundles from me. To me, too, that name seemed to be the final wrong.

I protested, but it did no good.

Sally and I watched the Singley pickup truck go down the drive and turn into the street.

"I am going to ask David," I said, glancing at Sally. There were tears on her cheeks, and she turned back into the house without speaking.

I went to my own house and sat down with the telephone. David was not in Two Bridges; he had not been there over that weekend — which was good, considering the weather we'd had. I didn't know if, even then, the roads were open.

But I felt I must talk to him, so I called his office in the city. I expect he was busy — I am sure that he was. But he was patient and friendly as always. I could picture him as he must have been sitting there in his office, the glint of interest in his eyes, the sweep of his pale hair across his forehead. One hand would be resting quietly on his desk or on his knee. And the dear man let me talk for twenty solid minutes.

I told him the whole thing; sometimes my voice was shrill, sometimes it trembled, once I cried.

"Take it easy, Lissa." His deep voice steadied me.

And I went on to the end. "Can they *do* that, David?" I begged him. "They can't, can they?"

"I'll explain all this when I see you," he told me. "But for now, yes, they can do it, Lissa. Sally knows they can or she would not have allowed them to take the baby. Mike Singley, legally, is the father, since the baby was born when Clare was his wife. When is the funeral to be?"

I looked foolishly at the telephone in my hand. "What?" I asked. Then I came to. *Clare!* Clare was *dead!*

David had thought of her. He was a compassionate man.

I was ashamed. And I answered him . . . I would go to the funeral, I said. I would send flowers . . .

I did those things in the daze which held me for almost that whole week. I could not think or even remember clearly all that had happened. I knew that Sally was heartbroken because she had not been allowed to keep the child. And I realized how much, how *much* she had wanted a child of her own!

I had to go back to Raj's office for therapy, and I did so with dread, though I must have known that Ward would be, as always, brusque, kind, talkative only about unimportant things, a fruitcake left over from Christmas, and the poor fit of seamless sheer stockings . . .

I didn't talk to Raj, but he was there, and cross — more than cross. He seemed to be in a perpetual rage. He slammed things — doors, drawers. He yelled at Ward . . .

Was he also upset and angry that the Singleys had moved in? I had studied Mike at the funeral. Raj did not attend. Mike behaved decently. He was soberly dressed, and he spoke quietly to people. I wondered if Raj had made any sort of protest about the baby. The thought occurred to me that Raj might have loved Clare. That would explain why he couldn't operate on her after she was dead. Wouldn't it?

I asked David. "No," he told me, "Raj is only furious at himself. But that, of course, is the worst rage that can inflict a man. Raj must face the truth that he has failed Sally in every possible way."

"Because he wouldn't operate and save the baby?"

"That, yes. But mainly because he has not given her this child."

"Oh, David!"

"Yes. Do you have a little pity for that man?"

I thought about this. "Yes," I said. "I can be sorry for him. Though I do deplore his heavy drinking."

"Is he still . . . ?"

"Not at the office. I mean, there are no signs . . ."

"Good."

"But I believe he has done some rather wild and irresponsible talking. At least, such things have been repeated to me."

"Keep out of it, will you, Lissa? Don't tell that you were there. And speaking of anger, *I* am furious that you were there."

"But, David — it was my own fault. I was told repeatedly to go home, to stay there."

"Did I say I was angry at anyone else?"

Perversely, his saying that made me feel better; at least, it was the turnaround point. I could pick up life again.

Until the night, a couple of weeks later, when I happened to be at the country club. The Langans were giving a party — Diane was, and that meant her mother and father were running it. Tee had been told to bring me, but I said I would go in my own car, and

I did, planning to leave early. It was the typical Two Bridges social affair. There were drinks and a buffet dinner, a crowd of people, and the deafening noise of talk and laughter. No one removed her panty hose that I knew about, but the women dressed in what I supposed was their best. There was a copper-colored lamé pants suit, there was a really smart white linen shift, there was a plaid taffeta poncho worn as a dress over a body stocking. This was the hit of the evening, but I was more intrigued, personally, by the woman who wore a black velvet dress — though the spring evening was warm— and had fastened all over it a score of rhinestone pins. There were butterflies, a flying bird, a pair of Dutch children carrying buckets from a shoulder yoke — a pin made of her own monogram. Her costume was as interesting as reading a book.

I smiled, but I was not criticizing Two Bridges. I could remember the weird things, the weird costumes, I had seen in Los Angeles and New York, and in places in between.

There was to be dancing after dinner, and I decided to go home while the tables were being removed and the chairs set back against the wall. More to dodge Tee than anything else, I took a short cut out through the bar. People stopped me to speak to me, and it was in that way that I overheard Raj, who was not a guest at the party, I felt sure, but who, as a member of the club, certainly had every right to come into the bar there. He was with two other men, one of whom I knew slightly. And I caught the tail end of the conversation as the crowd of people forced me closer than I wanted to be to Raj and his friends.

One of the men evidently had been speaking of the dramatic birth . . .

Raj said something about the event not being unusual, if one spoke medically.

"Yes, I have read of it. But to think that we, here in Two Bridges, are lucky enough to have a doctor of your caliber, one that could save that baby."

By then I was directly behind Raj. I could have reached out and touched his gold-colored sports coat. "Don't give me any credit I haven't earned," he was saying in his most engaging manner. "Sally did that Caesarean."

"I gather the mother could not be saved."

"No, she could not be. She had been in labor for thirty hours; I myself was exhausted . . ."

I hurried away. One of the friends was saying that he didn't know Sally was a doctor, too.

I was entirely too ignorant to realize what this interchange could mean, but I found out a week later when I was in the office and the Singleys came in to tell Raj that they meant to prosecute the doctor and his wife, charging them with Clare's death. They would demand heavy damages, enough to pay them for having to care for the baby . . .

I put my blouse on again and went quickly out to the telephone. I knew that David was in town, and I dialed his number.

He, at first, said for me to attend to my own business.

"But you have to do something!" I told him.

Finally he agreed to call Sally and ask if she and Raj wanted help. "And if you're still hanging around . . ." he concluded nastily, but I was prepared for that.

I was hanging around, all right. Mrs. Ward and I, between us, cleared the patients through. The Singleys had not stayed long. Mrs. Ward broke down enough to say to me that she was worried. Sally did not have a license to . . .

"But she didn't kill Clare!"

"Hush," said Mrs. Ward, "or Dr. Collier will stand you up right next to me when he shoots me for talking about office affairs!"

I went back to the treatment room and

turned on the heat lamp again and picked up my book. I had not closed the door into the hall, and David did not close the door of Raj's office when he and Sally went in there.

I could hear only a part of what was said . . . David said it was not important how he had heard of the threatened lawsuit. Sally said something about their evidently needing a lawyer — other than the medical-management one they had, or working with him.

David said this firm probably should be brought into the picture. Then there was quite a bit of talk about what had happened the night Clare's baby had been born. David asked questions, just as if he had not been told the whole thing. Once he lifted his voice angrily to ask Raj if he wanted his help or not. "I can step out this minute!" he said firmly.

Then he asked about witnesses. He asked who had brought Clare to the office, and he ended by telling the Colliers not to talk to the Prosecutor unless David, or some counsel, was present.

"If he comes around," said Raj. "The Singleys may have thought I'd pay them off on a threat."

"He'll be around," said David. And of course the Prosecuting Attorney did come.

He came that same evening; he came to Raj's home, explaining that he preferred to treat the whole matter as discreetly as possible. Before I left the office that afternoon, Raj had had the grace to thank me for calling David.

"David thought I was meddling."

"You were. But Sally and I are grateful. He might not have touched the case for us."

I thought that was probably true. David had fallen into a way of rescuing me from my involvements. Sally kissed me and asked me to eat dinner with them that evening. For an instant I thought she was avoiding too much talk alone with Raj, but I discarded the notion as ridiculous. I said I'd be glad to come.

So the Colliers and I were sitting at the dinner table in Mary Bridell's handsome home, surrounded by candlelight, lingering over coffee and the superb pumpkin custard pie, when the Prosecuting Attorney was announced.

"Will you ask Mr. Akers if he will join us for coffee and dessert?" Raj asked the houseman.

Akers. I had heard the name before . . . Yes! David had called the man by name when Denny had got into trouble during the summer, and — oh, *dear!* That had been the night when Bonnie had been so dreadfully hurt, and Raj and Clare . . .

I was devastated, and could scarcely acknowledge Raj's introduction of the Prosecutor to me.

But there the man was, seated in a high-backed chair across from me, refusing pie, accepting coffee, and saying that perhaps he and Dr. Collier should talk privately.

Raj smiled at him, and he smiled at me. "Lissa is one of the family," he said warmly. "Since I suspect the purpose of your call, I think she might stay. Sally, do you want to phone David?"

I went with Sally, and came back with her. David had said to hold the Prosecutor there until he could "get up the hill."

The men rose courteously at our return, and Sally suggested that we all move to the living room, which we did. And until David came we talked about the big piano and my "recent" career. Raj was holding a folded paper which I thought probably was a notice, or something, about the lawsuit.

When David came in, looking very handsome in a dark blue club coat and pale gray slacks, he took the paper and read it under the lamp. "Hmmmn," he said, sitting down, crossing his long legs, tapping the refolded document against his knee.

"Are you seriously contemplating an arrest?" he asked the Prosecutor coolly.

I jumped, and Sally made a sound of surprise and protest.

The Prosecutor said that he had thought it better to talk to Dr. Collier first, and get the story from his side . . .

"Mhmmmn," said David. "I am acting, of course, as their attorney, as well as Miss Bartels', under retainer. Would you explain whatever charge you have against Dr. Collier, and detail the claim the Singley family believes it has against him?" He lifted the paper.

The Prosecutor was a man in his fifties, a pudgy man with a smile I disliked. "Well, of course I have the Singley story, Masters. About the night Mike's wife died in Raj's office . . . and the baby was born . . . and if that story contains any demonstrable truth, I have grounds for a charge of manslaughter."

I pressed my fist against my lips. A glance at Sally showed her to be as white as cotton, her head back against the chair, her eyes closed.

"Now, look here!" said Raj loudly.

"Shut up, Collier," said David. He turned back to Mr. Akers. "A charge against whom, Fulton?" he asked in that calm way of his.

"Why, against Mrs. Collier!" said the

Prosecutor. "If she did surgery without a license . . ."

"Who told you such a story?" asked David, before Sally or I could speak. "The Singleys? They were not there, I understand. Who told you . . . ?"

Back in the house, the telephone rang, and while David continued to ask the source of Akers' information . . . I knew! Raj himself had told that Sally had operated. I'd heard him. But I would not speak. I would not!

The houseman came in to say that the call was for the doctor, and Raj went out, returning quickly, struggling to get into his topcoat.

"I wish," he said, smiling his boyish, charming smile, "that I could do as the TV doctors do — get one patient problem and put all my time and interest exclusively to it." He straightened his coat collar. "But before I leave," he said. "Before I go see how this man fell off a stepladder, and what he broke, let me say this:

"I was there in my office the Sunday in question. The Singleys had called me out to the farm on Saturday. I went, examined Mike's wife, and told the family to take her to the hospital; she had not been my patient. They wouldn't, or couldn't get out, and they brought her to my office about noon on Sunday. I was there continually until two A.M. Monday morning, a qualified, licensed doctor."

He picked up his medical bag, then he took a step toward the Prosecutor. We were all sitting silent, as if in a trance. David had a little smile about his lips.

"I had assistants," said Raj. "That woman was in deep trouble before I ever saw her. So I called in my office nurse, an R.N. of twenty years' experience. My wife was there; she often assists me, as you well know, Akers. Or have you forgotten the time your boy got a marble into his throat? It took Sally and me both to save his life." He leaned toward the Prosecutor. His lips were white with anger. "You didn't talk about licenses that day!" he reminded the Prosecuting Attorney.

Then he straightened and spoke more calmly. "Miss Bartels came down to the office, too, during that long day. She made hot coffee for us, and she saw that we had food. She cleaned up the stuff that got thrown around. *And*" — his finger shook in Akers' face — "she was still another witness as to what went on. You don't have to take my word for it!" He turned toward the door.

I thought he had given an admirable account of what was certainly a grave situation. David's face indicated that he agreed.

Raj stopped at the door, his black bag swinging from his hand. "It was a handicap," he said, speaking quietly and reasonably, "that Singley could not get Clare to the hospital. It was too bad that we had no hospital here, but Singley knew that — you know it. So — since the weather could be called an act of God, having told the family that she needed a hospital, and since they didn't take her to one on Saturday night — perhaps they couldn't — we had to battle several acts of God ourselves. Hers was a most difficult labor. We were not equipped to do surgery, but we finally, in the extremity, decided that we must try. And we all did the best we could. After Clare died, as she did die, the infant was delivered surgically, and an autopsy would show that it was delivered properly. The surgery was properly done."

"Will an autopsy show that, Raj?" David asked alertly.

"Of course it will. The incisions and the closings."

"Good," said David, seeming relieved. I certainly was.

Raj swung back to the Prosecutor. "My wife even brought the baby here to our home," he said, "and cared for it. None of the Singleys had stayed with Clare, and they showed no interest in the child until the thought occurred to them that there might be money in claiming the baby and suing us for malpractice.

"Now they have preferred charges, but I can prove everything I've told you tonight. If the family's action makes it necessary for any one of us — me, Sally — even Lissa here — to be put on trial —"

"There would have to be a hearing first, Raj," said David quietly. "But I think as you do, that you should be given that. And all of you permitted to testify."

"Me, too?" I asked, my voice squeaking.

"You, too," he agreed.

I knew that I would never survive having to testify. The Prosecutor took his paper away with him, Raj went on to his injured man, and David said he would go home. He was starved. Contrite, Sally had a tray brought for him, with coffee and a piece of that marvelous pie, some meat and bread.

Chapter Ten

David ate the food, though I wondered if he really had been hungry, and he talked quietly to Sally and to me about what he called "surmise only" as to the next move the Prosecutor and the Singleys might make. "I would say there would be no lawsuit at this time," he told us. "As for a criminal charge — perhaps Akers will leave that to a grand jury, perhaps call for a hearing — I couldn't say."

When he left, I shook my head at his suggestion that he would take me home. "I'll sit with Sally for a while," I told him.

He glanced at Sally, then stooped swiftly and kissed my cheek. This threw me into confusion; he had never done such a thing before.

"He wants you to bear with me," said Sally when we left the front door. "Come upstairs with me, Lissa, will you?"

At that minute, I would have done anything in the world for Sally. Well, I would at any time, but that night . . .

I could see that she was badly shaken. She had not let herself react too much all through the Prosecutor's visit and Raj's defense of himself — and her. But now . . .

Sally's bedroom, and Raj's, was a beautiful part of that beautiful house. The black walnut bed was a canopied four-poster, with curtains of gold and green and white English print. There were fresh flowers on the bedside table. Two green velvet wing-back chairs invited rest —

At last, Sally wanted to talk, to protest, and I let her talk to me. I tried to comfort her, to reassure her. David, I said, would not let any terrible thing happen to any of us.

"It isn't the police, Lissa," she told me, taking my hands in hers, "nor — that softie Akers making threats, nor any of the rest of this whole mess. It's just — well, listen . . ." She sat down on one of the chairs and leaned toward me. "I should not have done that surgery," she said. "No! I should have known how to do it. But, without knowing, I did it anyway. I chose to *do* it! Now, Lissa . . ." she spoke solemnly. "For the past ten days, and certainly tonight, I realize — I recognize — that all that has happened has brought me to the end of my voluntary life. I wonder if I can make you understand. But the thing is, now I must do something! Something about myself and who I am."

I didn't understand what she meant, not

that night. But I listened to her, and maybe that was what she needed. She knew that I loved her . . .

After about an hour — I don't really know how long it was — but, later, Raj came home. We heard his car, and he came upstairs at once. He glanced at me, then he looked around the bedroom.

"What in hell are you doing, Sally?" he asked.

Sally pushed her hair back from her face and went on checking the bottles in her cosmetic kit. "I'm packing," she said, not looking at Raj.

"Packing for what?" he asked. "Where are you going?"

Sally closed the case. "I am going where I'll never again find myself alone," she said. She came to stand before Raj, looking at him and speaking earnestly. He had dropped his coat and was slumped into one of the wing-back chairs; he was scowling. I sat on a low chest at the foot of the bed; I was putting Sally's shoes into flannel cases. I hoped I seemed separate and apart from the husband and his wife. I must have seemed so, because no one noticed me.

Sally sat down in the other chair and arranged the skirt of her red dress. The belt had a large brass buckle and she fingered it as she talked. That was her only sign of agitation. "I am going to the city, Raj," she said. "I shall leave tomorrow. Drive, if you want me to keep my car and use it. If not, I'll catch the bus. But I am going to the city. I am going to enter medical school and . . ."

He was on his feet. "You're going to enter medical school in *March?*" he asked. "Don't be ridiculous!"

Sally said nothing. She was pale, but calm. And beautiful.

Raj walked across the green carpet and came back. "Which school will you enter?" he demanded, his tone nasty. "Which one will you *honor?*"

Sally smiled a little and shook her head at him, patient with what she seemed to recognize as a reaction in Raj. "There are two good medical schools in the city," she said. "If neither will admit me, I can go elsewhere. But I'll find one. I'll find out what I need in the way of preparation. I can tutor, study, take any necessary examinations, and I hope I may actually enter next fall."

It sounded possible, and Raj heard that it did. "But why do you want to do it, Sally? *Why?*"

She had picked up a sweater; she folded it carefully and put it into one of the open bags. "Because our town needs a doctor," she said. She smoothed the sweater. "A good doctor." She did not look at Raj, but I did. He had gone stone white.

"That writes me off, doesn't it?" he asked tightly.

Sally faced him. "You made a pretty good story to the Prosecutor tonight, didn't you?" she said. "But the three of us were there the night Clare died. Then, and again tonight, you wrote yourself off, didn't you?"

She went around him to the closet, and took down a suit. She folded the skirt of it into the big suitcase. It was a dark red tweed suit; I had seen her wear it many times.

Raj picked up one of my bags of shoes. "It costs a lot of money," he said slowly, "to live in the city, to tutor, to enter medical school and stay there for three years."

"Five years, as I figure it," said Sally. "I'd want an internship and at least one residency. But I think I can manage it. I have some money of my own. I am pretty sure your mother would help me in this project. I might have to ask for a loan, but I think I could get one."

"But what about *me?*" he asked. I smiled, because he was believing her now, and he was feeling left out, abandoned.

Sally shrugged. "That's up to you, Raj," she said. "You can come with me, if you'd want to. Study, do some internships, things like that. Or you can stay here, work at the office as you have been doing, live here with Mary Bridell."

She turned to face him. "In either case, I hope you will behave yourself. You can, you know, if you want to."

Spring came then, and summer. I continued to live in my pretty house, and to do the things I had become accustomed to do. The Langans persisted in their determined way, but I had decided that I would not go to any more large parties, nor would I be upset by Tee, or about him. I saw him regularly, as I saw all my new friends and acquaintances. I missed Sally, but I still had Puddles and the Jimmies, across the street, next door, and behind.

That summer Bish took me on a trip to see the Missouri wild rivers and the springs that were among the state's treasures.

"A treasure that is threatened by progress and thoughtlessness," he told me sternly. "In an era of dying rivers and dead lakes," he continued, "a large region of pure and clear streams inspires many of us to a determination that they should always stay clean and swift-flowing. The Ozarks, as of today, present us a model of healthy rivers."

He showed me a patula warbler, and he took me down, and down again to an Ozark creek in its natural state. Stillness and green beauty were all about us. "It's an experience," Bish agreed. "Won't ever become stale or static."

He showed me several of the enormous springs that distinguish the Ozark rivers; I was delighted, excited by the boil and surge of these clear waters, green, sometimes blue, always cold.

"We have to keep them!" Bish said angrily. "We have to keep the quality of our rivers, and keeping that will depend on the careful use of the uplands which feed these springs." Beside him, I gazed at the rising face of the mountain, at the green trees, the vines, the heavy growth.

We drove over all that part of the state, we hiked, we floated down one river, we ate lunch on many riverbanks, and slept at tourist hotels. "I hope this expedition is a scandal back home," said Bish wickedly.

"If this is scandal, I'm loving it."

He nodded. "We'll do the Meramec tomorrow. There's a spring that some folk want to cover with a lake."

We saw that spring, rising below a vine-covered arch of natural rock, great forest trees shading it. "The spring water is colder than the river water in summer," Bish told me, "but it stays at fifty-five degrees, year round, which makes it warm in the winter months. The constant temperature allows year-round growth for some shore plants. It would be a sin to drown all that in a lake."

"Can we do something?"

He smiled at me. "Enough 'we's,' " he told me, "can do anything. Next time we'll make this trip on horseback."

I looked up at him in disbelief.

"Raj tells me you're going to be ready for a lot of things next summer."

I could imagine our horseback trip, and I laughed at the picture. So did Bish. "We'll go," he assured me.

He had mentioned Raj, and I wanted to talk to Bish about the doctor. So many things puzzled me in that situation. I continued to take treatments in the office, different treatment and exercises, and I didn't need them so often. I knew for myself that I was making good progress.

I continued to help in the office. I wanted to do that.

I would not talk about Sally, and certainly not about Clare, though many asked openly, or brought the subject up slyly. And I didn't talk about Raj, either.

"I help out down at his office," I would

say, proud of my cool manner, "so I can't discuss things that concern the Doctor."

My work was voluntary, but I liked doing it, and as often as not Ward or Raj would tell me I was useful. Even the lab technologist would depend on me to do certain things when his school duties kept him from coming to the office to do what we called "feeding the frogs." I would turn on sterilizers packed the night before, reverse test tubes in a rack, unpack shipments, put his test records into the files.

Oh, I did all sorts of things. Nervous about it, I was in the office when another o.b. problem arose, and I saw Raj handle it with meticulous care. When it went well, I was proud. And I wrote to Sally about his doing it.

She did not answer my letter, though she must know, as I did, that a milestone had been passed. Successfully. She would be pleased, and relieved, to know.

I told her, too, of the man who turned purple. This poor fellow — he was a college student, slightly on the hippie side, who was, he said, traveling across the United States during the summer months. He had run out of funds, and the owner of our largest drugstore had given him work. During one of our occasional "floods," the store basement had filled with water. Cardboard boxes stored down there had collapsed, allowing all sorts of empty bottles and plastic pill containers to spill out and pile up into untidy heaps. These must be gathered up, cleaned, repacked in fresh cartons which would be stacked in a room behind the prescription counter instead of in the basement. It was hard and tedious work, and for several days this large, bearded young man would regularly appear at the head of the basement stairs, carry his cartons of brown bottles through the prescription area and on to the storeroom.

Then one late afternoon, as I was told by Ward the next day, the druggist brought his helper to the doctor's office. He didn't know what had happened to the guy, he gasped, "but look at him, Doc! *Look at him!*"

Raj looked — and laughed, in spite of himself, for the young man's face, some of his blond beard and hair, had turned a brilliant purple. Raj examined the perspiring youth; he frowned, he asked questions.

"I can't figure," he mused, "why the back of his head or his hands have not turned blue."

He determined what the young man had been eating, he asked how long he had worked in the drugstore basement, what sort of drugs he had handled . . .

He agreed that the poor fellow was a sight to see. "If you'd just turn purple all over," he promised, "I'd get you a job with a carnival. I — Wait a minute!"

He asked Ward for some towels and a basin of water.

"Soap, Doctor?" asked the imperturbable Mrs. Ward.

"Bring soap, but —" He put one of the towels in the warm water, he wiped the purple man's purple cheek. A lot of the color came off on the towel. Raj nodded.

"Come with me," he said. "This may kill you, but I want you to strip and take a shower bath in here."

He and the druggist waited and watched with awed interest. The purple faded, washed away. The hippie came out bright and shining. Smelled good, too, Ward reported. "First time in months, maybe, he'd had a full bath."

"But what was it . . . ?"

"The dye? Oh, Raj remembered — the *doctor* remembered — that he'd prescribed some medication for a patient with acute dermatitis; it called for gentian violet. The druggist had it in powder form, he measured out a heap of it on his counter, and the helper must have got into some of the dust, blown by the little fan Mr. Gordon keeps back there in that room. Because the fella was sweaty, it stuck to his face, dissolved, and dyed his hair and skin. Simple . . ."

"After Dr. Collier figured it out," I agreed.

I told Sally about that, and David, too. He laughed, of course. So I told him about the successful delivery. "I think Raj is sticking close to business," I assured him, "and I find watching him very interesting."

David glanced at me. He'd taken me fishing — we had gone downriver in his boat, then, on foot, we had taken poles into a side stream. We were up on a little bridge over what the natives called a "slew" and had our lines dropped over the rail into the clear, brown water. We could see fish down there, but they didn't seem interested in our baited hooks.

"Do you . . . ?" he began, then broke off.

"Go on," I urged.

"Well, of course I will agree with you that no life can be so engrossing as that of a doctor. If it's done right . . ."

"Did I say that?" I asked in surprise.

"I can read your thoughts."

I laughed. "Then I think I had better not spend so much time with you."

"What do you call 'much time'? Here, I'm

309

home for the weekend . . ."

"The first this month."

"I had to go to Chicago, you know that. And that job took longer than I had guessed it would. But — where were we?"

"You were reading my thoughts."

He grunted. "I certainly was. And I find that your bragging vocally about our friend Collier wasn't a patch on what you were thinking about him."

"Oh, David, for heaven's sake! I've been worried about Raj ever since — well, last March. I'm just glad to see that he's doing good work. Because he can be a very good doctor . . ."

David straightened. "For God's sake, Lissa!" he cried. "Will you please watch it?"

I stared at him. He was angry. He really was.

"What did I say?" I asked. "David . . . I . . ."

"Look." He rested one forearm on the bridge rail and looked closely into my face. "I'll stand for Bish — your going out to his place, his taking you off into the woods for a week. I suppose we all are in love with you, Lissa."

I laughed. He was joking. He had not really been angry with me.

Though maybe he was. Because he went

right on to say, "I will not stand by, unprotesting, and see you fall in love with Raj Collier!"

I gasped. That he should think — for one minute —

But just then I got a bite. A big fish had seized my hook and was making off with the line. David grabbed for the pole. And in the excitement we forgot what we had been talking about, and the subject did not come up again.

In the fall, Sally entered medical school, having had no trouble in getting admittance. During the summer she had held a job in one of the medical center's hospitals, and she told me about it when she came home for a brief visit, as she did come at intervals. She was, she told me, an infection control technician.

"If that's a joke, explain it to me," I begged. "I find I'm not very quick at these things."

She smiled at me. "You'll do until a quick one comes around. But I'm not joking. That's how I'm listed on the payroll."

"Do they pay you in proportion to the title?"

"No, they don't. But it's enough to take care of the rent on my small apartment, buy my meals at the hospital cafeteria, and sometimes provide gas for the car."

"Do tell me about it."

"Oh, I mean to. I myself am fascinated. I didn't know there was such a job. You see, Lissa, I snoop, I sniff. I go into the kitchens and check the thousands of surfaces where infection-causing micro-organisms may flourish. I get down on my hands and knees in a hall and take readings off the floor."

"What kind of readings?"

"Oh, I use Rodac plates. They are small plastic dishes, you know . . ."

"Not me."

She laughed and drew her pretty legs up under her on the couch where we were sitting for our girl-talk. "They are small flat dishes filled with a medium — a gook — to which bacteria will adhere. I mark where they are gathered, and twenty-four hours later they are inspected for signs of growth."

"Do you find 'em? Those signs?"

"Oh, sure. Always. Some organisms always are found. Pseudomonas — always present. But the lab gets really excited when we turn up an unusually heavy colonization. Say more than fifty to the disc. Of course one staph aureus is too many."

"Are you the only one hunting these bugs?"

"Well, infection control is of course everyone's job. You're a housekeeper; you know what it takes to keep your house antiseptic. Well, my hospital multiplies that job. A hundred and fifteen bedrooms to your two, fifty-seven bathrooms to your two, kitchens, dining areas, lounges, miles of corridors used by ambulatory patients, and besides, there are the critical areas where diagnostic and clinical procedures are carried out."

"You go over all that every day?"

"No. Of course not. But I make the hotspots, the inhalation therapy facilities and apparatus, the instruments used in intravenous medication or feeding — though, in fact, we monitor all instruments used in the care of patients.

"Then there is the telephone, and drinking fountains, linen returned by the laundry . . ."

"Now how do you test the laundry? I suppose you mean sheets and towels and stuff."

"I do. Well, we test it this way. We test the disinfectant used in the laundry by cutting a small square from a sheet, impregnating it with bacteria, and watching to see if the disinfectant works."

"But are you the only one . . . ?"

"No. There is a committee of staff members headed by a doctor which meets regularly to study the results of our survey. That doctor is my boss."

"And he tells you what to do."

"Not only me, but the housekeeper, the orderlies everybody in the hospital. And do you know what he says most often, Lissa?"

"I haven't the foggiest."

"He tells everyone, 'Wash your hands. Wash your hands.' "

"That sounds simple. But I had no idea hospitals were so dangerous."

"Only because so many sick people with infections come in there. But we take care of things."

I looked at her glowing face. "And you love it."

"Of course I do."

"Will you continue after your school starts?"

"Parttime, maybe. Why?"

"I thought of applying for your job. It sounds like one I could do."

"I expect you could. But why should you? Aren't Tee and David and Bish keeping you happy here?"

I grinned at her. "Do you ever see David?" I asked. I'd been wondering that all summer.

"Oh, no," she said readily. "Well, yes, once I ran into him downtown, on the street. He said he was buying socks."

"You can't believe David, not a word he says."

"Oh, I expect he does buy socks."

"I'm glad you're happy, Sally," I told her. "I miss you, but I'm glad . . . We all miss you. Mary Bridell does. She told me that she did."

"She's been wonderful, Lissa. To me, and about me. We don't talk about — things. But she seems to approve of what I am doing."

I knew that she did. She didn't talk to me, either, nor to anyone, I felt sure, about anything connected with Sally's departure.

"How about you?" Sally asked me. "And your life?"

"Oh, I keep busy." I told her about my trip with Bish, and she laughed merrily. I said, yes, I saw David fairly often. He'd spent a month in Chicago. My arm and shoulder were better, right along. I did seem to be making a full life for myself, didn't I?

And I was. Telling Sally that I was made me examine what David would call the brief. Yes, I did have a full life. Without Sally's job.

And that was what I wanted, too. I had made that decision a year before when I undertook therapy. I knew that my life must change, I never again would be a concert pianist. But I thought I knew, as well, that I was too young to rusticate, to subside into the life and routine of semi-invalidism.

Certainly my year in Two Bridges had not been rustication. I could assess my present position and be a little smug about it. I was keeping myself busy with my home and my dog. I had begun to play the piano; I even had a few pupils. One was a local girl who played quite well, who attended college, majoring in music, and who wanted my guidance and criticism while she prepared her graduating recital. Her thesis, as it were. "I can tell you, I can't show you," I warned the girl.

My second pupil was Jimmie across the street. The one who didn't count because he was twenty-five. This pleasant young man could play the piano. He wanted to learn to play the organ. When he heard that I sometimes played for service in our church, he asked me . . . I enjoyed working with Jimmie across the street.

Then, Jimmie next door's mother suggested that I might teach the little boy.

"If he wants to learn to play the piano," I agreed.

"I think he should learn."

"It will depend on Jimmie's wanting to," I

specified. "So far as I am concerned." We were going to start the experiment in September.

Another thing I did which gave me satisfaction, and filled the rest of my days, was the work I did in Raj's office. I was working there regularly, and often I took over therapy for people who needed it. I became expert with the machines, I knew how to make a person comfortable while spending a half hour using the diapulse . . .

I was part of the crew, and I also began to take Sally's place in the watchdog department.

Raj was the first to tell me that I was checking on his behavior. "You sound like Sally," he would tell me. "You act like Sally."

He was right. I would hear myself protest about drug dispensing; I sent an abortion case elsewhere. And it was Sally speaking in me.

To do those things, I thought, was good.

I argued that point with David when he undertook to tell me what I was doing.

"But, David, I am there. These things come up. What else should I do?"

He was stretched out on the carpet before my fireplace; he and Puddles had been playing. Now the little dog was sleeping with his long nose pushed into David's hand. This was the first open fire of the autumn, and we all were enjoying it.

"Now let's see," said David, "what should you do besides substituting for Raj Collier's ethical conscience? Well —" His eyes lifted to my face. "Maybe you could marry me and keep busy shaking rugs out over the balcony rail."

My heart stopped. Thudded, then raced on. If I only could . . . But, of course, he was only being kind to me. Just as a year ago he would have been kind to Clare when he thought she might need his help.

I was wistful. To love, to marry a man like David — to marry David himself . . .

But he was Sally's. I'd known that from the first. Now he was lonesome for her. And I would not take advantage of a lonesome man. I would not do that to him, nor to Sally.

I gazed into the fire, dreaming of what it would be like to shake the rugs out over the rail of his house . . . I *could* marry him! I would really have a life then. David, my little dog, later a child . . .

It would be wonderful.

He reached out and grasped the toe of my slipper, shook my foot a little. "Wake up!" he said. "I put a proposition to you."

I smiled down at him. "Yes, you did," I

318

agreed. "Have you stopped waiting for Sally?"

He didn't answer me; he jumped to his feet, got his raincoat and left. He was angry, and for all that winter I thought he was angry because he didn't want me to work in the doctor's office. He wouldn't come out and say so, of course.

Though all winter he would say biting things, like asking me if I were still building Raj's ego, or telling me not to get myself into another near-mess with the law. He still resented what Raj had let Sally in for. I knew he was serious about his feeling, but I was sorry for Raj, as well.

He was lonely, too. Mary Bridell spent her usual winter weeks in Arizona, and in Florida. Raj would often drop in at my house for an hour or so in the evenings when he did not hold office hours. He didn't need the food I would offer him, nor the drink. Those things he could have up the hill. But he did seem to want companionship, and of course he was interesting, charming company for me. He would draw me out to talk about myself; he would enjoy the anecdotes I could tell of my life as a virtuoso. The term became a joke between us. In turn, Raj talked to me about the hospital he wanted to have, that he needed to have. David said that

I was foolish to let him come to the house —
what with Raj's reputation, and my living
alone. Bish, too, asked me if I thought it was
wise.

I told them both that my reputation
would have to stand on its own merits. I believed Raj Collier to be a troubled man.

"I should think so!" said David.

"Let him seek counsel elsewhere," suggested Bish.

"He doesn't seem to want counsel. He
wants to talk about a hospital. He seriously
wants to have one. I think the town needs
one and I stand ready to help him get it in
any way I can."

"He's going at it the wrong way," said
David. "He should have done what Sally
wanted him to do, or at least what she suggested to him. He should have gone back to
school, gone through ranks, and learned to
do things as they should be done."

"You don't like Raj," I pointed out.

"That's right. I never have liked him.
He's a spoiled boy. Things have always
come too easily for him — his profession,
the girls . . ."

"His mother knows that. She knows that
she has spoiled him. That is why she is good
to Sally now, and admires her."

"But neither of them is ready to pitch him

out on his ear. Nor are you."

I looked at him in protest. "Because I talk to the man, and am civil to him . . ."

"If you dare say that you let *me* come around on the same basis, Lissa . . ."

"I won't say that," I promised. "You are different. Your coming to my house is different."

He turned quickly as if to say something or to ask some question. But he didn't speak.

"Go on," I urged. "Say it."

He shook his head. "I've said my say on Collier, Lissa. You know how I feel about the guy."

I did know how he felt, and had felt for ten years and more. But now — wasn't he ready, ever, to give Raj a chance? David was a tolerant person on other matters, about other people. I was puzzled about his feeling toward Raj, his refusal to consider anything about the doctor except from his own jealous viewpoint.

That narrowness was not typical of David as I thought I knew him. Once I considered trying to find out how Raj felt about David. I didn't do it, and on later, more quiet thought, I was glad that I had not.

It was at this point that I began to think seriously of ways to help Raj — I mean, beyond the little helpful things I did at his office. If the man wanted a hospital, if the town needed one — and it did! — could I help?

I would have liked to talk to David about it, but he himself had closed that door. He'd think, or at least say, that it was the *man* I was interested in, not the doctor, not the town.

He was wrong. And I would prove him wrong if my plans worked out. I decided I must get outside help. I knew literally hundreds of people. And of those hundreds, there must be a dozen who would be able to help me get a hospital for Two Bridges. Through money, through influence, through personal and professional know-how, they would help.

It was a good idea, a workable one. I spent hours making notes, listing arguments for the project, planning strategy. I would use my friends, but it would be for a worthwhile purpose. I repeated my arguments. The location was perfect. We did need a hospital in the district. Two Bridges was the center of many small communities, resorts and industries where a doctor and a hospital were vital. The place was beautiful. Who could deny that? The river, the hills, the forest trees . . .

So I was not unduly attacking my friends. I knew doctors who would be interested, I knew specialists from my own recent experience, and they would know others. I knew politicians and show people whom I had helped in the past, and who would now listen kindly to me. I selected certain ones — key names — among these friends. And I began, during the spring, to invite them to Two Bridges for a weekend. I used the friends I had made in the town — I gave parties. I invited Raj to each one, telling him of my scheme. I invited David and Bish to meet Dr. Kohl; after that first party David refused my invitations. But I kept on with my idea. I shamelessly used the Langans. They offered to entertain some of my weekend guests, reveling in the names they could drop.

Raj helped. He was at his most charming, and deprecated what he had been doing, carrying the medical load alone . . .

David watched his performance, he found my notes, my schedules and charts, and studied them, with no comment except a lifted eyebrow and a flat refusal to come to my next "fish fry."

He said very little, really. I suspected that Bish kept him informed, and there was of course that strong and efficient grapevine maintained by the good black folk who worked in our kitchens, who served our drinks and our dinners, who heard the talk, and seemed not to note what was said. But — later —

The word went around town. I was working to get a hospital in Two Bridges. Yes, it could be done! Oh, we'd get doctors. We had Raj — If Sally actually took her degree, there would be two doctors, right there!

How long would it take Sally . . . ?

About as long as it would take to build and equip a hospital.

Where would the money come from?

Well, we had some in town. There were wealthy people . . .

The Langans?

And the Bridell money. There were others, less wealthy, but solid citizens who believed in the community. Raj enthusiastically listened to that talk. He said he had patients and former patients . . . The mines would like to have a good hospital right there! He spoke enthusiastically of these things, and furnished me with information on government help. Since we had no hospital in our county, that was a distinct possibility.

He went off for two or three days, and returned with stacks of plans and pictures. He favored one special hospital. He put the picture of it on his office wall. The government had helped local people build that low white building; they started with thirty beds. Kitchen, o.r., laboratory — we'd need just about the same thing.

He was fired up. And I was.

A week later, he had lost all interest. Just that quickly. "Don't bother me just now, Lissa. I'm swamped, and I want to get away for this weekend."

He did get away. He came back, worked hard for ten days, and then went to Baja California to fish.

I was dismayed. After all I had done, the groundwork I had laid. David was right. He was a spoiled boy, and I was impatient with him. Tired of a new toy, he was ready to discard it . . .

But the hospital project was *not* a new toy! It meant lives saved, people comforted and helped. I would hold that man to his obligations! I would, if it killed me.

"It won't kill you," David told me. "But it will exhaust you. And the town still wouldn't have your hospital."

"You think I'll have to give up the idea?"

We were driving out to Bish's for a barbecue. David turned the car into a side road and stopped under a tree. A horse thrust his long head over the fence and studied us. "You'll get your hospital someday, I think," David said kindly. "But don't count on Collier. He makes a leaky egg basket. However, if the town could get in another doctor, Lissa . . . Maybe you should start trying to accomplish that."

I considered the idea. "Is there enough work for two men?" I asked.

"Gee whilikers, Lissa! You thought there would be work enough for a hospital, and for at least two Colliers!"

Yes. I had thought that. "When Raj goes off . . ." I mused.

"The other fellow could cash in. Why, even Diane Langan might take her kids to the second man. I'd go to him myself, instead of driving back to the city for a runny nose."

I looked up at him, laughing. "You do that?"

"I sure do. I wouldn't trust my sinuses to Collier. He'd put arsenic into my nose-drops."

"Oh, David."

"He doesn't like me any better than I like him. And do you know? I do like my second doctor idea. I have wondered about Sally's training and coming back here . . . Could Raj take the competition?"

"But they'd work together."

"I don't believe that has been Sally's idea. Not exactly."

"Has she said that?"

"I haven't discussed the matter with her. Nor any matter, for months. Now answer my question. Could Raj . . . ?"

I nodded. "Take competition. I remember. Wouldn't it be good for him, David? Wouldn't it?"

"I don't know if it would be good for Raj. But I do think it would be good for the town. Especially if he were a good doctor. Though even if he were not so good — Of course we don't need another bad doctor." His big hand fell to my knee. "Yes, he is, too, a bad doctor, Lissa. Doctors and lawyers can't be both good and bad. So we could get in another baddie, but even that kind might make Collier pull up his socks and get to work."

"It will take too long to wait for Sally?" I asked.

"She'll be competition for Raj, all right. When she comes back."

I sat thoughtful. The horse went to sleep with his head resting on a fence post. Puddles wanted to get out, and David opened the car door, then sat filling his pipe, gazing off across the field and the trees beyond it.

Bees hummed in the warm evening air.

"Is that why . . . ?" I began, speaking slowly.

"That Sally went to med school?" David took me up quickly. "Certainly it is."

"So he'd pull up his socks?"

"Oh, she wouldn't recognize her motives that clearly, Lissa. No, she's doing just what she said she wanted to do. To give the town better medical care."

"Socks and all," I agreed, satisfied. "Call Puddles. We are expected at Bish's ten minutes ago."

David whistled and Puddles came running, a golden streak of satin across the horse's pasture. Then, of all things, he decided he could not get through or under the barbed-wire fence.

He whined and looked at us, his big eyes pleading.

"Of all the dumb dogs," said David, getting out of the car. "Just like your mistress," he told Puddles. Standing on the lower wire, Puddles went through, prancing. "Gets into a fix — friends have to bail her out."

I was indignant. "What fixes have you bailed me out of?" I demanded.

David got into the car seat. "How long will it take you to think of something?" he asked.

"I'm sorry," I murmured. "Of course you have helped me. Many times. Thank you."

"I like helping you, Lissa. You make life interesting."

"Even if I still want to help Raj?"

He groaned. "I hope you're joking, but I'm afraid you are not. Though — I do wish I could be sure of one thing, sweetheart."

"You can be. What is it?"

He laughed, shook his head, and started the car. "I'd like to think," he said when we were back on the main road, "that you would not fall in love with the man. You should know that he's a woman eater."

"I also know how to take care of myself."

He looked at me in some alarm. "Don't tell me you already . . ."

"Of course not!" I said vehemently. "And watch the road."

I thought he had told me why he had not wanted to cooperate on the hospital plan. I even thought Sally might have suspected my schemes, though she had said nothing except "Well, good luck, Lissa. Maybe you can accomplish the impossible."

Then, even Mary Bridell . . .

Bish was there that evening in my garden. When I first came to Two Bridges, I decided that I would have a rose bed. I planned its location, its size, and I ordered two dozen roses from a catalogue, handsome plants with the promise of lavish blooms. I read the directions, I bought the recommended fertilizers, plant food, sprays . . . Denny and I set the plants in place, and I rejoiced when the first bloom appeared. I was lyrical when the whole bed burst forth in color. And this, the second, spring, I was desolate when a mole — oh, surely a score of moles! — decided that my rose bed should be their happy hunting ground.

Bish comforted me and said he would bring a trap. The evening he did, Mary Bridell came down to watch "what was going on."

"You two make a picture," she assured us.

"Beauty and the beast," Bish agreed. He was studying the ridges and furrows made by my mole.

"Don't fish for reassuring compliments," Mary told him. She sat down on the garden bench and urged me to follow her example. "I worry about you," she told me.

"For heaven's sake, why?"

"Ever since, early in the spring, you took up your project of getting us a hospital . . ."

"That's dying a natural death," Bish told her.

Mary glanced at me. She was wearing a white cardigan sweater over her dark blue linen dress. "Has it died, Lissa?" she asked.

"I hope not, but I wouldn't suggest that Bish would tell you anything untrue."

"Of course he wouldn't. Lightning would strike — And, anyway, I want to believe him."

"I am greatly disappointed," I assured her. "I thought I could help get a hospital for us."

"I know you thought so, dear. But when I saw the way you were working at it, house guests and parties — I was so afraid you would wear yourself out and accomplish nothing besides."

I decided not to repeat all my arguments, not speak of my hopes.

"I'm stronger than you think," was what I found to say. Bish chuckled. Mary did, too.

"A hundred pounds of muscle and yellow linen," she agreed.

"*And* determination," I reminded her.

"Oh, I'll acknowledge that. But, don't you see, my dear, that you'd do much better to spend your energies and talents on David Masters."

I gasped a little with surprise. I can still see us as we were that evening, the late sun casting long shadows across the lawn, flashing in the sprinkler as it whirled. Puddles was playing with a bit of old carpet, growling at it, running with it, shaking it. Bish in his white shirt and khaki trousers, his bald head sunburned to a rich walnut. Mary and I, seated on the white bench. She was smiling gently at me, and I was wishing that I knew what to say.

"If you have something you mean behind all that . . ." I began uncertainly.

"I have a great deal behind it, Lissa. My fondness for you, my desire for your happiness, not to mention the fact that you are in love with David."

I looked down at my hands, and I was no longer afraid I would blush. I could have tried to deny — I knew I was not able to conceal anything of that size or nature.

"So what are you supposed to do?" Mary asked the question for me. "Well, I'll tell you what you are supposed to do. You should go after him, and get him."

I ran my thumbnail over the welted seam of my yellow culottes. I might have told Mary that David had already proposed to me — in his fashion. Would she be surprised?

Instead, I asked her, "With a man like David, would going after him do me any good?"

"Oh, yes, it would," said Mary Bridell heartily. "Though I doubt if either of you would ever thank me when you got him."

I turned in surprise. "Why not?" I asked. "What do you mean?"

She smiled at me and patted my arm. "Maybe I didn't mean anything; maybe I was wrong."

"You were," said the Bishop from the rose bed. "They'd thank you. It would do that smart young feller a lot of good to get a woman like Lissa. She'd be loyal, and honest . . ."

"You're a newcomer to these parts, Bishop!" cried Mary. "But even then — you should know that David has always been in love with Sally."

"I know that!" said Bish and I, in unison.

"All right, then. So he loves her, and he's a one-woman man."

"Rats!" said Bish.

I laughed.

"I see him as one," Mary said with great dignity. "And it's too bad, because there is no future for him there. There never was; there never will be."

"Women get wiser as they get older," said Bish in a detached tone.

"That doesn't feature in this case. Because the big point is, Raj needs Sally much, much more than David would ever need anyone. So she stays with Raj, and will stay."

I agreed with her on that.

"Therefore . . ." Mary turned to face me. "You marry him, Lissa. You fill that house of his with little redheaded boys. He'll like that."

I didn't much enjoy her laying out my life plan. I could do that for myself. "And," I said softly, "then Sally will be safely Raj's wife."

"She *is* his wife!" Mary pointed out firmly.

"Yes, she is. And you're his mother, aren't you?"

I felt her stiffen; I saw her do it. Her head lifted; her shoulders squared. "Yes," she agreed. "I am the mother you claim me to be, Lissa. But I don't think one needs to be a mother to see this situation."

"A four-sided triangle," said Bish, standing up to look down at his shining mole trap, which looked like a dangerous piece of machinery.

"Could Puddles catch himself in that?" I asked.

"Not unless he digs a tunnel under your rosebushes."

So the conversation changed. Mary Bridell went up the hill. I took Bish back to the screened porch for a cold drink.

And after he'd left, not having mentioned Mary's remarkable conversation with me, I sat on in the dusk, Puddles on my lap. I was thinking about Bish and his four-sided triangle. Mary was right. David had never had a chance with Sally, and never had had since her marriage. Raj needed her, and she would stand by him. And David knew that, too. He'd seen it almost from the first.

And I should have seen it. But I had not. Not through our growing friendship, not when he'd told me I had better marry him and shake rugs . . .

I'd be so happy, too, shaking his rugs over his railing. I'd always thought any woman would be lucky to be David Masters' wife. And if I could be . . . Even if, even when I knew that I would be second choice.

Weren't a lot of women "second choice"? Few men, I thought, married their first love. Circumstances changed, people changed. Things happened. My thoughts drifting, I was reminded of Clare, and the tape which David had made. In it, from it, the conclusion was drawn that a woman could go on, if she were lucky . . . Clare had not been, but of course I wanted to be. I certainly did!

"Let's go inside," I told Puddles. "David will be home for this weekend. It is already Wednesday."

I was leaning toward my next chance of seeing him again.

Chapter Eleven

But before I could see David again, there had to be Thursday, and on Thursday . . .

I wanted to see him again, to look at him in the light of what Mary Bridell had said, and of what I had thought out for myself. Certainly I wanted to decide what I would say and do, or wait for David to speak and do. Hoping . . .

On Thursday, Clare Thomson's little boy was brought to the office by her father-in-law. The man came in — I was at the desk that afternoon freeing Ward to help Raj with some examinations. Alvin Gordon, the technician, was busy in the lab, spinning test tubes, using Bunsen burners, three at once, counting on his little machine that looks like an adding machine, but is not one, rubbing slides together and peering through his microscope — Oh, any or all of the things he does in the lab.

The car pulled up right to the front door; the wheels must have been on the sidewalk. The car, really, was a pickup truck, yellow, with a piece of machinery in the bed of it, a pump or something.

The waiting room still had a few people in it; the afterschool crowd had not yet arrived. This great tall man came in. I recognized him. I'd seen him the day he had come to the Collier house and claimed Clare's baby. I hadn't liked him then. I wasn't happy to see him on that September afternoon. He was a big, rawboned man, his skin coarsened and reddened by the weather. He wore rough clothes, clean, I think, but showing old stains of paint and oil. His hair was sandy, and getting thin. His eyes were blue, and I thought cold.

That afternoon he carried a child, Clare's child, in his arms, and the baby was sick — very sick. In fact, he looked dead to me. I stared at the man holding that baby — the infant whom I had seen born! I had been the first one to hold and wrap him warmly, to love him. For months that child had haunted me day and night. Several times I had driven past the Singley farm; during this past summer I had seen the tow-headed baby, fourteen or sixteen months old, toddling about the dooryard. I had not dared go closer than the road, but I had seen him, usually dressed in a diaper and a striped T-shirt, barefooted, his hair tousled.

But that day, brought into the office, the

child was no longer playing, no longer a bit of happy babyhood. The grandfather told me he couldn't walk — though I had seen him walk! Today his hair was as lifeless as old straw; his skin was the color of ashes, though blotched; his eyes were closed, though I knew he was not asleep. As I watched, his limbs straightened, stiffened, and his head fell back. I made a small sound of protest. I was alarmed, though Ward had told me I was never to show alarm.

"Is Doc in?" Mr. Singley asked me.

"Yes, sir." I stared at the baby.

"I gotta see him."

"If you will sit down . . ."

"I can't sit down, ma'am. This here kid's sick, and Doc has to see him right off. Anyway, you don't want him in the waitin' room, because my wife and I, we think he's got polio."

I jumped. The waiting patients jumped. I waved my hand at them. "Nobody gets polio anymore," I told them, my voice too loud.

"Well, that makes me feel better," said Mr. Singley. "But I still think the Doc . . ." He shifted the child in his arms, and I picked up the intercom phone.

"Doctor," I said. "Mr. Singley is here with the baby. He thinks it has polio."

I could hear Raj's shout, *"What?"* through

the phone and from down the hall.

"Have him come back to my office, Lissa," he said then, speaking quietly.

Mrs. Ward came to get the man and the child. I heard her tell him to wait in there — meaning Raj's comfortable office — the doctor would see him soon.

I stayed where I was, at the desk, though anxious to know what was happening. The patients talked excitedly, one to the other. "It might not be polio, but that's one sick kid!" I agreed.

"They shouldn't bring a kid sick like that out . . ."

One woman decided to leave. I was ready to agree that she should, and crossed her name off the book.

I listened to the patients. I tried to hear what Ward was saying to Raj out in the hall. She seemed to have been trying to start the baby's record card. "I can't even weigh him," she said.

"I'll go see . . ." said Raj.

After five minutes, he himself came to the waiting room. He looked at the three remaining patients. A cut hand to be dressed, a pregnant woman for a routine visit, a man — an old man — who needed company more than medication. Raj smiled at them all. "Look," he said in his warm, personally friendly way. "I have this very sick child — would you be able to come back tomorrow? I'd appreciate it. Lissa, if you could cancel my other appointments . . ."

I could. Half of them were school kids for physicals. I got busy on the telephone, calling the high school first.

All the time, things were busy back in the examining room. Gordon came from the lab to get blood.

"If he has any," said Raj. "The kid's so dehydrated . . ."

I saw Mrs. Ward carry an i.v. bottle down the hall. I stood in the waiting room door, watching as well as listening.

"How long has the boy been sick?" I heard Raj ask Mr. Singley.

"Temperature one hundred four degrees," said Mrs. Ward.

"He's been sick for a week, maybe ten days," said Mr. Singley.

"Looks more like poisoning than anything else," said Gordon.

I shivered.

"How did it begin?" asked the doctor again. I could imagine him bending over the child.

"It began," said Singley. "His stomach was upset. Just exploded sick at supper one night. Kids do that way. I thought he'd maybe got some castor bean seeds. Mike did that one time when he was a kid, made him God-awful sick!"

"They're poisonous," said Raj, his voice cold.

"Yeah, I've heard that. But we plant 'em to keep the moles away. Then I decided that Wayne here couldn't reach the beans, and they weren't ripe enough to fall. But he stayed sick, couldn't hold a thing on his stummick, and he messed himself all the time. I decided maybe he'd got hold of some of the spray stuff we use. You gotta have it, Doc, on a farm. Dust and liquid both, and a kid that age is into everything."

"But you didn't take him to a doctor to see if he was poisoned."

"No, I reasoned a good cleaning out like he was getting would get rid of anything."

"You mean his vomiting and the diarrhea."

"Yeah. He was in a mess *all* the time. We knew it wasn't anything special he ate. I told the wife just to give him milk, but he threw that up, too."

"That was a week or more ago?"

"Roughly. Several days."

"What gave you the idea he had polio?"

"Don't he, Doc?" Singley sounded eager.

"I don't know, Singley. But when you

came in, you said . . ."

"Well, the preacher said it could be that. He'd seen a case or two. He was at the house, and he saw the way Wayne here would stiffen his legs and the way he'd stare."

"This was . . . ?"

"Well, Sunday the preacher suggested it." Now it was Thursday.

"And you still didn't take him to a doctor?"

"We got into a sort of hassle about that, Doc. First, because the kid was — well — who he was. And since you're the only doctor in town . . ."

"But, if you thought the child had polio, man!" Raj sounded angry.

"Yeah. Well, that entered into it. You see — I knew right off, and I told the old woman, that if it was polio, the kid would have to go to the State Medical Center, and we'd be quarantined."

"Too bad," said Raj dryly.

"Yes. Well, we were ready to send him to the Medical Center — we knew we couldn't take care of him . . ."

"You did, eh?"

"Well, I mean, if he was crippled, and all. But then we heard that you'd have to be the one — you, or some doctor, I mean — to send him to the Center. Is that right, Doc?"

"Yes, oh, yes, that's right. A case has to be referred. So you let this child become dehydrated, a victim of acute malnutrition, rather than bring him to me . . ."

"Well, I know there's been hard feeling in the past, Doc."

"There is hard feeling now!" said Raj. "There surely is. So, Mr. Singley, if you will come with me, there are certain things we have to do. Mrs. Ward will stay with the child."

I stood where I was. Raj and Mr. Singley went to his office, and then Gordon came down the hall toward me.

"Tell me!" I whispered.

"Kid's got hold of some poison. From the urine, it's arsenic or something of that kind. I've seen arsenic poisoning. Doc's restoring some body fluid. He's got a job ahead of him. After he kills Singley, I mean."

"What can I do?"

"Just hang loose. I expect he'll send Singley back for a sample of the insecticides the kid might have got hold of."

"I'll bet they know."

Gordon smiled at me, patted my arm, and went on to the lab with his test tray.

Mr. Singley came out of the office; he didn't even glance at me, and went out to his truck, which he drove away. Raj stayed in his office. After five minutes I took him a cup of coffee. He glanced up at me from the thick book he was studying. "Thanks, Lissa," he said. "I guess you've an idea of what's going on."

"Yes. Will the little boy . . . ?"

"I don't know. He's an awful sick kid. Gordon thinks he may have got into some arsenate of lead — and he could be right. If Singley brings back some of that, we'll proceed along that line. I have to do something, and quick!" He reached for another book.

I took Mrs. Ward some coffee, and she gestured to the child. There were great blue patches on his temples and his sunken cheeks.

We waited for Singley, who finally came with a box full of cans and bags of dry powders. There were bottles and jars of liquids.

He wanted to leave. He said he had cows to milk.

"Just wait a little," Raj told him. He and Gordon were reading the labels.

"Every damn one says to keep out of the reach of children and pets!" the technician growled.

"Now, look here, young fellow . . ."

Raj stood up. "Shut up, Singley," he said wearily. He held a square box toward Gordon, who took it.

Then he turned to me. "Lissa," he said, "see if you can locate Sally for me. Her medical school center has a poison unit. Someone there can tell me what I should be doing."

I went back to the desk in the reception room. A patient walked in and I told her that the doctor had an emergency and could not see anyone. I found the numbers, and I dialed, my hand shaking. Still, I was glad to have something to do.

I had to call three numbers before I reached Sally. But when I did, I listened shamelessly to what Raj had to say to her. First thing, she offered to come home. He told her no, but to get the information he needed, to find someone to tell him what to do. "I'll handle it, sweetheart," he told her. "Ward and I — and Lissa. Yes, she's here. Has a right to be, I figure. Don't you?"

I softly put my phone down.

"She's working on it," said Raj, coming out of his office. He examined the baby, then he came out to Singley.

I began to shake again. Raj's face was pale; his eyes were, too. "Singley!" he said angrily. "You can go home now. Tell your wife that, between you, you have criminally neglected and abused a child. You've let him get into poison, and you waited to bring him to a doctor until he was, maybe, only minutes from death. I should call the police. I could call them. Because I want to tell you that it is my turn to go to court. You can't mistreat a child in this state . . ."

Singley stood up. "If I done all you say, Doc," he drawled. "It was your kid. Maybe you could do better."

"I could," said Raj. "And you are right. He is my child. I am ready as of this minute to claim him and take care of him. With God's help and my wife's, we'll save his life. Then we shall adopt him and raise him. And if you, your wife, or Mike should have any crazy idea that you could interfere or get money from us on any basis, think again!

"There were three people besides me in the office this afternoon who saw the condition the boy was in. They heard what you had to say. They are hearing the talk now. They heard me make my promises. So, clear out, will you? And I don't want to hear one damn word from you ever again."

It was seven o'clock when Raj decided to take the baby to his home. The child was responding to care; they'd used the stomach pump, they'd administered stimulants and anodynes, Ward told me. His temperature and color were improved. There no longer were any spasms. Mrs. Ward put various things into my car. Gordon and I closed the office, and I drove up the hill, following Raj's car. I unpacked the boxes of supplies; the yard man helped carry them into the house. Ward had taken the baby upstairs.

Raj was out on the sun porch, talking to Mary Bridell; evidently he had been telling her what had happened, and he was angry again. "I brought him here, Ma," he was saying. "I had to do that. I told that skunk Singley . . . I've arranged for Hattie Hopson to come. She'll nurse the boy and stay on to be his nurse. Will you come upstairs and see him?"

Mary Bridell said something which I could not hear. Just the ripple of her voice.

"Masters is in town," said Raj. "Yes, he is. I saw his car this morning. He'll get things lined up. Though Singley won't make trouble for us. I put the fear of God and the courts into him. Besides, I think he's tired of taking care of the kid.

"So come on, Ma. See him . . ."

I was standing beside the front door. They both saw me. They came down the hall, and Mary smiled faintly. "Lissa," she said softly, then she and Raj went to the stairs which curved beautifully upward. I watched the tall woman in her immaculate white dress. There was an embroidered monogram in blue on the front of it. Raj, on the other hand, showed considerable wear and tear. He had left his white jacket behind at the office, but his white shirt was rumpled, still open at the throat, the sleeves folded back. His thick hair was untidy.

He continued to talk earnestly to his mother. "I'm counting on you, Ma," he was saying. "I am counting on you to take care of your grandson, at least until Sally comes home."

They had reached the landing, and now Mary Bridell turned to face Raj. Her blue eyes were stern. "Home to you, Raj?" she asked. "Or to David Masters?"

I put my fingers up to my mouth. I thought she was cruelly attacking him.

Raj extended his hand to his mother. "She's coming home to me, Ma!" he said firmly.

"Why should she?" asked Mary Bridell. "Why should she come home to you?"

Raj brushed his hair back from his face. The late sun came through the window at the head of the stairs and shone like a spotlight upon him and his mother. "She'll come home, Ma," he said assuredly, "because she loves me. She has always loved me. And she knows I need her." He put his foot on the first step. "Besides, Lissa down there has first claim on David."

Mary, too, had turned to mount the last few stairs, but she stopped and leaned toward Raj. "Are you sure of that?" she asked.

"As sure as I can be," said Raj, his voice happier than it had been for hours. "He's asked her to marry him."

I was startled. How did he know that?

"He told Sally," Raj was saying. "He asked her why she supposed Lissa had not taken him seriously."

I had not. I had not believed . . .

His mother stood gazing at him, then she stepped to the railing and looked down at me. "Is that true, Lissa?" she called. My face must have answered her. "When did he do that?"

"Oh, last winter," I said. "I think it was winter. We had a fire . . ."

"And you didn't say you would marry him?"

"No."

"But why not?" She was as stern with me as she had been with Raj.

"Well, you see — I didn't believe he meant it."

She straightened. "You should know David better than that!" she told me.

I nodded. "I do now," I said humbly.

"Then go tell him so. While I go on to see

my grandson." She glanced at me again. "Hurry up," she bade me.

I laughed and opened the screen door behind me, feeling that I was opening, and then closing, a door on a room in my life. I no longer needed therapy; I would no longer go to Raj's office and help. I would see him and Sally, Mary Bridell and the baby, but I would be living my own life, full and happy, and —

I ran down across the Collier lawn and my own, picturing Mary Bridell's grandson, a healthy, happy baby again, playing in our flower beds, the sunlight bright upon his golden hair, a daisy in his chubby hand . . .

I burst into the house, as happy as Puddles was to see me. I let him out while I changed my rumpled skirt and blouse for a green linen shift which David liked. I ran a comb through my hair, and called to Puddles as I came outside again. "We're going for a walk," I told the little dog, waving his leash at him. He knew the leash meant a real walk, and he came bouncing.

Both of us feeling fine, we ran down the hill. The sunlight was still bright on us, me and my little dog, his shining coat the color of my own hair.

"You two redheads make a picture," said Tee Langan, pulling his car up at the curb.

"How about letting me have some fun, too?"

I was already past him. "Can't!" I called back. "I have an appointment."

I did have — one long overdue. I was remembering and saying under my breath something which David had said to me months and months ago. "Never marry anyone you don't like, and don't want to share every detail of your life." Well, for me that would be David!

And for David? Oh, he had been sincere when he'd said I'd better marry him. So he, too, wanted to share life with me, rugs to shake, four-minute eggs, children to give loving care. I would tell him about the baby and Raj and Mr. Singley. I would tell him about me, and what a mistake I had made. I would . . .

Through the trees below me I could see the soaring roof of David's house.

"David," I would ask, "do you have room in your house for my little piano?"

His gray eyes would smile. He would say "Yes," and —

"Let's run!" I cried to Puddles. "Let's *run!*"

We hope you have enjoyed this Large Print book. Other Thorndike Press or Chivers Press Large Print books are available at your library or directly from the publishers.

For more information about current and upcoming titles, please call or write, without obligation, to:

Thorndike Press
P.O. Box 159
Thorndike, Maine 04986 USA
Tel. (800) 257-5157

OR

Chivers Press Limited
Windsor Bridge Road
Bath BA2 3AX
England
Tel. (0225) 335336

All our Large Print titles are designed for easy reading, and all our books are made to last.